THE JOURNEY
Song of Life – Book 2

I0665987

Tony Chandler

THE JOURNEY
Song of Life – Book 2

DOUBLE DRAGON

Dedication

For Becky and Leonard 'Tex' Vann -- my second parents.

Chapter One

Bluesky awoke alone and freezing.

Every fiber of his body ached with excruciating pain, as if a suffocating cloak was wrapped around his very soul. It sucked away his breath and pressed against his heart so hard it threatened to stop it.

He desperately needed relief.

He contemplated dying; perhaps then he would know relief. However, he quickly realized he was too tired even for that. Bluesky was drained in every way -- emotionally, physically, and mentally. He sat on the frozen branch, completely sapped of his life's energy.

He had not eaten in over twenty-four hours, and anything the intense stress and sadness had not drained out of his body, the night-long battle to stay warm had taken.

The one-legged Mockingbird slowly leaned forward and looked down at the ground far below. The grass looked so soft from up here.

He leaned further.

Without warning, the small bird fell off the branch.

He opened his wings, but his muscles screamed with pain. He couldn't fly; he couldn't even glide.

He fell to the ground with a thud, his feeble wings outspread on the brown grass. The frozen ground instantly began to suck the last bit of warmth from his body.

He realized if he simply lay there he would die.

He didn't have to do anything else.

Of course, if the cold didn't kill him, the two cats that lived at this house would probably finish him off. He changed his mind again when he recalled that a more dangerous yellow tabby also hunted here because seed was abundant and attracted large numbers of birds. Bluesky decided it would be the yellow cat who would take his life, the cat with the burning green eyes.

He didn't care.

All he knew was that he needed relief from this overwhelming pain. And if death were the only way to get relief, he welcomed it.

He would just stay there and die.

No one would care anyway.

The one-legged Mockingbird closed his eyes for the last time.

In the next moment, a sudden burst of noise distracted him.

Bluesky turned his head toward the excited chirps and whistles.

A small group of Sparrows and Doves hopped on the ground eating seed a short distance away. Their entire attention was focused on feeding in order to keep warm.

Bluesky shivered.

He laid his head back on the grass and closed his eyes, hoping against hope his end would be swift and painless. A soft sigh of resignation escaped into the chilly morning air.

The morning sky was laden with low, gray clouds. Suddenly, strong winds parted a group of the thick clouds, and shafts of golden sunlight streaked through from the burning orb of the sun.

One of the shafts of light glowed brighter than the others. While that particular ray of light shot to the earth below, its brilliance increased tenfold -- like a shining beacon of hope. Down, down the beam of shimmering sunlight came, like a mighty arrow shot from a heavenly bow.

The brilliant beam of light reached the earth and now surrounded the unmoving Mockingbird in a tight circle like a spotlight. The world outside the bright spotlight remained cold and unforgiving. The area within glowed with a comforting warmth.

And then something else happened...

At first, Bluesky noticed nothing while he continued to lie there with his eyes tightly shut. Because of his total exhaustion, he fell into a deep stupor somewhere between wakefulness and slumber, that mystical place where dreams and reality mix and combine into one until the dreamer is unsure if he is dreaming or really awake.

Bluesky dreamed, but this time his dreams were pleasant ... even happy, filled with noise -- so much noise ...

A great number of birds flocked all around him.

An instant later, even more birds arrived ...

A myriad of birds filled the air all around him, and ... and they sang to him! They sang of joy and happiness.

Even more shocking, they sang of their friendship -- to him, Bluesky!

Somehow, he knew he was no longer alone.

In fact, he realized that all of these birds were his friends. Yes, Bluesky the one-legged bird, had hundreds of friends now!

Somehow ...

Oh, how he yearned for friendship.

He wanted a friend; he needed a friend -- even a single friend would be great. But these birds were innumerable! There were hundreds ... and then there were thousands ... and then tens of thousands, and now hundreds of thousands! More and more kept singing out to him ...

A sudden realization of the sheer numbers sent a shock throughout his being.

Every bird in the world was his friend ...

A new feeling grew inside him, a feeling of intense delight, a feeling of such exquisite happiness and of such unimaginable joy that he felt alive as if for the very first time. This wonderful glow inside his heart grew and grew until it filled him completely. This burning feeling nourished him; it gave him strength. It gave him a new life.

It gave him warmth ...

Yes, he felt so wonderfully warm ...

Bluesky groaned, and his eyes fluttered open.

He looked around quickly, at first not realizing where he was. He grimaced when he realized the sad truth -- he had only been dreaming. Suddenly, he felt the wonderful sensation of the dream fading away.

"No!" Bluesky protested. "Please, let me go back into my dream. Please! Please! Please!"

The cloak of sadness flooded back into his mind and heart, and he cried out at the terrible, excruciating pain.

And yet, something was still there deep inside. He felt the smallest surge of energy rejuvenate his soul. In a flash of recognition, he realized he felt better -- it was the warmth giving him strength.

Lying there within the beam of sunlight, he felt the burning glow caress him deeper and deeper.

Next, he felt hungry.

A movement caught his eye.

A juicy bug crawled within the circle of light, drawn to the warmth that now healed the bird's body. Bluesky eyed it carefully while it crawled closer and closer, almost as if it wanted to be eaten!

With a swift lunge of his curved beak, Bluesky took the morsel and chewed it with unimaginable joy. After he swallowed it, he actually felt his body absorb the vital nourishment. He was amazed at how much his pain lessened simply from eating a single bug.

Now fully awake, he looked around again.

The shaft of light quickly thawed the ground of winter's icy grip. Even more quickly, the feathers that covered Bluesky absorbed the heat; it quickly penetrated to his skin and even seemed to make him glow inside. It felt so good to feel the sun's warmth after the long night of freezing cold. It was like ... it was like hatching out of the egg again, being freed at last from the confinement of the shell and emerging to find a new world.

Suddenly, more bugs crawled straight toward him.

Bluesky shook his head in dumbfounded amazement. His motion alone should have scared them away. He didn't realize that they too were drained from the cold of the night, and the only thing they could focus upon was the light and its promise of removing the icy chill -- that was how close to death even these insects were now.

Again and again Bluesky lunged and ate. It was almost as if dinner were coming to him. It was so easy.

A funny thought struck Bluesky. Lying on the ground, still weak but feeling better by the moment, it seemed like he was back in the nest and his parents were feeding him.

But there were no parents that he could see, just these bugs willingly coming to him so he could eat.

A personal favorite of Bluesky crawled slowly toward the edge of light. This one, however, crawled with more authority than the others, and when Bluesky cocked his head to one side for a better look, this bug did react and turned.

With wings spread, Bluesky chased after him with a burst of energy. His curved beak stabbed the juicy bug on his first attack.

He chewed the bug slowly, appreciatively, enjoying the flavors that sent more surges of energy throughout his being.

Bluesky now began to hunt in earnest. It seemed the bugs were literally coming up out of the ground in every direction. In just a few minutes, he'd eaten enough for two meals!

While he stood and carefully wiped each side of his beak on a fallen branch, he looked over at the Sparrows and Doves still pecking at the fallen seed. The Sparrows moved with quick, jerky motions of their bodies, as if they were in a constant state of high energy. The Doves moved more slowly, more deliberately. When they walked, their heads bobbed forward and backward in rhythm with their steps.

Bluesky chuckled at the sight. He'd never seen a bird that walked so funny.

The patch of light he stood within now widened until it encompassed the entire yard and every bird. One of the Doves stopped eating and glanced over at him.

With a surreal whistling sound, the Dove took wing and flew straight toward him. The gray-brown bird landed right beside him and looked him over carefully with soft bobbing motions of her head.

Finally, she spoke. "Are you all right, little Mockingbird?"

Bluesky looked at her with puzzled surprise.

"I don't understand?" Bluesky asked.

The female Dove walked all around Bluesky, her head bobbing back and forth with every step. She carefully checked him over with obvious concern.

"You seem to be fine, but are you in pain?" she asked with feeling.

"Why?" Bluesky paused, still in a quandary. "Why do you ask?"

"My flock and I saw you fall from the tree earlier. We thought at first you had succumbed to the cold of last night. You fell pretty hard and didn't move for a long time." She looked deep into Bluesky's eyes. "Many birds have stopped flying the last two nights. It's been a real struggle for all of us to stay alive against this bitter cold."

Bluesky still couldn't grasp why this bird was interested in his health. He looked from her back to the four other Doves still pecking at the seeds scattered on the ground. Finally, he turned back at her.

He could tell from her eyes and from her demeanor that she was an older bird. She carried herself with the experience of many seasons.

"You seem to be better now. I just wanted to warn you that a yellow cat hunts here, and you need to be careful. Don't stay in one spot for too long, or he'll eat you."

"I want to die."

The Dove bobbed her head up and down a few times in total surprise.

"Why? You're such a young bird, and you have your entire life before you. You're a Mockingbird. You've got lots and lots of happy songs ahead of you."

"My father has left me. He took my brother and sister. Now, my mother has left me."

"A mother never leaves her baby."

"My mother left me."

"I don't believe it." The female Dove's expression now changed to puzzlement. "What is your name?"

"Bluesky."

"Well, your parents gave you a name of great honor. That alone shows their love for you."

"They left me. They were ashamed of me."

"Pshaw! Why would they be ashamed of a good-looking young bird like yourself!"

Bluesky's surprise deepened further at the Dove's words. It seemed she spoke them with complete honesty in spite of his deformed condition.

"Haven't you noticed? I -- I only have one leg."

The old Dove glanced down at his leg. "Well, I hadn't really noticed until you mentioned it. You know, we all have our little imperfections. As I've gotten older, some of my feathers no longer fit together like they used to. See, these on my right wing stick out and look pretty ugly." She turned and displayed her wing, where indeed several feathers stuck out with ragged edges, no longer smooth like the others.

She chuckled merrily a moment. "You might've guessed by now, my eyes aren't that good either. I don't see too well -- probably why I didn't notice your leg." She leaned closer and whispered to Bluesky, "That's why I need younger birds in my flock. They're my eyes now."

Bluesky was shocked that this bird had shared such personal information with him. No other bird had ever done that. Even more surprising, she shared her own imperfections and even laughed about them.

"What is your name?" Bluesky asked in a soft whisper.

"My parents called me Fallingleaves. My dad always did love that time of year. Not me though -- it always reminds me that the warmth of summer is over and the cold of winter is on the way." She shook her entire body for emphasis and fluffed out her feathers.

"I like your name." Bluesky smiled shyly.

Fallingleaves laughed with a twinkle in her black eyes. "That's a nice thing to say, young bird. A nice bird like you must have lots of friends. I'll

15

remind you again, your mother didn't leave you. Where was the last place you saw her?"

Bluesky briefly related how he and his mother lived after Treetop left with Songjoy and Cloudshadow. He poured out his heart, fears, and emotions at being ostracized by all the other Mockingbirds -- the pain and hurt it caused him. He especially emphasized the pain he felt at seeing his mother so sad and knowing he was the reason. He spoke of how she'd urged Bluesky to eat and prepare for the cold, but how he saw his mother pining away and not eating and seeming to grow sadder each day.

Finally, he told Fallingleaves of his mother's promise to never leave him. He spoke about the final night they spent together just two nights ago.

"I'm afraid I have some bad news for you, Bluesky." Fallingleaves' expression softened.

"What could be worse than being abandoned by your family? And being ostracized by all of my kind? And being totally alone?"

"Your mother didn't leave you, not really. I can tell that she loved you with all her heart. I'm afraid your mother most likely has ... *stopped flying*."

The thought that his mother had died that night had never occurred to Bluesky. On waking up that morning and finding her gone, he'd just assumed she had left in the night like his dad. But he did recall how she seemed so weak that night ... and she was having trouble staying warm ... and she hadn't eaten like she should have ...

Bluesky raised his head and cried out, stricken with grief once again. His single, forlorn note pierced the air just like it had all the previous night. A single note filled with melancholy and sadness echoed through air. Slowly, that single, sad note faded away on the wind.

"Was that you crying out all night?" Fallingleaves asked in surprise.

"Yes. I couldn't sleep. I-I hurt so bad. I kept waking up afraid and sad and so alone." Bluesky looked down at the ground. "The sadness hurt so bad, it made my whole body hurt. I felt so helpless ..."

"If you cry out like that again tonight when the night is warmer, something will come and take you. A possum or a cat -- they'll hear you and come for you in the dark."

"My heart hurts so bad ..."

"It's okay to grieve," she whispered comfortingly.

"It hurts so bad, I don't know why my heart keeps beating ..."

Bluesky's tears streamed down his feathered cheeks, and the sadness and the loneliness overwhelmed him again.

Fallingleaves watched silently a moment. Her aged eyes studied the Mockingbird while he trembled and stood on his single leg as if in the midst of the most terrible of storms. Perhaps it was true, but this storm raged inside his heart and soul. She stepped beside the sobbing Mockingbird and gently caressed his neck with her short beak.

In Bluesky's mind, it felt like Sunshine had just comforted him. He jerked his head up in surprise, but when he saw the Dove, his heart sank with bitter disappointment.

Fallingleaves saw his expression of hope change back to despair.

"I want you to call me by something else -- by the nickname my flock calls me."

"T-t-they don't use your name?" Bluesky sobbed.

"They call me, Ol' Gray Mama." The Dove opened her beak and smiled at Bluesky's obvious surprise. "I'm the matriarch. Yes, it's only a little flock. At times some of the birds fly off and join bigger flocks. And sometimes they come back. Some are my relatives, and the others are just my friends."

"Why-why do you want me to call you that?"

"Because you're going to join my flock, Bluesky. It's not good for a bird to be alone. Besides, you can help me keep warm tonight. I want you to roost right next to me. I need help staying warm too!" She laughed merrily.

"I thought that only 'birds of a feather, flock together'?" Bluesky asked.

"Pshaw! We can flock with whoever we want. We're all birds, aren't we?"

Bluesky nodded in puzzled silence.

"Good, it's settled," Ol' Gray Mama said.

"But I don't know anything about Doves." Bluesky's eyes widened with surprise.

"Ah, we're just a bunch of old birds. We fly kind of slow. We eat kind of slow. Shoot, we do everything kind of slow. C'mon, let's fly over there, and you can meet the others." Ol' Gray Mama took wing with a whistling sound and flew over to where the four others pecked at the ground in search of seed.

Bluesky took wing, amazed at how much better he felt. The healing warmth of the sunshine and the nourishing meal had rejuvenated him. He flew with strong strokes of his wings and followed Ol' Gray Mama to her little flock. He landed a bit behind her, still feeling a bit awkward in the company of these new birds.

"Well, I declare, Ol' Gray Mama, what have we there?" The Dove that spoke was also an aged female. She looked questioningly at Bluesky.

Bluesky quickly noted that all five Doves had gray-brown feathers all over their bodies, though when the sun hit their feathers at a certain angle they seemed to shimmer with color. Mostly, they were simply plain birds -- just as he had heard.

Still ...

"This is a young Mockingbird named Bluesky. He lost his mother to the cold and is all alone. So, I invited him to join us."

The four Doves gazed at Bluesky a moment in obvious surprise.

"He ain't no Dove! We're a flock of Doves!" the lone old male protested.

The other Doves, all females, nodded in agreement.

"You remember how cold it was the last two nights?" Ol' Gray Mama asked with a twinkle in her eyes.

The Doves all nodded slowly.

"The more birds we have perched together nice and comfy on a branch, the easier for all of us to stay warm!" Ol' Gray Mama laughed out loud.

They all nodded agreement enthusiastically.

"Tarnation -- I hadn't thought of that. I hope he don't mind flocking with a bunch of dried-up old birds like us. Remember this, young fella, we ain't no fancy singers like your kind either." The old male chuckled with a mischievous glint in his black eyes.

"Now, Pops. Don't be makin' no trouble for this Mockingbird. Lots of Mockingbirds don't think they're all high and mighty like some of them do."

"Don't mind Pops," Ol' Gray Mama whispered. "We call him Pops, but his name is Redsky. He's Firstflowers' hubby, her mate." She nodded at the two Doves who had just spoken.

"My name is Foggymorning."

This female Dove seemed a bit younger than the first three. She coo'ed soothingly. However, Bluesky remained silent and unsure. He didn't know what to say, really. He'd never met so many new birds all at once.

"Foggymorning is my daughter from three seasons past," Ol' Gray Mama clucked proudly. "She's a widow like me now. She likes the company of all of us old birds."

"Hello, Bluesky. My name is Treeshadow."

"That's my niece."

Bluesky nodded silently at each in turn.

"He don't say much for such a hoity-toity Mockingbird, does he?" Pops laughed.

"Be nice, Pops. He's a sad little bird," Treeshadow said.

"That was him singin' so sad all night long," Ol'

Gray Mama added.

All five Doves coo'ed softly over and over again. The soft, forlorn sound filled Bluesky with a strange, comforting feeling -- not quite sad, but not quite happy either.

"Why I declare, that was the saddest sound I ever heard in my entire life," Foggymorning coo'ed.

"He'll fit right in with us." Pops laughed.

"Yeah, you know what they say about us Doves." Ol' Gray Mama opened her beak and smiled at the others.

"What do they say?" Bluesky peered at her curiously.

"If it wasn't for sad songs, we'd have no songs to sing!"

"Yep, we love them sad songs." Pops uttered a series of melancholy cooing calls for emphasis.

"I guess I might fit right in with you guys," Bluesky said.

The old doves all smiled at him.

For the first time in two days, Bluesky smiled.

Chapter Two

Bluesky woke up huddled close beside Ol' Gray Mama.

He felt her nearness, and it gave him a sense of comfort. He wasn't sure why, for he had only met her the day before. And yet, just the simple act of perching next to her along with the other Doves in this tree made him feel much better.

He wasn't alone any more.

The next few days were busy for him and his new flock. When the Doves flew from place to place in search of seed, Bluesky flew along with them. During the time they searched the ground for seed, he searched nearby for bugs. If ever Ol' Gray Mama or the others strayed too far away, Bluesky hurriedly flew closer, even if bugs were nowhere near the Doves.

He'd rather go hungry than be alone.

Still, as much as he liked their company, he couldn't stay with them all the time. They were so loud searching for seed that they scared away any bugs nearby, so he would fly a little way off and hunt among the grass and leaves for his nourishment, always keeping the Doves in sight.

Ol' Gray Mama seemed to take a special liking to him, which made him feel good too. When he would return from foraging for insects, she would always ask if he had gotten enough to eat and chide him if he hadn't eaten enough. And if he was gone for longer than she deemed fit, she scolded him and wouldn't allow him out of her sight until she realized it was time for him to eat again. Then she'd send him on his way again with a firm reminder not to stray too far.

Bluesky got used to the routine. He even enjoyed it.

It was a nice feeling, knowing that someone cared.

He didn't mind that they were a bunch of old birds either. He didn't mind if they repeated the same stories again and again. As long as they allowed him to flock with them, he'd put up with just about anything.

He marveled at how content they all seemed to be, even though they complained about their aches and pains and other common infirmities of old age. He was most surprised at how they could laugh at themselves.

A week soon passed. The cold air warmed under the strength of the southern sun until the days and nights moderated. In fact, it grew so warm that birds no longer needed to fluff out their feathers in order to stay warm at night.

One sunny morning after Bluesky had just finished a meal of crunchy bugs, he flew back to his flock of Doves and surprised Pops.

"What? Where'd he come from?" The expression on Pop's face grew deeply puzzled. He blinked inquisitively in Bluesky's direction.

"That's Bluesky, Pops. Don't you remember? He's the Mockingbird that came to stay with us," Foggymorning said.

"Oh yeah. I thought he looked a might skinny fer a Dove." Pops looked Bluesky up and down with a keen eye. "What's he standing like that fer? Looks like he's trying to balance himself!"

"He only has one leg, remember, Pops?"

"Why, he has two legs -- I see them."

"Now, Pops," Ol' Gray Mama said with a chuckle. "That's your eyes playing tricks on you again. You get that blurry vision at times. He's only got one leg."

Pops looked at Bluesky closer.

"Why, I guess that's so, it looks like he's got two heads, and I guess that can't be right -- heh heh heh. Guess my eyes are playing tricks on me again." Pops looked at the ground and picked up a piece of dirt in his small beak.

"Pops, you just ate some dirt!" Firstflowers, his mate, shouted in shock.

"Hmm, I thought the seed around here tasted kind of bland."

"How many times we got to remind you, Pops! If you see two seeds on the ground, always eat the one on your right!"

"Yeah, yeah. I keep fergettin. Doggone eyes, I hate it when my vision gets blurry."

"That's why you need us gals to help you out. Listen to us."

Pops waddled away from the others, mumbling under his breath about harping old Doves and the vagaries of growing old.

"He's a deary, you know. He does get a bit confused when his eyes act up though." Firstflowers sighed.

"That's' all right," Bluesky said. "I don't mind."

"Didn't he ask you about your leg yesterday?"

Foggymorning smiled with mild embarrassment. "He's getting forgetful too."

"It doesn't bother me, really. I don't mind when he tells me the same story over and over again either."

"Well, that's most of us does that, eh?" Ol' Gray Mama laughed. "I guess we're fond of our favorite stories and love to tell them again and again."

Bluesky smiled at her and the others. The female Doves chatted happily away about all kinds of things -- days gone by, birds they had once known, and especially family. Their words flowed like a steady breeze washing over the tall grass.

The days were filled with the happy chatter of the old Doves. A lot of times, Bluesky couldn't get in a word edgewise. In fact, Pops had trouble getting in a word himself. He and Bluesky contented themselves in listening and marveling at the breadth of subjects and the infinitely detailed memories of times gone by that the old Doves lovingly told.

Bluesky learned the details of Ol' Gray Mama's life. She shared the memories of her mate, who'd died two seasons ago. She talked about each of her babies and how they grew up and flew away in order live their own lives. Most of all, she talked often about her youth and other precious memories of her childhood.

He liked her stories. She had lived a grand life and made many friends. Each of the other female Doves shared similar tales. Soon, Bluesky knew many of the details of their personal lives. It seemed to him that they got a certain boost from remembering their past.

They also discussed recent events and talked about the concerns and joys of their lives now.

When they reflected on days gone by, Bluesky noticed how their eyes got a certain glow and how they spoke with more powerful emotions. Sometimes when they talked about themselves and their long-lost youth, it almost seemed as if they were speaking of someone else and not themselves.

Bluesky realized that their stories were more precious than any treasure.

Bluesky, being a true Mockingbird, soon was able to imitate the coos and calls of the Doves until they exclaimed that he was really a Dove in a Mockingbird's body.

He liked that.

The shortened days of winter slowly faded. Another cold front swept down from the north, but like all winters in the deep south, as soon as the sky cleared, the southern sun quickly warmed the air until it seemed that winter had never come.

On one of those warm winter days, Ol' Gray Mama and the others foraged near a scattering of seeds while Bluesky hunted near a stand of trees. In fact, the dogwood tree in which Bluesky had been born stood in this very backyard just across from them. The Doves visited this particular yard often because seed appeared here at regular intervals.

Bluesky stabbed at a bug and nabbed him with his slender beak. He was chewing with rapt appreciation when a bird broke out in song in a tree above him.

He looked up at the branch and spied another

Mockingbird.

In the next instant he realized it wasn't just any Mockingbird -- it was Funwind.

Funwind was perched in the highest branch of the tallest tree in sight. He sang out with a clear and powerful voice. He twittered a jolly phrase, repeated it, and then he sang out with a new, lilting tune.

Bluesky chuckled to himself a moment. Then he sang out and repeated Funwind's songs with detailed finesse.

Funwind paused a moment and cocked his head, looking around for the bird who dared sing back to him.

Bluesky couldn't help himself. He only did what was a natural for a Mockingbird. Singing with a fellow Mockingbird was the most natural thing in the world.

Finally, Funwind spotted Bluesky standing on the ground underneath him.

"Are you trying to play the 'Singing Game' with *me*?" Funwind called out in challenge.

Bluesky realized Funwind didn't recognize him from above; he couldn't see his leg from that angle. In addition, it had been many days since they last saw each other.

Instead of replying, Bluesky sang out and repeated Funwind's last melody again. Then he added an extra tinkling sing-song dash right at the end.

Funwind lowered his long tail and held his head up with beak wide open. He boldly answered Bluesky's challenge with more song.

Bluesky let the notes fade on the wind a

moment. He lowered his own tail, raised his head high, and sang out again. His snippet of song, however, was totally different.

Funwind barely let Bluesky's last note fade before he sang out in perfect imitation. Without pausing, he launched into a five-minute-long chorus made up of dozens of snippets of songs. Funwind sang with bravado and passion, daring the challenger below to try and match this mighty effort.

Bluesky flew up to a lower branch in a nearby tree in the midst of Funwind's solo. He too launched into a seemingly endless variety of song snippets and twinkling melodies. Bluesky let forth with all his heart and soul, matching Funwind's own passionate singing note for note.

This contest continued for almost ten full minutes. Neither Mockingbird paused, nor did either slow down. Indeed, it seemed that neither slowed even for a breath.

Most surprising, neither bird repeated themselves even a single time.

Song after song burst forth from both Mockingbirds, and with each new tune they sang out with even more energy and more passion than before.

Finally, and almost simultaneously, both birds stopped in silence and mutual respect.

Funwind stared down at Bluesky.

Without warning, he flew down and landed right next to Bluesky.

Bluesky noted how Funwind's expression quickly changed from intense interest to surprise and finally outright shock.

"What? It's you!"

"Hello, Funwind," Bluesky said almost in a whisper, noting Funwind's condescending expression.

"Why were you singing with me? Don't you realize that no self-respecting Mockingbird wants to sing with you, much less be seen with you?"

Bluesky felt the sting of Funwind's words and hung his head sadly.

Ol' Gray Mama flew up beside Bluesky. Seconds later, all the other Doves of the flock flew into the tree with them.

"What's this bird saying to you, Bluesky?" Pops said, weaving unsteadily on the branch. It was obvious his blurry vision had returned.

"What are you saying, old bird?" Funwind said angrily. "You're nothing but an ugly old Dove. Nobody cares what you say or think."

"Now listen here!" Pops tried to hop toward Funwind, but he lost his balance and flew down to a lower branch with a cry of surprise.

"You leave our Bluesky alone," Ol' Gray Mama said with a threatening tone.

"Who are these old Doves, Bluesky? Why do they care about you?"

"I-I flock with them." Bluesky spoke with hesitation, his tone unsure. After all, it was well known that 'birds of a feather flock together.' In spite of that proverb, he was flocking with Doves.

"A Mockingbird flocking with ugly old birds like these? Why, they can't even sing!"

"I-I flock with them. And ... they can sing."

Bluesky looked away with embarrassment.

"Next thing you know, you'll be making friends with the Sparrows! I mean, they're like Doves -- they all look alike, and they're all just plain and ugly!"

"Didn't your mama teach you no better?" Ol' Gray Mama said in an angry tone. "Didn't she teach you that if you don't have anything nice to say, then it's best to say nothing at all?"

"Shut up, you old bird." Funwind sneered.

In a flash of feathers, Ol' Gray Mama flew up over Funwind, and before he could react, she pecked right him right on top of his head.

"Owww! That hurt!"

She hovered right above him and pecked him two more times for good measure.

Funwind leapt away. A few of his feathers floated away on the air he left so quickly, but he managed to shout back over his shoulder in his hasty retreat, "I guess if none of your own kind will have you, you'll have to flock with a bunch of old Doves!"

Bluesky watched him fly away with sadness in his heart.

The Doves looked forlornly at Bluesky while he flew slowly back to the ground and went off to be by himself.

Later that night, Ol' Gray Mama perched beside Bluesky on a branch. The stars sparkled like miniature diamonds in the black sky above them.

"I don't fit in ... not with you ... and not with anyone ..." Bluesky closed his eyes and sighed.

"Sure you do. We all enjoy having you in our

flock. It's nice to have some youth mixed up with all of us old birds." She chuckled cheerily.

"But I'm so different. I don't mean just because I'm a different kind of bird than you. I-I only have one leg. Other birds think --"

"Pshaw! Who cares what other birds think. You're okay by us, kid." Ol' Gray Mama winked at him.

"I don't fit in." Bluesky sighed.

"Do you like being part of our flock?"

Her words caught Bluesky by surprise.

"Of course I do."

"Still, it is a bit odd that a Mockingbird flocks with Doves." She seemed to pause in deep thought.

"I don't mind. Really."

"And we're all old -- lots older than you. The tribulation of old age is catching up with us too. We'll stop flying one day." Ol' Gray Mama peered into Bluesky's eyes a moment. "Even I will stop flying one day."

"I hope not for a very long time," Bluesky said with an urgent tone.

"You're a young bird -- this is your hatching year, your first year of life. You've got your whole life ahead of you."

"I-I guess so."

"You need to find your place in the world, don't you?" Ol' Gray Mama's voice suddenly filled with hushed excitement.

"I guess so."

"You need to know where you belong. Nobody owns the sky. The sky is for every bird, even a one-legged Mockingbird. I think you need to find out what it is you want out of life, and more importantly you need to know where you're going." Ol' Gray Mama peered at him with a twinkle in her eyes.

"I-I don't know exactly what I do want. I just want ... I just want to be happy. I just want a friend."

"That's what we all want. But all the other Mockingbirds have shut you out. It's not right."

"No, it's not."

"Birds of a feather flock together. That's what they say!" She opened her beak and smiled.

"Other Mockingbirds won't even speak to me, much less flock."

"Still, birds of different feathers do flock together."

"Really?" Bluesky said with surprise.

"Sure, haven't you noticed how Titmice will flock with Chickadees in the cold weather? Even some Sparrows and Finches will flock along with them."

"Why?"

"Chickadees are friendly little birds, although a bit too chatty for my taste. Still, they're usually the first to find fresh seed, and they're so happy they can't keep from spreading the happy news to every bird within earshot. Better yet, since they are such small and nervous little birds, they're usually the first to recognize danger and graciously cry out a warning, again benefiting any birds close by."

"Is that why the other birds flock with them?" Bluesky smiled.

"Yep. They're useful that way."

"Well, maybe I'll be useful to you Doves in

some way?"

"Could be," she said cheerily. Then a serious look came into her eyes. "And yet, I think your journey is only just begun. You still need to find your place in this world."

"Can't I be part of your flock?"

"Of course you can. You can stay as long as you want." She peered at him. "But you're young. You have your entire life before you. One day you'll want to go out on your own and find your own niche, your own place in the 'Song of Life.' This coming spring, you will feel that very urge."

"I don't want to go out on my own!" Bluesky exclaimed. "I will just stay with you, Ol' Gray Mama. I'm happy to stay with all of you."

"All birds leave the nest, Bluesky. One day, you will grow up and go out into the world. It is the way of life."

"W-where will I go?"

"Let me think ..." She paused a long time. Bluesky realized she was meditating, pondering deeply.

"I know it!"

Bluesky jumped at her unexpected outburst.

"I don't know the answer, but I know a bird that will."

"Who?"

"The wisest of all the birds." She smiled with a mischievous twinkling in her eyes.

"Who is the wisest of all birds?" Bluesky asked.

"The Owl."

"Oh."

"And I know just the Owl."

"Really?"

"Yes. He's an old friend of mine. He's lived in these parts since before I was born. He's the wisest bird I've ever met."

"What's his name?"

"Nightwind."

Chapter Three

Ol' Gray Mama searched long and hard trying to track down Nightwind. Since Owls were nocturnal, it was even more difficult than to find a sleeping bird. When most birds were roosting and asleep, Owls were awake. Under the star-filled skies they flew alone except for a handful of other nocturnal birds.

More than that, Owls led solitary lives.

They perched high in the treetops in silent contemplation. Since their large eyes were some of the most sensitive in the entire world, an Owl could spot a mouse on a moonless night from over a quarter mile away. Combined with their extraordinary vision, their long hours spent in quiet meditation made them the wisest of all birds.

Over the next few days, Ol' Gray Mama assured Bluesky many times that not only would Nightwind help him, but he would gladly share his great wisdom and show him how to find his place in the world.

Bluesky grew more excited each day. His yearning to meet Nightwind grew with each sunrise.

Finally, the great day arrived.

"I've found him."

"Where?"

"He's living in a large poplar tree not far from here."

"Should I go now?"

"No, wait until the sun is almost set. Owls come awake with the setting of the sun."

"But I'll have to fly back in the dark."

"We will fly together to a nearby tree. You will leave me and fly on and meet with Nightwind alone. When you are done, you'll make the short flight back to me, and we'll roost there together through the night."

Bluesky nodded slowly, but he had an expression of apprehension on his face.

"Don't worry," Ol' Gray Mama said comfortingly. "I'll be close by."

Bluesky smiled with trust, although a twinge of fear rose inside his heart at the thought of leaving her behind and flying alone to meet the wise Owl.

Right after the sun set, it happened just like Ol' Gray Mama said it would. Together they left the small flock and flew into another patch of woods located within the subdivision of homes. She alighted upon a branch, and Bluesky perched right beside her. With a silent nod toward a tall tree, she urged him to fly on alone.

Bluesky's heart pounded inside his chest as he left. Now that he was actually going to meet the wise Owl, he felt afraid.

He wasn't quite sure why. It wasn't that he was afraid the Owl would hurt him. He just felt afraid.

He tried to analyze the jittery fear that caused his heart to beat so rapidly. No, he wasn't afraid of meeting the Owl. He was afraid that even a wise old Owl would not be able to help a one-legged Mockingbird.

Maybe the Owl would decide he wasn't worth helping. In fact, he was more afraid the Owl would laugh at him and make fun of him like the other birds.

Worst of all, perhaps he might tell him he had no place in the world.

Bluesky swallowed hard as he approached the tree. He flew up to the forest giant and landed on one of the higher branches. He slowly looked around, but he didn't see any birds in the fading light of the early evening.

He looked down the entire length of the branch on which he sat and then looked up to the topmost branches. He gazed along every branch, but he couldn't find the Owl anywhere.

Bitter disappointment filled his heart, and the young Mockingbird turned to leave.

Suddenly, a sharp whistle split the air.

Bluesky's heart pounded harder and faster than it had ever before. It sounded as if the bird was right beside him, but there was nothing ...

"You must be Bluesky."

"Wha? Where are you?" Bluesky quickly looked around, trying to find the source of the unseen voice.

"I am here, on the branch just above you."

"But I looked for you there."

"Ah, yes. You looked, but you didn't see."

"I don't understand."

"Look up now."

Bluesky looked up at the branch. He looked again and again, but he saw no bird anywhere.

Suddenly, a part of the tree trunk moved!

It was the Owl.

He was smaller than Bluesky imagined -- and he was different.

Nightwind was an Eastern Screech-Owl. His feathers were mostly gray like the trunk of the tree, with patterns of black feathers interspersed with the gray feathers, creating a perfect camouflage. The Owl blended so well that he seemed to melt and become a part of the tree.

Now that Bluesky could make him out, he marveled at his shape. Although he was about the same height as a Mockingbird, the Owl's body was thick and wide, like his huge face. He was almost as wide was he was tall!

Two feather-pointed ears rose straight up on either side of his wide head. A streak of solid gray feathers ran down from both ears and formed a 'V' shape, effectively dividing his face into two parts with the bottom of the 'V' ending at his short, curved beak.

As Bluesky stared in awe, Nightwind slowly opened his huge, yellow eyes. The Owl peered at Bluesky a moment; then he blinked and slowly closed his eyes until they were almost shut again.

However, Bluesky noted, the Owl still watched him carefully between the slits of his eyelids.

"Come closer, Bluesky."

Bluesky flew up to the branch and perched near the Owl.

"I've heard a lot about you."

"H-how?" Bluesky stammered and then suddenly lost his balance. He fluttered his wings wildly trying to regain it so he could stand on his lone leg. Finally, he crouched low on the limb until he steadied himself.

"Don't be nervous, little Mockingbird."

Bluesky's face grew warm with embarrassment because he had almost fallen off the limb. He fluttered his wings again, although he was perfectly steady.

"I-I'm not nervous. It's hard to keep my balance sometime ... I ... I only have one leg." Bluesky looked down and sighed.

"That's all right, I understand," Nightwind said with compassion. "I'm very pleased you've come to visit me."

"Why?"

"I've heard about you. I've heard how your own kind has shunned you and how they even fear you. It has recently come to my attention that you perch with Ol' Gray Mama and her elderly flock now." Nightwind smiled benevolently. "I've wanted to meet you for quite a while now."

"Why do you want to meet me? I'm -- I'm just a one-legged bird."

"And that is exactly the point."

But poor Bluesky didn't understand at all.

Nightwind laughed. The Owl's laughter was a deep, joyful bass sound, like his voice.

"Now tell me, why have you sought me out?" Nightwind's large, yellow eyes blinked solemnly. This time, he opened them wide and peered deeply at Bluesky.

Bluesky's fear evaporated.

Bluesky could tell from Nightwind's eyes that he was a good bird and a bird of deep thoughts -- a wise bird indeed.

"I-I have come to you ..."

"Yes ..."

"I've come to ask you a question."

Nightwind chuckled again, his bass vibrato seeming to shake the branch on which both birds perched. "Ask away."

"I don't know what to do. I cannot flock with my own kind -- they've ostracized me. My own father abandoned me." Bluesky looked down in shame. "And ... I like flocking with Ol' Gray Mama. But she says I'll grow up and fly out on my own one day. And ... and neither of us knows what I should do then. I don't know where to go or what to do sometimes ..."

"Difficult questions, Bluesky. Even a wise bird like me cannot answer all of them."

Bluesky felt his heart drop in despair.

"However, I may be able to help you in a different way."

He looked up with hope.

"Do you have any friends, little Mockingbird?"

Bluesky let out a forlorn moan.

"Ah, I perceive that is a problem. I suspected as much. But you do have some friends, don't you?"

"I don't have any friends, wise Owl." Bluesky shook his head sadly.

"Hmmm. Are you certain of that fact?"

"Oh yes, quite certain."

Nightwind peered at him with his large unblinking eyes. "How do you know?"

"I've always wanted a friend -- and just one friend would be enough. I want a friend like -- like Treehopper. I just can't find another Mockingbird who wants to be a friend with me."

Nightwind blinked his eyes solemnly. "Oh yes,

from the Song-Tale."

Bluesky nodded.

"What would you do if you found a friend like Treehopper?"

Bluesky smiled with a burst of enthusiasm. He looked off in the distance a moment, his eyes glistening with eagerness.

"We would play every day and have fun. He would fly high up into the sky and touch the clouds, and I'd follow him. He would sing with me and hop up and down every tree in the forest with me. Most important, he would be my best friend!"

Nightwind peered steadily at Bluesky. "Is that everything you would do?"

"I-I would play with him. And sing with him. I guess ..." Bluesky looked questioningly at Nightwind.

Nightwind's eyes slowly closed until they were almost completely shut.

"Why couldn't you see me the first time you looked for me?"

The question took Bluesky by surprise. "I don't know."

"You looked directly at me several times."

"I guess, well, I couldn't see you."

"And yet, you were looking for me. You knew I was close by."

"Your feathers blend so well with the tree and the shadows in the bark ..."

"You looked, but you didn't see."

"I don't know what you mean." Bluesky's beak fell open with puzzlement.

"You looked, but you didn't observe. You

looked, but you didn't comprehend. You didn't see me, but I was here the entire time."

"I'll look better next time, I guess."

Nightwind blinked several times in thought. Finally, he gazed hard at Bluesky. "How do you make friends, Bluesky?"

"I don't know, I guess that's one reason I've come to you."

"The first step in making friends is to learn a bird's name."

"I know the names of lots of birds," Bluesky said quickly.

"Then, you have taken the first step."

"I still don't have a best friend like Treehopper."

"To have a friend is a great responsibility. Friendship is not simply joy and fun as you envision it. But the happiness true friendship brings is worth it. Are you ready for such a responsibility?"

Bluesky looked around nervously. It seemed to him that the wise Owl talked in puzzles.

"I want a friend..."

"Good!"

"But all the birds I meet treat me funny, like there's something wrong with me."

"Yes, I imagine that is true. They only see the empty place where your other leg should be. They don't really see you."

Bluesky felt dizzy inside his mind. He gripped the branch tighter so he wouldn't fall. With a start, he realized it was getting dark -- very dark.

"Will I make friends, wise Owl?"

"Yes," Nightwind said emphatically and without the slightest hesitation.

"I don't understand. How can I make friends when every bird I meet treats me as if I have a disease?"

"It is up to you, if you are to make friends."

"I don't understand. I want to make friends, but I can't!" Bluesky pleaded in a high-pitched voice.

"Treat others the way that you want to be treated."

"I do!"

"If you want them to be nice to you, you must be nice to them -- first. If you want them to care for you, you must care about them -- first. If you want them to like you as a friend, you must treat them as a friend -- first."

Bluesky shook his head again and again. He couldn't understand the Owl. Hadn't he told him over and over how all other birds treated him? Didn't he realize it was out of his control? How could he make friends when he wasn't even given a chance?

"But I'm doing that! When I treat others nice, they're just mean to me in return!"

"Not every bird," Nightwind replied, his tone matter-of-fact.

"All the Mockingbirds treat me that way."

"Not the Doves of your flock. Ol' Gray Mama doesn't treat you that way, does she?"

"But ... but ..." Bluesky swayed unsteadily on the branch while his thoughts swirled like a whirlwind inside his head. "She's old. She's ... she's not a Mockingbird."

"Oh, so your friend must be a Mockingbird. And your friend must be someone your own age."

Nightwind peered inquisitively at him.

"Birds play with their own kind. That's what birds normally do ... right?"

"I see more clearly now." Nightwind sighed.

"You see what?" Bluesky looked around hurriedly -- had some new bird flown up without him knowing it?

"I see in that I understand."

"Wise Owl," Bluesky cried out with tear-filled eyes, "I am afraid I must be too stupid. I don't understand what you're trying to tell me. I want to make friends. I try to make friends. But ... nobody wants to be my friend. They all hate me!"

"If you treat a bird with kindness and friendship, and they treat you that way in return, they are showing you that they are your friend."

"Then I don't have any friends. No one treats me nice, no one cares about me. Anyone I've ever loved has left me -- in one way or another. I keep trying to tell you that I don't have any friends!"

Nightwind slowly shook his head, and his expression grew more thoughtful. "You have had a difficult life, Bluesky, a more difficult life than most birds have experienced in an entire lifetime, but I will help you."

Bluesky jumped with joy, flapping his wings excitedly. "I am so glad. Tell me what I must do."

Nightwind peered at him a few moments in contemplation. "You must go on a journey of discovery."

"That sounds kind of cool," Bluesky said with feeling. "Where am I going?"

"A journey has no destination."

Bluesky felt the dizziness returning.

Nightwind chuckled again. "You live with a small flock of Doves, right?"

"Yes."

"Most birds believe that Mourning Doves are simple and plain birds -- nothing special about them. Isn't that right?"

"Yes."

"Go back and observe them -- *really see them*. Like all living creatures, they bring a distinct beauty to this world. I want you to discover what that beauty is and return and share it with me."

"Okay ..." Bluesky said hesitantly.

"After that, go to the Sparrows. Many claim that Sparrows are the least of all the birds in the world. Go and meet a few of them; learn their names, talk with them. Listen carefully when they talk -- learn who they are. Discover the subtle beauty that they add to the world both as individuals and as Sparrows."

"They're just little brown birds." Bluesky paused a moment in thought. "I was told that all Sparrows look alike."

Nightwind's eyes narrowed. *"I want you to disprove that gross lie."*

Bluesky stared fearfully at Nightwind a moment. He could tell the Owl was angered by his last statement. Bluesky stood very still while he waited for Nightwind to speak again.

"Seek out what is good and beautiful in every bird you meet," Nightwind said earnestly. "That is what this journey is all about."

Bluesky nodded silently.

"When you learn how to do that, you will begin to understand how to make real friends."

"That's how to make friends?"

"That is what this entire exercise is all about, my young Mockingbird."

"Huh? I thought it was a journey of discovery?" Bluesky shook his head in total confusion.

"That too," Nightwind chuckled.

"I will try," Bluesky said without conviction.

"Never try, Bluesky. Do your best. Always do your best." Nightwind smiled. "If you do, you will always succeed in some measure -- perhaps more than you hoped."

"I will do my best." Bluesky said cheerfully.

"Now, go forth on this journey of discovery! Discover the beauty of Doves and Sparrows. And most important, look for the good in everyone you meet. If you look, you'll always find it."

Nightwind opened his tiny, curved beak and smiled.

Bluesky turned to leave. Now that it was dark, he wasn't sure if he could find the tree where Ol' Gray Mama perched, but it gave him comfort knowing that she waited somewhere nearby for him, even if she was just an old Dove.

"And Bluesky ..." Nightwind blinked with a gentle expression on his feathered face.

"Yes."

"I enjoyed meeting you today. Please, come back and visit with me any time you like."

Chapter Four

"We're going to help Bluesky make friends with the Mockingbirds," Ol' Gray Mama coo'ed happily.

"Everybody needs friends," Treeshadow added.

"Especially the young," Foggymorning said.

"What?" Pops jerked his head up and looked around with a puzzled expression. "Someone needs a friend?"

"That nice young Bluesky -- we're going to help him find a friend," Firstflowers coo'ed softly.

"Why does he need help making friends?" Pops blinked repeatedly.

"He's only got one leg," Ol' Gray Mama whispered. "Remember?"

"Only got one leg! Did he have an accident?"

"Hush, you old bird," Firstflowers said sharply. "Don't you remember anything? He was born with one leg."

"Born with one leg? How did he learn to walk?"

"He hops, Pops. He hops on one leg. See him over there."

Pops blinked repeatedly at Bluesky. "Oh yeah, I remember that bird. But why would he want to make friends with the hoity-toity Mockingbirds?" Pops leaned forward and blinked at Bluesky some more. "Why, he's not a Dove, is he?"

"He's a Mockingbird. Remember, he's been living with us for the last couple of weeks."

"Well, I guess that's why he wants to make friends with the Mockingbirds -- he's one of them!" Pops laughed.

"Do you remember him now?" Firstflowers asked.

"I don't know, birds come and birds go. He's welcome to flock with us, if he likes. We'll treat him nice."

"He is ... he has ..." Firstflowers shook her entire body in frustration. "Oooooo, you old bird. You drive me crazy at times!"

"Heh, heh, heh, I do get kind of crazy when you talk real sweet to me."

"Oooooooooohhh!"

Bluesky stifled his laughter while Firstflowers and Pops flew over to a nearby tree. He could hear her frantic tone in the distance as she tried explaining everything to Pops before he forgot any of it. Pops seemed to have a special knack for getting everything confused and mixed up.

"Did that wise Nightwind mention how we could help you make friends with the other Mockingbirds, Bluesky?" Ol' Gray Mama coo'ed softly.

"He told me I needed to go on a journey." Bluesky shook his head with a puzzled expression.

"A journey! What kind of journey? I'm a little too old to go on much of one."

"Well, not like real journey, I think. He said I needed to find out some things."

"What kind of things?"

"He said I needed to discover what makes Mourning Doves and Sparrows beautiful."

"Ha! That's a good one," Ol' Gray Mama laughed. "I'm afraid we're mostly just plain birds. I can say that because I am one!"

"Nightwind seemed positive I could find something beautiful about you."

"Maybe he was thinking about my cousins who live on islands far away in the middle of the great western ocean." She bobbed her head excitedly, walking in circles around Bluesky. "Yes, there are some beautiful Doves there. They don't eat seed -- they eat fruit!"

"How are they beautiful?" Bluesky asked.

"One of our cousins has beautiful orange feathers all over its body. Another has bright green feathers. Can you imagine that? An orange Dove!"

"Wow, they sound beautiful. Have you ever seen one?"

Ol' Gray Mama laughed with a twinkle in her black eyes. "No, child, I haven't even flown up to the mountains much less the great western sea. From the Song Tales I've heard, once you reach the great western sea a bird would need to fly many more days over nothing but water to reach the tiny islands."

"I doubt I'll ever fly that far myself," Bluesky whistled.

"Now, now. You're still young. You might fly that far."

"Maybe." Bluesky smiled broadly. "At any rate, I need to start my journey here with you birds."

"I'll do everything I can to help you, Bluesky. We all will. Each of us thinks you're a right nice bird. I'll go tell the others, and we'll try to figure out if there's anything beautiful about us plain old birds!" She took wing and flew over to the others.

He focused his attention and listened quietly

while Ol' Gray Mama talked to the other Doves and exchanged ideas how they might help Bluesky make friends as well as what they thought was beautiful about themselves. Their ideas and suggestions started out simple, but soon it seemed all the Doves were talking at once. Bluesky couldn't make sense out of what they were saying, so he quietly hopped away.

He ate a couple of bugs and thought about what Nightwind had told him.

Bluesky carefully observed the Doves. They continued talking among themselves, some pecking at scattered seed on the ground while a couple sat on a tree branch.

His first impression still held true -- Doves were covered with drab, gray-brown feathers. They bobbed their heads in rhythm with each step they took. He noted that their eyes were small and black ... their beaks tiny as well.

Bluesky knew Nightwind wouldn't accept that. There had to be something more. He hopped a little closer.

He must have startled Foggymorning, because she suddenly took wing and flew away as if something were chasing her.

A familiar whistling sound cut through the air.

Bluesky knew the whistling sound was created by the Doves, and it only occurred when they took wing. At first he thought it was one of their cries, but now while really observing them, he realized Foggymorning's beak had been closed when she took flight.

In a flash of understanding, he realized the

whistling sound was caused by their feathers when they took off in haste!

Almost as he finished his thought, Treeshadow took wing and confirmed Bluesky's deduction.

He searched his memory, but he had never heard of any other kind of bird that could make a whistling sound with their feathers. Here was something unique about Doves, although he wasn't sure if it would qualify as something beautiful. Still, it was kind of cool!

Maybe it would qualify as beautiful -- a beautiful sound! He felt a surge of excitement that seemed to confirm his observation.

He watched Treeshadow fly between the tree branches and farther into the little patch of woods.

He noticed something else!

Her tail, like those of all Doves, was long, tapered in shape, and boldly edged with white feathers. He focused on the shape of the tail. Yes, all along the edges as the tail tapered to a point, he now noticed bumps, or semi-circles, giving the tail a very unique -- even a beautiful -- shape.

Doves had a uniquely shaped tail!

Inside his rapidly beating heart, Bluesky knew this was something Nightwind wanted him to notice. Their tails were beautiful -- in shape!

Feeling flushed with excitement, he flew up to the branch above Pops and Firstflowers. Maybe he could observe something else to triumphantly share with Nightwind. After all, he had found two beautiful things about these birds -- a beautiful sound and the pretty shape of their tail!

He observed first one Dove and then the other,

slowly and carefully.

Once again, his impression was confirmed -- a medium-sized bird covered with gray-brown feathers. Doves had no other color ...

Bluesky froze.

Something had sparkled on Pops' slender neck when the sunlight streamed suddenly between the clouds.

Bluesky looked closer.

Yes!

He noticed sparse patches of feathers that seemed a darker shade on his neck. When the sunlight hit these patches, they sparkled. Male Doves had very small patches of iridescent feathers.

It was truly beautiful -- though difficult to detect.

Bluesky continued to observe them the rest of the afternoon as they chattered among themselves. After the afternoon shadows had lengthened and the world slowed down in preparation for another night of rest, he discovered another subtle beauty about them.

He focused on the soothing sound they made while they coo'ed to each other.

It was indeed a gentle and melancholy sound. It suddenly struck him that their soft cooing made him feel relaxed. It was enjoyable to hear, although it was nothing like a regular birdsong.

And yet, he liked it.

He spent another night perched close to Ol' Gray Mama and the other Doves. He felt good because he had discovered so many beautiful things about Doves.

The next morning, after the sun rose in the east, he waited on the ground for the Sparrows. He knew he wouldn't have to wait long. Like the Doves, Sparrows frequented this place because of the abundance of seed.

In that instant, he wondered why this yard always had such an abundance of bird food. He decided to use that question to start up a conversation and get to know a Sparrow.

While he waited on the ground, Bluesky noticed a small brown bird land on something that resembled a straight branch hanging down with tiny branches sticking out from its sides -- except it wasn't made of wood.

He watched while the Sparrow ate some seed while sitting on one of the tiny branches of the bigger, strange-looking branch. It hit him that perhaps the seed originated from this weird thing.

He looked at the patterns of brown and black feathers, seeking to find something beautiful about them. He stared a long time, but nothing really stood out.

It suddenly occurred to him that he had forgotten to look for the good in each of the Doves yesterday. He had only quietly observed them from a distance. He remembered Nightwind's words about discovering something good about each bird he met; he'd forgotten that part yesterday.

He would have to do better today.

He wanted to go forward and meet some of these birds, but he remained frozen. His heart beat rapidly, and a familiar fear gripped his soul, a fear that sent a chill throughout his being.

He hesitated to approach new birds because he feared rejection.

Somewhere in the depths of his mind, the words of Nightwind echoed. While he stood frozen in place, the words grew louder -- *'treat others as you want to be treated.'*

Bluesky wanted so much for the Mockingbirds to like him and treat him with kindness, and yet he still didn't see how it would help him make friends with them by seeking out these tiny Sparrows.

He watched other Sparrows flying down and mingling with the Doves. They all searched the ground for seed. He observed how they acted toward each other -- sometimes a Sparrow and a Dove even smiled at each other. Sometimes they sang out brief snippets of songs to each other in greeting. Mostly, however, they all concentrated on eating peacefully together.

Bluesky glanced from bird to bird, but one Sparrow in particular kept drawing his attention.

He noticed that she always smiled at any bird that came near her, and every few minutes she let out a happy whistle as if she wanted the world to be happy along with her.

He liked her for that.

His fear slowly melted away. The joy that emanated from this little bird struck a chord deep inside his heart. She treated others the way he wanted to be treated. Perhaps if he smiled at her, she would smile back at him.

He watched her closely. He noticed when she flew back up to the strange seed branch.

Bluesky hopped closer until he was directly

underneath the strange branch. He whistled joyfully up at her.

She glanced down at him with a wary eye.

Bluesky smiled.

He noticed her glance at the emptiness where his other leg should be, and suddenly his heart beat rapidly with fear, but she looked back at him almost instantly. Her eyes looked directly into his, and then she smiled at him.

"Hello! Uh, I hope you don't mind, but could I ask you a question, please?" Bluesky asked politely.

"You want to ask me a question?" she asked, somewhat surprised.

"Um, yes. I mean, if it's okay with you."

The Sparrow laughed out loud as if something were quite funny, but after she noticed that Bluesky was serious, she spread her wings and flew down beside him.

"Well, this is quite a shock -- a Mockingbird wanting to talk with a Sparrow. I hope this isn't some kind of a joke?" She peered at him with a twinkle in her black eyes.

"I don't mean to offend you."

"Oh, no. You're fine -- nothing wrong with the way you're asking. I'm ... I'm just surprised."

"Why?"

"Mockingbirds don't usually want to talk to Sparrows. We're beneath them, you know."

"I don't think like that," Bluesky said.

She laughed out loud.

"I really want to speak with you." Bluesky smiled shyly a moment and added, "Please."

"I've heard everything now!" The Sparrow

laughed merrily. "Okay, Mockingbird, what's your question?"

It occurred to him she didn't know his name.

"Let me introduce myself. My name is Bluesky. And yours?"

"Ah, proper introductions even." She bowed her head a moment in thought and then looked Bluesky directly in the eyes. "Hello, Bluesky. My name is Treeflower."

"You have a pretty name. Why did your parents name you that?"

"Oh my ... and now compliments!" She laughed.

Bluesky felt embarrassed, and he wasn't even sure why.

"Yes, then, my name," Treeflower said. "When the first trees bloom in spring they're completely covered with white flowers. My parents built a nest near a grove two years ago, the year I hatched. They named me Treeflower since I was born in one."

"I like your name."

"I like your name too, Bluesky. Is that your question?"

"No. Actually, I wanted to know why this place always seems to have seed when other places don't."

"That's an easy one -- there's a seed-nest here. More than one, in fact."

Bluesky felt the dizziness return. It seemed every bird he met lately talked in mysterious code.

"What's a seed-nest? I've never heard of them before."

"It's a man thing. See it up there. It looks like it sits on a tree with no limbs, but if you touch it, it is hard like rock!"

"What's that hanging down from the top of it?"

"That's the seed-nest."

Bluesky looked at the Song Sparrow questioningly. "Do you mean the man lays seed in that nest?"

Treeflower laughed merrily a moment before she replied. "He doesn't lay the seed like a bird lays an egg, no, but the man will bring the seed and fill the seed-nest when it is all gone. That's why all of us come here so often!"

"You mean the man actually provides food for birds?" Bluesky whistled, trying to comprehend. "Why would he do that?"

"He wants us to sing for him. At least, that's what most of us think. And so, we do!"

"Does he provide bugs?" Bluesky asked excitedly.

"I don't think so, but this place is full of bugs too."

Bluesky knew she was right; he had come here often to hunt bugs. In fact, this was the place where he had been born and left the nest. He looked around and quickly spotted the dogwood tree and the very branch that still held the remnants of his birth nest.

He still couldn't quite comprehend this concept of a seed-nest. He was still gazing in awe at it when a Cardinal lighted on its edge and started pecking at the seed. While the red bird eagerly sought for a black sunflower seed among the smaller seed, it sent a shower of the smaller seed flying through the air. This seed fell on the ground around the other Sparrows and a couple of Doves, who quickly moved forward to eat this new supply of food.

"I want to see this."

Before Treeflower could reply, Bluesky opened his wings and flew up and landed on the seed-nest.

"What?" the Cardinal exclaimed. "I've never seen a Mockingbird eat seed before!"

"I-I'm not here to eat. I just want to find out what this seed-nest is!"

The Cardinal's crest stood straight up as he stared at Bluesky. His expression changed from puzzlement to outright surprise, and then, with a flurry of red feathers, he flew away without another sound.

Bluesky analyzed the seed-nest. It was true; an abundance of seed was inside it -- he could see right through it. It was sort of like a nest, the way the edges held the seed inside. Still, he couldn't fathom how the seed got inside in the first place. It all seemed so -- mysterious!

At any rate, he now knew why so many birds came to this place. When he looked around, he noticed another seed-nest hanging from the man-house with other birds eagerly eating from it. All around the yard, he saw seed scattered while dozens and dozens of birds hunted among the grass for morsels.

He quietly observed the birds a moment. Suddenly, he noticed Treeflower fly over and join a group of other Sparrows on the ground.

They all had their backs to him.

In that moment with all their backs turned to him, they did all look alike!

Each Sparrow was covered with brown feathers

interspersed with black feathers. As he looked closer, he noticed they also had a few patches of white feathers all over their backs and wings and tails.

Bluesky shook his head. It seemed that Funwind was right. And yet, Nightwind had gotten so angry when he mentioned that all Sparrows looked alike.

Bluesky's thoughts whirled in a flurry of conflicting emotions. In the end, he decided that contrary to what his eyes told him, he could never believe anything Funwind said over Nightwind. He decided he had to investigate further, and he flew down for a closer look.

No, he flew down to observe ...

He landed near Treeflower, who glanced up at him after he landed.

"Oh, you're back? You certainly are a curious Mockingbird. Most times, Mockingbirds simply ignore us."

"I have a task."

"A task?" Treeflower asked inquisitively. "What do you mean?"

"Well, it's more like a journey. Anyway, Nightwind the Owl asked me to discover the beauty of Sparrows. He wanted me to disprove the lie that all Sparrows look alike."

All around him, the other Sparrows stopped searching for seed and looked up at him with startled expressions. Bluesky felt some of them staring at him -- and some of them stared hard at the place where his other leg should be.

He felt nervous inside. He started to feel very warm and uncomfortable too. Suddenly, he felt his sense of balance slipping away. He started to fall over. Bluesky fluttered his wings frantically and quickly righted himself. He now crouched low to the ground so he could more easily maintain his delicate balance.

He groaned inside. He felt so embarrassed when he had to flutter his wings to keep himself from falling over.

Most of the birds hopped farther away from him. Most pretended to hunt for seed now, but they continued to cast furtive glances at Bluesky.

Three Sparrows, however, remained close by along with Treeflower. They seemed unaffected by his disability.

Bluesky felt shame and embarrassment because of the murmuring and stares of the others that had hopped away, but Nightwind had sent him on a journey, and he was determined to complete it.

"I hate that myth," the nearest Sparrow said.

"Me too. It's degrading."

"Well, you know how most birds feel about us," Treeflower added.

"How do they feel?" Bluesky asked.

They looked at him a moment in shock. "Why, they think we're just little brown birds. Even worse, they think we're the least of all birds," Treeflower said with a hint of sadness.

"Yeah, they've thought that for all time," another said.

Bluesky felt their sadness inside his own heart. He knew what it felt like to be treated in that fashion -- to be looked down upon and viewed as something ugly, as something different.

"I don't feel that way about you," Bluesky said emphatically.

"Really?" Treeflower said with surprise. "You are different from other Mockingbirds."

"Yeah, most of the time you Mockingbirds are so haughty" Before the male Sparrow could finish, Treeflower shoved him with her wing. He looked at her in surprise but noticed her stern expression.

"Okay, okay," he said. "It's wrong for me to stereotype Mockingbirds by saying they're all haughty. That's what the other birds are doing to us when they say we all look alike. I can see that this Mockingbird isn't that way."

The four Sparrows nodded agreement.

"So, Mockingbird --"

"Bluesky, that's my name. I'm sorry, I didn't introduce myself."

"My name is Littleclouds," the Sparrow to his right said. He was the one who had spoken first, almost calling Bluesky haughty.

"My name is Seedfinder," another Sparrow to his left said.

"My name is Treesinger." The last Sparrow nodded happily.

Bluesky looked from one to other and smiled, and each smiled back at him.

"And guess what?" Seedfinder asked. "Each of us is a different kind of Sparrow. Can you tell?"

Bluesky felt his heart suddenly beat rapidly. Seedfinder's words felt like a test of some kind, and Bluesky was never good with tests, especially when put on the spot. But that was part of his journey, to determine that all Sparrows didn't look alike.

He hopped closer to Seedfinder.

"Hey, why don't you put down your other leg?" Seedfinder asked. "It looks like you might fall over at any minute."

Bluesky felt his old fear return. He felt that once he told them the truth, they would reject him just like all the other birds, but he saw no way around it.

"I-I only have one leg." Bluesky hung his head in shame. "That's why Mockingbirds look down on me. That's why none of them will play with me. That's why none of them will be my friend."

Treeflower walked up until she was right beside Bluesky, who continued to stare at the ground, preparing himself for their rejection.

"That's all right. We don't care if you only have one leg."

"Really?" Now it was Bluesky's turn to stare at her in amazement.

"C'mon, see if you can tell how I'm different from Treeflower," Seedfinder prompted with a smile.

Both Treeflower and Seedfinder hopped in a circle, displaying their feathers to him. Once again, his attention was drawn to the fact that both birds were primarily covered with brown feathers with patterns of black feathers interspersed with a few patches of white feathers, especially white wing bars.

From the back, they looked alike -- but Nightwind had firmly stated this was a lie!

Bluesky looked closer.

At just that moment, Treeflower hopped around to face him again with her beak opened in a happy smile. He glanced from her to Seedfinder, who also faced him.

He noticed a difference!

Treeflower had brown streaks of feathers all over her breast and belly, but right in the center some of the streaks converged into a small brown spot. On the other wing, Seedfinder had a chest and belly of gray feathers!

Treeflower was larger too. In fact, she was almost twice the size of the other three.

He realized something else: Seedfinder's head was crowned with alternating black and white stripes. In addition, he had a patch of bright yellow feathers between his eyes and the back of his beak while a patch of bright white feathers graced his throat.

Treeflower on the other hand had a gray eyebrow stripe and two brown stripes of feathers on her throat.

Happily, he told them what made each of them different from the other.

"Yes! Seedfinder is a White-Throated Sparrow. They come south during the cold months to feed with us here. I am a Song Sparrow." Treeflower congratulated Bluesky heartily on his keen observations.

"What about us! Do you see how Treesinger and I are different from them!" Littleclouds chirped excitedly.

At first glance, Littleclouds looked exactly like the White-throated Sparrow. Then Bluesky he looked harder.

Yes! He saw it.

Littleclouds had two stripes of black feathers on his head, similar to Seedfinder, but on the top of his head, Littleclouds sported a white crown of feathers. Unlike Seedfinder he didn't have a white throat nor a small spot of yellow. Otherwise, they were very nearly identical!

Still, he noticed how Littleclouds jumped around with more energy than Seedfinder. He stood with a different posture as well.

Bluesky proudly described how Littleclouds was different.

"Right!" Littleclouds twinkled. "I'm a White-Crowned Sparrow."

"What about me!" Treesinger sang out.

This time the difference literally jumped out at Bluesky -- or maybe it was because he knew how to focus and distinguish the subtle differences between these Sparrows now?

Treesinger also had a clean, gray breast like the White-Crowned and White-Throated Sparrow, but he was different in that he had a chestnut cap with a black eye stripe and directly above it a white eyebrow stripe of feathers.

"You're right!" Treesinger sang gleefully after Bluesky related his discovery. "I'm a Chipping Sparrow."

Inside his heart, Bluesky felt gladness. He could now easily discern the differences in these four types of Sparrows. He felt certain that he could explain it to Nightwind.

He still wasn't sure how this was going to help him make friends with Mockingbirds, but at least it was fun.

Now he had to find something beautiful about Sparrows and something good about each of these particular birds.

Immediately, he felt the feather patterns and stripes of Treesinger, Littleclouds, and Seedfinder were each beautiful in their own way. But Treeflower was just kind of brown all over ...

Still, he had noticed some beautiful things about Mourning Doves. He watched Treeflower closer as she hopped around on the ground searching for more seed.

Several minutes passed, and Bluesky still couldn't discern anything.

Suddenly, Treeflower took wing and flew up to a high branch in a nearby pine. She threw her head back, lowered her tail, and sang out.

While her beautiful trills and chirps and twitters laced the wind, Bluesky realized why they were called Song Sparrows.

Yes, her singing was beautiful!

Bluesky listened a moment in rapturous appreciation. Finally, he did what any self-respecting Mockingbird would do -- he sang back to her, imitating her song.

For a few minutes, Treeflower and Bluesky sang out to each other with happy songs. When Treeflower realized it was Bluesky singing with her, though, and not one of her own kind, she flew down to him with a scowl on her face.

"Are you mocking me?" she said with an edge to her voice.

"No, no. I felt so happy, I wanted to sing *with you*," Bluesky explained.

"Why didn't you sing a Mockingbird song?"

"Haven't you heard 'imitation is the sincerest form of flattery'?"

Treeflower laughed out loud. "You sure are different than most Mockingbirds, Bluesky. Most of the time, they only want to show off and prove they can out-sing any bird alive, but you're not like that."

"I just want to sing with you and have fun. You sing pretty, and, and ... I wanted to sing with you. It's more fun to sing with another bird than all by yourself."

"I like singing with you too. I hope you come back again so we can sing some more."

"I-I will try," Bluesky said, pleasantly surprised at her invitation.

He was impressed at how nice she was to him. In fact, he realized she was nice to every bird. She seemed to exude kindness and made any bird feel at ease when in her company.

Bluesky liked her even more.

In fact, all the Sparrows talked with him as if he were one of them -- another Sparrow!

Bluesky thoroughly enjoyed the company of these little brown birds. He stayed with them for quite some time. He hunted for bugs close by while they hopped on the ground searching for seed. And if any of them sang, he would fly up to a tree branch and sing with them, imitating their Sparrow songs with joyous appreciation.

The afternoon shadows slowly lengthened as evening drew near again. Bluesky had lost track of time in the happy company of these birds. While he continued to observe the birds around him, he failed to notice the fading light and lengthening shadows. The shadows grew darker, and the bushes and trees blurred together.

Somewhere in a tree high above, a Chickadee squeaked its warning urgently.

Suddenly, several more birds whistled and twittered with the same sense of urgency.

A few moments later, Bluesky realized they were crying out a warning of danger!

Just as Bluesky focused to listen, his whole world turned upside down.

A terrible pain pressed against his side, and as he clenched his eyes shut he realized to his horror that he couldn't breathe!

The sharp pains pressed harder until he felt his skin pierced.

Bluesky tried to scream, but he couldn't utter a sound -- he couldn't even breathe. He was being crushed to death!

He gasped finally after the pressure surprisingly eased and sweet air rushed into his burning lungs. Bluesky groaned and swooned as everything went out of focus.

Without warning, the pain completely subsided.

As he slowly regained consciousness, he realized he was lying on the ground. At least the terrible pressure and sharp barbs were gone!

All above him, he heard birds crying out more and more warnings of danger.

A shadow suddenly covered Bluesky.

When he opened his eyes and looked up, a large, yellow-striped cat with piercing green eyes peered down at him.

"Yes, you've been caught, stupid bird. And not by just any cat either."

With a sickening dread, Bluesky realized this was the cat that every bird in the neighborhood feared most.

"Yes, I see you recognize me." The cat purred arrogantly. "I am called Tiger, but the birds know me as the 'Great Hunter' because I catch so many of you!" The cat laughed with an evil hiss.

"W-what are you going to do with me?" Bluesky gasped under the pressing weight of the cat's forepaw after Tiger placed it on him again.

Tiger's green eyes flashed dangerously. He closed them until they were mere slits and then purred his answer with deadly earnestness. "I'm going to play with you. And when I tire of that -- I'm going to kill you!"

Chapter Five

Mark drove down Anneewakee Road with his friend Walter sitting in the passenger seat looking out the window at the trees.

They were trying to make contact for the third time with a man on their list. The man's name was Charles Marcion. The reason he was on the list provided by the county office was that he had owned a fertilizer distribution business from 1985 up until 1992.

More interesting, and the main reason he appeared on the list, was that his business had been part of a class-action suit due to a 'bad batch' of fertilizer. The resulting litigation had been enough to put him and his small company out of business.

Part of the ruling against Marcion and Company had required the proper disposal of the toxic materials.

"Toxic fertilizer!" Walter exclaimed. "How could fertilizer be toxic?"

Mark looked over, and Walter shook his head for emphasis. "I have no idea, Walt. I've never heard of it before. I just hope we get to talk to this guy today."

As they rounded a curve, the forest of trees on each side grew denser.

"You know, I'm sure glad we don't live in one of those newer subdivisions where they clear-cut all the trees first and then build the houses." Walter rubbed his chin.

"Builders can put in more houses that way. Still,

trees would help the homeowners keep their cooling bills down in the summer," Mark said.

"Sure -- my house is totally in the shade by three o'clock each day. I bet my bill would be double without the shade."

"I like it because it seems like our houses are islands amid a sea of trees." Mark smiled.

"You've got nice little stretches of wood on two sides of your property, right, Mark?"

"Yes. It almost feels like I'm not in a subdivision except for the house to our left and across the street."

"Slow down -- here it comes." Walter sat up and peered ahead.

The gravel drive appeared. The other two times they'd tried to make contact, a metal gate had been locked tight across the driveway and prevented them from going any further.

"Maybe this time," Mark said with a faint twinge of hope, but when he turned his car off the road, he stopped with a crunch of gravel right before the closed metal gate.

"I can't believe it," Walter groaned. "Isn't this guy ever home?"

"He's got an unlisted number too." Mark tapped the steering wheel with his fingers in a rapid rhythm, staring with frustration at the gate. He suddenly realized the gate was simply to keep cars out. The gate was standalone and not attached to a fence on either side. He came to a decision.

"Walt, you stay with the car. I'm going to walk around the gate and down the drive. I'll leave the keys here."

"You think he locks the gate behind him whenever he leaves?"

"I don't know."

"But you can't even see the house from here."

Indeed, as they both stared down the gravel drive, they could see that half a mile away it curved to the right and seemingly disappeared into the forest.

"I bet this guy's got a mansion sitting nice and pretty surrounded by woods." Walter chuckled.

"Perhaps." Mark stepped out of the car. He walked up to the gate, around the right post, and onto the other side. He turned back to Walter, who remained in the passenger seat.

"I bet it's a just an old double-wide trailer that doesn't even have A/C."

He and Walter laughed.

"Anyway, I'll let you know when I get back." Mark's shoes crunched over the gravel as he started down the drive.

"I've got my cell phone on. Call me if you get in trouble." Walter smiled when Mark glanced over his shoulder.

"What kind of trouble can I get into? I'm just walking up to a guy's house." Mark continued forward at a brisk pace.

Mark looked around at the dense stand of trees on either side of the gravel driveway. He guessed this guy must own at least fifteen or twenty acres. After all, there were no other houses near this drive. Mark wondered if Marcion appreciated living in the midst of nature like this. He continued down the gravel path and enjoyed the silent woods on either

71

side.

When he approached the curve a good half mile from the car, he turned again and waved back to Walter. He could just make out Walter's wave from the open car window.

With a deep breath, he rounded the curve, and his car and friend disappeared from view.

Just as he feared, the drive stretched on another full half mile with no house in sight, curving back to the left further up. It almost felt as if nobody lived out here, but utility poles with wires paralleled the drive, so he knew someone lived back there somewhere.

Mark suddenly felt very isolated. He wondered now if this was such a good idea or not. He pulled out his cell phone and checked the signal. He was down to two bars already, and as he reached the second curve, it dropped down to the last bar.

Mark placed the phone back on his belt. He marched around the bend and stopped dead in his tracks.

A rusted-out pickup truck, something from the seventies, sat silent on the left side of the gravel drive. All four tires had rotted off the hubs, and most of the windshield had been busted out. The driver's door lay on the ground beside the dilapidated wreck.

He walked closer, and now he could see that the seats had been ripped up by a knife; even the dash was sliced open in dozens of places -- shredded in anger or disgust. The floor board was covered by a layer of broken glass from the windshield in addition to broken shards of countless bottles of beer.

Mark walked along the wreck, looked inside the truck bed, and stopped in surprise.

Broken beer bottles, crushed aluminum beer cans, and countless crushed cigarette packs filled the bed of the truck almost to the top. He now noticed the broken glass and other trash that littered the ground all around the wreck.

It seemed Charles Marcion used this rusted truck as a kind of garbage can, perhaps throwing them into it when he walked by.

Or drove by?

He shook his head. He certainly hoped this man wasn't drinking and driving on his way out toward the main road ... or coming back!

He now noticed dozens of holes spread all across the rusted metal body of the truck -- bullet holes.

He looked around carefully, but he still didn't see a house, though now the forest faded into a grassy field on either side of the drive. In the far distance, he saw a tall tree line, and just beyond them he recognized the tops some metal electric towers. He guessed those metal towers were the same ones that stood next to the new subdivision just down the road from his own neighborhood.

In reality, this place was only about three miles from his own home -- as the crow flew. By staying to the roads, however, he had driven over twice that distance to get here.

He stepped forward with a crunch of gravel.

Several dogs howled angrily, and Mark felt the hairs on the back of his neck stand up.

They sounded like large dogs -- and suddenly he heard them running on the gravel and coming for him although he couldn't see them!

He froze with his heart beating like a jackhammer, realizing he had nowhere to run for protection.

As he looked around for somewhere to retreat, he heard a man's voice shout in the distance. "Bear! King! What is it, dogs?"

After a second's pause, the next words caused a chill of fear. "Go get it, big dawgs! Go get'em!"

He heard the dogs begin to run in earnest and realized with a sickening feeling that he was completely vulnerable, with no place to hide and no where to run. The dogs would be on top of him any second.

Mark stood his ground, his heart feeling like it would leap right out of his chest while he chided himself.

Suddenly, a German shepherd and a huge, black Rottweiler rounded the corner.

The dogs slowed and then stopped when they realized Mark wasn't moving. He noticed how their eyes became slits and that the hair stood up on their necks. Even worse, their howls and barks now changed to ominous growls.

Slowly, the two hunters spread out and closed on Mark with bared fangs.

The two dogs were stalking him now, planning their attack.

He pulled out his cell phone and glanced down at it -- all the bars were gone. He put the phone back and stared from one dog to the other, never letting his eyes stay on one too long in case the other decided to attack.

His racing heart skipped a beat when another distinctive growl came to his ear -- a growl so powerful it vibrated the air ...

This ominous growl was more powerful than the others combined. The terrifying sound rolled through the air again.

In his mind, Mark imagined something huge was about to come into view around the corner. He felt his knees begin to wobble while electric bolts of panic and adrenaline shot through his body. He staggered backwards.

The terrifyingly ominous growl reverberated again.

Suddenly, he saw it.

It was the largest and ugliest dog he'd ever seen.

The dog was huge. Its massive head rose chest high; powerful muscles rippled across its shoulders and back as it came steadily toward him.

Mark stared in silent awe; the animal must weigh as much as he did.

As it drew near, the dog lowered its head and laid back its ears. Mark couldn't tell what breed it was. In fact, the closer it came, the more it seemed like some kind of horrible, canine abomination.

Its short fur was mingled brown and black over its entire body. It gave the dog a 'wild' look, as if it was feral.

And then Mark saw the scars.

An old scar crossed its face from just above its right eye and down its cheek. A number of smaller scars crisscrossed its face and neck, each a hairless and jagged of line of bare flesh that told of past battles.

Mark somehow knew that this huge dog had won them all.

The big dog closed fearlessly.

The other two dogs continued to encircle him. All three animals growled so ominously that the sound flicked some kind of switch inside his mind. An overpowering urge to run filled every fiber in his being like a thousand volts of raw electricity.

He knew that would be the worst thing he could now -- run from them. He stood completely still, clenching his fists as beads of sweat dripped down his face.

Mark was so intent looking from one dog to the next he never heard the approach of the man.

"Whut do yew want?"

He jerked with surprise at the unexpected words.

The man laughed at him. "Guess yew'll think twice next time before yer come up a man's private drive now, eh?" he said with a condescending tone.

Mark stared at the large pistol holstered on the man's hip.

The German shepherd, sensing Mark's helplessness, suddenly charged forward.

Mark turned and put up his arms up in self-defense.

"King! Down boy!"

The shepherd stopped immediately on command.

The man turned to the Rottweiler. "Bear! Down boy," he commanded with brutal authority. The

Rottweiler stopped growling and sat down, though his black eyes never left Mark.

The monster bulldog uttered one last, ominous growl and then stood stoically beside the man.

"Good dog, Jack."

Mark stared at the man and spoke. "Are you Charles Marcion?"

"Whut of it?"

Charles Marcion was a tall man, probably six-foot-three. He was too thin for a man that tall, though. His clothes hung off him as if several sizes too large. His gaunt face and bone-thin arms made him look like a living scarecrow. With his pale, almost translucent skin and the emotionless look in his eyes, he seemed more dead than alive.

Marcion wore a red plaid shirt, discolored with countless stains. His jeans were also covered by untold layers of dirt, grime, and ancient stains that appeared to have been washed over and over until they were now part of the very fabric.

Mark looked up at the man's face.

Based on a few sparse patches of color, his short hair must have been jet-black back in his youth, an untold age ago. Now, it was mostly a dirty gray. A solid gray goatee etched his chin into a sharp point while the rest of the man's face was grizzled with about two days' growth of matching stubble.

His face and neck were lined with a spider web of wrinkles like a jigsaw puzzle.

He laughed again, and Mark noticed his yellowed teeth, discolored no doubt from decades of smoking cigarettes.

But it was the haggard man's eyes that sent a

chill throughout Mark's body. They were wild and bloodshot. They were so red it gave him an unnatural appearance, almost as if his eyes had no white at all. They were just bloody red and ...

"I'll ask ya agin, meester. Whut'cha want here?"

A terrifying thought made Mark's heart freeze with fear. *This man was crazy ... and he had a gun.*

Charles Marcion rubbed his chin a moment. Right as he opened his mouth to speak, Bear bellowed forth.

"Shaddup, Bear!" He spat at the Rottweiler and laughed when it leaped aside to avoid the wet missile.

"If you don't mind my asking," Mark asked. "What kind of dog is that?" He nodded at the mongrel bulldog.

"He's a special one, ain't he?" Marcion chuckled with pride. "He's a cross-breed twixt a mastiff and a pit bull. Ol' Jack here, he's my big dawg!"

Mark shook his head in disbelief, though the facts fit the dog's terrifying form.

"Now, why are yew here. Ya ain't from the guv'ment, are ya?"

"No," Mark said with surprising calm.

"Good. Ya ain't selling nuthin', are ya?"

"No."

"Good. Then what'cha doin' on my property?"

"I-I came to talk ..." Mark hesitated to add that he wanted to ask him about the court case twenty years ago.

"Talk? Whut about?"

"I'm your neighbor."

Charles Marcion's red eyes stared, unflinching.

"I wanted to make sure you've heard the warnings," Mark continued.

"Warnin's?"

"You've heard about the babies who've died? And the miscarriages? There could be danger for all of us living here if we don't find the source soon."

Marcion scratched his gray stubble a moment. "Yeah, I heard sumthin'."

The monster bulldog yawned with boredom, showing off his fangs as saliva dribbled down each side of his sagging lower lips.

This seemed to settle things for Charles Marcion. "C'mon then. Yew kin tell me what you came to say."

He turned and started walking away.

Immediately, the three large dogs lumbered to their feet and trotted after him as if Mark no longer existed.

Mark stood a moment in total shock, wondering if he should just turn and leave.

No, he'd come this far, and Charles Marcion was the last man on the list provided by the County Commission to the citizens group working with them.

Mark walked forward with a determined step.

Rounding another bend, they came to Charles Marcion's home.

It was the filthiest trailer he'd ever seen. Every window was either boarded up or had broken glass. The windows with broken glass were crudely taped over in a hopeless attempt of repair. He couldn't even tell what color the trailer had been originally because a thick coating of dirt covered it completely.

The door hung open at a precarious angle on its lower hinge, the only hinge still holding it to the trailer.

Outside the front door, several chairs sat in a semi-circle under a small shade tree. Just on the other side of the tree, three more rusted-out truck bodies rested in various states of ruin, each one filled with broken bottles like the first. Everywhere, litter and trash of every description was strewn.

It was if Charles Marcion and his dogs had perfected life amid squalor and filth.

When they stepped closer toward the door, a morbid scent of filth emanated from inside the trailer.

Mark stopped in his tracks, hoping against hope that Marcion didn't want to go inside and talk.

Marcion glanced back at him and caught Mark gaping at the trailer. "Home sweet home, eh."

Mark closed his mouth, still speechless.

"Let's sit here under my shade tree. It's warmed up nice today. I'm glad we don't believe in winters here in Jawja." Charles bared his yellowed teeth in a crooked smile, sitting down in one of the rickety chairs.

"Yes." Mark started to wipe the dirt off the chair but figured it might be coating something worse below it, so he just sat down. He looked around at Marcion's land. "How many acres do you have here, Mister Marcion?"

"Eh? Oh, call me Charlie." Charlie reached inside his shirt pocket and pulled out a pack of cigarettes. After he struck the match and held it up, both his hands shook so badly it took him three tries to light the end of the cigarette dangling from his pale lips. He took a deep drag and blew out the blue smoke. Charlie then coughed so hard it seemed he would go into convulsions.

Mark waited, wondering if the man was ever going to stop coughing.

Charlie finally hacked up some phlegm and spit a wad twenty feet away. Satisfied, he took another long drag. As he spoke, blue smoke filtered out of his mouth and nostrils.

"About twenty acres. Been in mah family a long time. Almost everyone I know round here has sold off to the builders and moved away -- but not me."

"I know -- I didn't think anyone owned this much land around here any longer," Mark said.

"I hate it. Ten, twenty years ago, I knew almost everyone who lived in this county. All of 'em from the South, all of 'em lived their entire life here." He took another drag. "Now, it seems half the folks are furriners. Most from overseas or from out west. Or worse..."

Mark paused, afraid to ask who worse might be.

"All them stinkin' yankees have moved down here."

"Atlanta's seen an influx of people from all over the world since we hosted the Olympics," Mark agreed. "I like it. Atlanta feels like an international city now."

"I hate it." Charlie's hand shook as he brought the cigarette to his mouth again. He took such a long drag that the ash curved down from the end. He flicked it off and continued. "I go to buy sumthin' and can't hardly understand what they say. And they're always talkin' on their cell phones in a furrin language like they're tryin' to hide sumthin'." He shook his head angrily. "Too many furriners."

"I don't judge anyone by the color of their skin or what language they speak," Mark said. "As long as they're decent people, that's what important."

"Huh?" Charlie grunted. He finished the cigarette, pulled out another, and lit it with the first one before he discarded the original on the ground.

"Yew ain't a Southerner, are ya'?" Charlie asked.

Mark sat up in his chair. "I was born in Charleston, South Carolina, and grew up in Summerville. I lived my early life in the Lowcountry. I moved to Marietta, Georgia, when my company transferred me in 1985. I moved to Douglasville a few years later." Mark peered unflinching at Charlie Marcion a moment.

A look of intense distaste filled Marcion's face.

"I'm from the South -- born and raised." Mark smiled.

"Yew ain't no *true* Southerner." Charlie spat out. "Anyway, I don't care about no Atlanta, it's just a big city. I jest care about here, my place. And me!"

Mark decided to change the subject and get to the reason for his visit. After all, Charlie Marcion was obviously someone stuck in the past and only concerned with his selfish priorities.

"I'm here because the county fears there could be some kind of poison or some kind of pollution that's causing the deaths."

"Whut's that got to do with me?"

"You were part of a fertilizer business that

operated in Douglasville back in the eighties. There was a court case about some toxic fertilizer --"

Charlie Marcion jumped out of his chair.

Mark sat very still, since all three dogs, up to this point all lying down as if they were asleep, now raised their heads and started growling again.

"I thought you said you weren't from the guv'ment?"

"I'm not. I'm part of a civic group helping --"

"Listen!" Charlie's voice shook with anger. "I lost a lot of money over that stuff. I almost lost my home and land, Gawd forbid!"

Mark glanced around at the filth and trash of Marcion's home.

Charlie now erupted into a long tirade of curses. Mark tuned out the words and tuned out the man's anger. He did his best to maintain his composure. After all, if he got angry in return, things could quickly get out of hand, and he didn't want that. He wanted information -- that was all.

Finally, Charlie's anger lessened until the foul language dissipated to every fifth word he uttered. Almost in an apologetic tone now, Charlie continued.

"Listen, I had no idea about that toxic stuff! Me and my brother were distributors of fertilizer they made up in the Midwest. We sold it mainly to the farmers down in south Jawja. We had the contacts on both ends -- bought it cheap and sold it at a good price. We had no idea it would kill all them cattle and ruin the land like that!"

Mark's mind reeled a moment. Once again, he tried to fathom how fertilizer could become toxic enough that it could kill animals and ruin land.

"I guess the farmers sued your company?" Mark asked, trying to think of what to say next.

"Sued us for everything. And we had to 'properly' dispose of the stuff on top of that, though the fertilizer makers paid fer the most of it." Charlie took another angry drag of his cigarette.

"Which landfill did you put it?"

"Couldn't use any of them here! We had to put them up in special barrels and then get'em ready for the trucks. Guv'ment folks took it ... let's see, yeah, took'em to sumthin' called a Super Site. Yeah, that's what they called it." Marcion paused a moment, and smiled with a twinkle in his eyes.

"They dumped it sumwhere in L.A.," he said cryptically.

"In Lower Alabama," Mark replied without a pause, familiar with the acronym.

"Yep." Marcion chuckled as his bloodshot eyes twinkled crazily.

Mark rubbed his chin in thought. "So none of it wound up in any of the local landfills in Douglas County?"

Charlie Marcion's face grew puzzled a moment while his red eyes stared off in the distance. Suddenly, he started pacing in a circle around the German shepherd. After Charlie circled King once, the dog jumped up and scurried off behind the tree. The other two dogs, sensing a change in the air, joined King.

"I got rid of it all. Even if it did cost me dearly."

"Where did you store it before the trucks came for it?"

"We had a warehouse up by the railroad tracks, next to Bankhead Highway near downtown."

"None of it is here in Douglas County now?"

"Not one barrel!" He shouted angrily and then coughed before he continued in a more calm voice. "I was ordered to have it packed up in metal barrels, and then we shipped it all out. A hundred and forty-four barrels. We had to wear masks and gloves and everythin'!"

"Would you be willing to come with me to the next meeting --"

"I ain't going to no meetin'!"

"I just want --"

"Nope! Ain't gonna get involved. You tell'em so at the meetin'."

"Charlie," Mark asked in a pleading tone, "in a time of crisis, all the citizens need to help one another. All I'm asking is for you to review the records and --"

"It's not my concern."

"It should concern you. You live here."

"I got everythin' I need here. Ain't nobody dyin' on my place."

"We need each other, Charlie."

"Cheap beer, cheap cigarettes, and cheap women. That's all I need."

Mark sat speechless.

He tried to think of another way to reason with Charlie, to reach his heart and touch his compassion.

"Time fer you to leave." Without another word, Charlie stormed away and disappeared inside his trailer in a cloud of dust.

Mark watched him a moment and quickly realized he wasn't coming back out. In another second, he realized that all three dogs were eyeing him suspiciously from the other side of the tree.

He rose carefully, watching the dogs.

All three dogs sat in total silence, watching his every move.

Mark decided to walk slowly and steadily back down the gravel drive.

He glanced over his shoulder from time to time to make sure none of the dogs got up to follow him. After he rounded the first bend and out of sight of the dogs, he felt a huge sense of relief.

He kept his pace steady and listened out for any movement from behind. After what seemed an eternity, he made it back to the car.

"How'd that go?" Walter asked.

Mark rolled his eyes. "I met him."

"What was he like?"

"He's a little strange..."

"I bet. Did he tell you about the fertilizer incident?"

"Yes, he did. He got very angry about it."

"Did he dispose of it like the reports say? None of it's here?"

"He said that he did. And that's what the county records report."

"Well, I guess that's that." Walter rolled his window up, and Mark started the engine.

Mark felt a twinge of disappointment. Walter was right. Charles Marcion had been the last name on their list. He knew the others on the team were near the end of their research as well. And although some of the field tests of the air and water had shown a few spikes, none had been conclusive enough to focus a thorough search in any specific locale.

Whatever was killing unborn babies and causing deformities in others was still out there somewhere.

And it was a threat to everyone - especially the children.

***

Our Feathered Friends of the Southeast
A. C. Wages

Eastern Towhee
Latin: *Pipilo erythrophthalmus*

(excerpts)

At first glance, a novice may think they've spotted an American robin.

But observe closely ...

The eastern towhee is smaller and slimmer than a robin. Though its feathers are similar in color and pattern, a keen eye quickly detects the differences.

This handsome bird sports a hood of jet-black feathers over its head and also over its back, wings, and tail. Rufous brown feathers cover its sides and flanks while its chest and belly are solid white. The most distinctive feature of the towhee is its eyes -- these are a striking red.

The female is patterned exactly the same with the sole exception that she wears brown feathers in place of the male's jet-black feathers, and, yes, her eyes are the same fantastic red color.

The towhee is one of the largest members in the sparrow family, a surprising fact to people new to birdwatching.

Being quite shy, the towhee is oftentimes heard long before it is seen.

Like most birds, the towhee has both its own personal call and its own personal song. Its call consists of two notes, each note drawn out and often transcribed as *toe-weeee* (hence the name of the bird). A towhee will repeat this two-note call in rapid succession with only a brief pause in between.

This author has personally whistled back in reply to its call, and almost every time the towhee has answered. In fact, most birds will call back if you whistle in imitation, almost as if it is some kind of game to them.

The towhee's song is sometimes transcribed as *drink your tee-eeee-eeeee*. The first note is a fast-rising whistle while the second note is drawn out and descending. The last part is a tinkling trill (or perhaps a wavering warbling).

This wonderful creature is a bird of the thick brush. It also has a quite peculiar way of scratching through thick piles of leaves in search of seed and insects. Again, you are likely to hear its eager foraging long before you spot a towhee. However, if you are patient, you are likely to spot a towhee exhibiting its famous two-footed scratching technique as it searches for seed among loose leaves.

Its diet consists of wild fruit, seeds, insects,

grubs, and worms. Although this author has never seen a towhee eat birdseed directly out of a bird feeder, if you spread birdseed on the ground, a towhee will come and eat it there.

Alas, there are no famous quotes specific to this wonderful bird of the brush. References by Native American tribes are also lacking. The only historical reference this author found stated that the naturalist Mark Catesby first studied the towhee in 1731 in the Carolinas and named the bird after its famous call.

Even more surprising, not a single American state has designated the eastern towhee as a state bird. Perhaps one day this beautiful bird will be honored with such a distinction.

This author can truthfully say that this common but timid bird is one of his personal favorites. Listen for its distinctive call and observe them for yourself; perhaps you will soon share my humble opinion about this handsome bird.

Chapter Six

"Leave that bird alone!" a new cat said in a serious tone after it suddenly appeared.

"Go away, KC. And take Buddy with you, before somebody gets hurt." Tiger growled threateningly.

Bluesky watched in surprise while the three cats eyed each other angrily.

KC uttered a low growl to emphasize her intentions. On the other side, Buddy snarled his own displeasure.

Bluesky's heart hammered fearfully. Now he was surrounded by three cats, and they were about to fight in order to figure out which one got the pleasure of killing him. He knew without a doubt he would die. He tried to close his eyes, but the fierce growls and chilling hisses kept him mesmerized.

He watched the cats almost unwillingly.

"This is my bird. I caught him. And I'll kill him." Tiger lashed his tail angrily as he flattened his ears and hissed back at them.

"This is our yard, and we don't want you here," KC growled. She also flattened her ears.

"KC, how can hope to fight me? You're so much smaller. Besides, you're a girl." Tiger laughed.

"She won't fight you alone."

Tiger whipped around and hissed in surprise when Buddy hissed threateningly.

"What is it? You want to steal my trophy? It'll take more than both of you to defeat me!" Tiger snarled.

"No, I don't want the bird," KC said in a matter-of-fact tone.

"What?" Tiger and Buddy said together in surprise.

"You're crazy, KC," Tiger crooned sarcastically. "And I won't leave this yard. It's part of my territory."

Crouching and flattening her ears, KC uttered a low, threatening growl.

Tiger prepared for her attack.

Instead, Buddy attacked first.

Tiger howled wildly and lashed out with his claws.

Buddy shrieked with a mixture of anger and fear as he faced the larger cat. He lashed with his claws, but Tiger used his superior size and closed with the smaller cat.

Buddy now wailed in fear after Tiger shoved him to the ground. The two cats clawed and bit at each other, each one sending small patches of fur flying into the air.

Tiger opened his mouth and hissed loudly, revealing his fangs. Buddy half-heartedly hissed back from the ground under the shadow of the yellow cat.

Tiger lunged at Buddy, but he stopped short when KC attacked from the side.

He turned and howled at her in surprise as she closed.

Both cats clawed wildly at each other, each aiming their blows at the other's face. But each cat was fast, moving and avoiding direct blows although their sharpened claws sent more fur into the air. Surprisingly, although the air was full of growls and hisses and fur, no blood had been drawn.

"Enough!" Tiger growled. "Now feel the wrath of my teeth and claws, puny girl!"

Tiger leapt at KC in order to bring her down and bite her savagely.

KC backed up slightly, and then to Tiger's utter surprise she lashed out!

Tiger howled in pain when her claws struck across his sensitive nose. Two bloody wounds dripped crimson streaks, and Tiger pulled up short.

The big cat rubbed his foreleg across his wounds. He looked down in surprise at the blood on his foreleg. Tiger's howls now changed into a low, angry growl. He crouched low in order to attack with his ears completely flattened against his head.

"I'm going to kill you for that," Tiger hissed.

KC faced the bigger cat and hissed back. "I am the black and white panther. Attack me if you dare!"

"And I am the black lion," Buddy growled from behind Tiger. "That's a panther and a lion against one tiger!"

"You're not a fighter, Buddy. Go away, or I'll kill you too."

Buddy lunged and bit at Tiger's shoulder, but Tiger had expected such a foolish move. He turned toward the attack, and Buddy's teeth bit into nothing but fur.

Now Tiger bit down through Buddy's long, black fur until his sharp fangs found flesh.

Buddy's piercing howl of pain sent birds flying away in all directions from where they had been watching the fight in morbid fascination.

Tiger gnawed angrily, trying to sink his fangs deeper. He used his superior weight and pushed Buddy down onto the ground.

He jerked his head and bit deeper.

Buddy shrieked horribly. Although Buddy was more of a lover than a fighter, his instincts took over. Using the claws on his hind legs, he kicked and clawed with all his might. One of Buddy's fierce kicks sent his claws into Tiger's soft belly.

Tiger howled with pain and he loosed his hold on Buddy's shoulder. Blood dripped on the ground from where Buddy had slashed him across his belly.

"I'm going to --" Tiger didn't finish.

KC lashed out with her claws, slashing at Tiger's bleeding nose again. He tried to move back but felt Buddy again kicking out at him. Tiger jumped away from Buddy's blows.

Unfortunately, he jumped right into KC's attack.

KC and Tiger fell together, biting angrily at each other. KC avoided Tiger's teeth again and again as she sought to sink her teeth into him!

She clawed at Tiger's left eye. When he twisted away, she lunged at his right ear and bit down hard.

Tiger pushed her away, hissing in pain, but KC held on, her teeth ripping his ear.

Buddy lunged and bit into Tiger's hind leg.

Tiger hissed louder, jerking himself away from both his attackers.

He ran for the fence and cleared it in a single bound. He landed hard on the ground and rolled over in a heap. He jumped up an entire foot into the air as if he expected both KC and Buddy to be right on top of him. When he realized he was alone, he wiped his foreleg across his bleeding ear in an effort to ease the terrible pain.

When he withdrew his foreleg, it was covered in crimson.

"I'm going to get you for this, KC and Buddy!" Tiger howled, more in pain than anger.

KC charged for the fence.

Tiger turned tail and ran for his life. He ran into the cover of the small patch of woods and never looked back.

"Well, I hope he understands this is our territory now." KC sat and licked nonchalantly at a couple of minor scratches on her leg. Pleased with her efforts, she started cleaning herself with a gentle air of confidence.

"Owwww," Buddy said after he tried to stand. He lay back down and licked the wounds on his shoulder.

"Are you hurt badly?" KC asked, stopping her personal cleaning.

"My shoulder -- it hurts!"

"You need to go inside and show Dad. He will make it better." KC licked her foreleg and rubbed it gently across her cheek.

Buddy rose unsteadily. He placed his weight on his right foreleg to test it.

He winced. "I think I'm all right."

"Go in the house and let Dad look at you."

Buddy took a few painful steps toward the house. "It hurts worse when I walk."

"Go inside."

Buddy limped toward the front of the house so he could look in the window, hoping someone

94

would see him and let him inside.

KC watched Buddy, trying not to put weight on his injured right shoulder, limp away.

Bluesky had watched the entire battle lying helpless on the ground. Now, he waited for KC to come over and finish Tiger's work.

The black and white kitty continued her efforts to clean herself for several long minutes. She seemed almost unaware that Bluesky was even there. He decided this might be his chance to escape. He slowly raised himself up on his leg.

"You're that one-legged Mockingbird, aren't you?"

Bluesky froze.

He knew there was no escape now. He didn't even know if he could fly, because his right wing still throbbed with pain from Tiger's teeth.

"Yes, I see you are," KC said in answer to her own question. She looked him over with her green eyes a moment. "Can you fly?"

Bluesky said nothing.

"Go on -- you can fly away if you like."

"You just want me to try, so you can catch me and kill me," Bluesky said sadly.

"No, I want you to fly away. I really do."

"You're a cat, and cats love to kill birds."

"Not me. I like birds."

"Yeah, right!" Bluesky said with total disbelief.

"No, it's true. You see that window there?" KC nodded toward the kitchen window, where one of the seed nests hung.

"Yes."

"I like to sit there and watch birds flying around

and eating seed my dad gives them."

"You're kidding!"

"No, I really like birds."

"I don't believe that," Bluesky replied.

"I saved your life, didn't I?"

Bluesky remained silent.

"And I haven't attacked you."

"I don't believe you."

KC began cleaning herself again. After a few moments, she walked over to the patio and sat down in the shade of a bush. She looked over at Bluesky.

"Does your wing feel better now? Try it out, but before you fly away, I would like to ask a favor of you."

"What's that?"

"Come back tomorrow and fly for me."

Bluesky looked at KC with a shocked expression.

"I'll be sitting inside the window looking out. When I see you, I will put my paw on the window and wave at you. Then, you can fly in circles and do some acrobatics and show me how fun it is!"

Bluesky shook his head in disbelief. What a strange request, especially from a cat.

The one-legged Mockingbird spread his wings tentatively.

He winced.

Something was wrong with his right wing. He looked at the bottom and top of it. Yes, several painful scratches were evident, and some of his feathers were torn.

He tried to fully extend his wing but folded it back quickly when the pain grew too much. He slowly moved it, trying to ease out the soreness.

"If you can't fly, you need to hop into the bushes and hide. Although I won't hurt you, Buddy does have a bad habit of catching birds."

"You said he went to your dad. I guess there's another cat around?" Bluesky asked.

"No, Dad is the man who feeds the birds. Cats perceive humans as our parents when they take us to live with them. They feed us, they pet us, and they provide us shelter -- just like our original parents."

"Your dad is a man?"

"Yes."

From a gap in the privacy fence, a small Jack Russell terrier erupted into a series of excited barks. KC and Bluesky looked over at the small dog jumping up and down while it barked continuously at them.

"Dogs perceive their owners as one of the pack or the leader of the pack. We cats, we look at them as our mom and dad who take care of us."

"Why?"

"We're domesticated. We've learned to live with them."

"Why don't you want to kill me -- like most cats?"

KC chuckled a moment. She rose and walked over to Bluesky, who took a single hop backwards in fear.

KC lay down before the Mockingbird and smiled broadly.

"*I wish I could fly.*"

"You what?"

"That's why I like birds. You can fly, and I wish

I could fly. It must be so fun to be able to fly through the air!" KC sighed. "Sometimes when I sleep, I dream that I'm flying!"

Bluesky cocked his head to one side and stared at KC.

"Listen, I need to go inside," she said. "I heard the front door open, and Dad is going to find out Buddy and I have been fighting. He'll call me soon."

Bluesky peered at KC inquisitively.

"I want you to hop on my back, and I'll carry you over to the big bushes. My dad doesn't trim those bushes, and they reach up to the lower branches of the trees. You'll be safe there and can hop on up into the trees until your wing is better," KC meowed.

"You're kidding, right?"

KC licked her front paw and calmly cleaned the other side of her face without answering.

Bluesky took this to mean she was serious. He thought it over a minute and tested his wing again. Although he could now flap it without too much pain, it throbbed with too much soreness to fly.

"Okay, how do I do it?"

KC smiled. She stood up on all fours. "Hop up on my back, just behind my shoulders. Hang on tight -- you can't hurt me."

Bluesky rolled his eyes a moment, but if this cat was going to kill him, he wouldn't be able to stop it anyway. With a shrug of resignation, he hopped up to KC. Then with wings spread he flapped his wings and landed on KC's back. He struggled for balance a few moments, flapping his sore wings to get himself centered. It was hard to keep his balance on KC's soft skin and fur. Finally, he clenched his toes tight for a better grip.

"There you go. A cat's skin is thick -- your little claws only tickle a little. Hang on tight. I'll walk slowly so you don't fall off."

Bluesky's eyes opened wide in amazement.

While he held on, KC ambled toward the big bushes. He flapped his wings a few more times when he found himself leaning too far to one side, but very quickly he learned KC's motions and found himself crouching steadily.

"Wow, this is ... kind of fun." Bluesky looked down at KC's back. He noticed her shoulders rising and falling and learned to lean in rhythm with her movements.

KC meowed gently. "I never thought I'd give a bird a ride on my back!"

"I never dreamed I'd talk to a cat, much less ride on one!" Bluesky laughed.

The birds in the trees began to sing and whistle and squeak louder and louder in sheer surprise. Down below, they were witnessing a sight that seemed completely unreal, but their eyes told them true -- a cat was giving a Mockingbird a ride on its back.

Bluesky started to enjoy it. The cacophony of whistles increased with each step KC took.

He looked at the back of KC's head and whistled out a short, happy song.

"I love to hear birds sing when they're happy," KC purred.

Finally, KC stopped before the branches of a large bush. Bluesky opened his wings and leapt for it. He grabbed it and again got off-balance as the branch swayed crazily. Once it slowed, he hopped onto a stronger one. Standing within the protective embrace of the branches, he turned back to KC.

KC sat on her haunches peering intently at him. She smiled a moment and then turned to leave. After a couple of steps, she turned back and spoke. "I do hope you'll come back and fly for me. I'll be looking for you."

Bluesky remained silent a moment, still filled with amazement. Finally, he replied. "I will come back. I come here often anyway, but I'll look for you and ... I'll do some acrobatics and show you how fun flying really is."

KC laughed. "I'm glad I saved your life, and I hope Buddy and I have scared Tiger off for good."

Bluesky thought a moment. "I-I have forgotten something important, KC."

KC smiled and waited patiently.

"Thank you for saving my life. I-I still can't believe a cat would save a bird's life."

"Maybe we can become friends." KC purred happily.

Bluesky's beak fell open in shock. "What did you say?"

"I would like to be your friend," KC replied.

"Wow!" Bluesky said in total disbelief.

"KC! Kitty, kitty, kitty!"

With a swish of her tail, she turned as the man called for her from the back door.

Bluesky watched in stunned awe while the black and white cat ran toward the house. He remained in the bush a long time with his thoughts in a jumble and his heart pounding wildly. Finally, he hopped higher in the bush until he made it to the lowest branch of a tree.

He turned back to the house.

He wondered if such a thing was possible -- a bird and a cat becoming friends ...

Chapter Seven

Ol' Gray Mama was beside herself after she had almost seen her little friend killed right before her eyes. She was consumed with worry until she found Bluesky huddled in the tree above the bush where KC had taken him. The Dove looked him over carefully, cooing comfortingly the entire time. Satisfied he was not hurt too badly, she perched right beside him.

Bluesky nestled against her reassuring warmth.

The night grew darker, the moon slowly rose above the trees, and the two birds now began to talk to each other in low, soothing tones. They were both restless and unable to fall asleep.

They talked of about many things. Not too surprisingly, Ol' Gray Mama focused on Bluesky and KC.

"Well I declare, I've never seen such a sight in all my born days!" She said with awe, "A bird sitting on a cat's back. Who would have ever thought it possible? I mean, bird and cats -- they just don't get along and never have!"

"She seemed like a nice cat to me," Bluesky said.

"It's unheard of! I just knew that cat was going to throw you down any minute and eat you clean up right before my eyes!"

"She told me she likes birds."

"Likes to eat birds, more like it!"

A gentle silence settled between them.

In the dark, Bluesky knew she was deep in

thought. He nestled closer against her comforting warmth. It made his hurt wing feel better too.

He hoped that with the rising of the sun he would be able to fly again.

"I'm just glad you're all right. I don't want anyone hurting my little Mockingbird." Bluesky could hear her smile through the darkness.

Bluesky smiled back.

They both grew still and eventually fell into a sound sleep.

The next morning, Bluesky still felt sore. He remained on the branch while the Doves flew off for breakfast. After the sun rose higher and its burning glow lit up the world, its soothing warmth caressed his sore wing and eased the pain. After a couple of hours, he found he could move it without too much discomfort. Finally, when the sun had passed its zenith in the sky, he took a short test flight over to another branch in the same tree.

It still hurt.

He made it, although his landing was quite awkward even for a one-legged Mockingbird. After a while, he flew to another branch with more success and less pain.

Finally, his hunger overcame what pain was left in his wing. From the branch, he could see a few juicy bugs crawling in the grass below. Without thinking, he flew down and gobbled them up. After he gulped down the last one, he realized he had just flown!

Bluesky laughed at himself.

Soon, he was flying almost normally. He flew around the branches and through the trees deeper into the woods while the shadows grew longer and the sun settled lower on the western horizon.

He realized these trees were familiar; in fact, the tree to his right was the one on which Nightwind had perched when he first met him. Bluesky flew up toward the branch where he had first met the Owl. He hoped he might be awake already.

He spotted Nightwind the first time he looked for him this time. Bluesky perched on the branch, silently watching the sleeping Owl and wondering if he should wake him, when Nightwind suddenly opened his eyes.

"Ah, Bluesky. You've returned." Nightwind smiled. "What did you discover about our friends the Doves and the Sparrows?"

Bluesky related to Nightwind his careful observations of both Doves and Sparrows. He was very glad to tell him about the beautiful things he'd been able to observe in each bird. He felt very proud after he finished relating to the wise Owl everything he'd discovered.

"I see you missed something."

Bluesky stared at Nightwind in surprise.

He had missed something? How could that be? He had observed closely and was positive he'd discovered everything beautiful about those birds.

"I don't understand? How did I miss something? I believe the tails of Doves are quite beautiful"

Nightwind blinked his large eyes slowly. "Indeed, they are. And everything you said is correct."

"But I missed something?"

"You missed something obvious."

"I don't know how I did -- I really looked hard." Bluesky sighed with resignation.

"Perhaps my original request was misleading in a way." Nightwind closed his eyes and meditated a moment. "I did ask you what unique beauty each family of bird added to the world. And you did answer that correctly."

Bluesky felt better.

"Let's see ... did you enjoy meeting those birds and talking with them? Did you learn their names?"

"Yes!" Bluesky replied enthusiastically. "It was fun. I had fun singing with Treeflower too."

"Good. So, they were friendly to you. Perhaps they want to be your friend?"

Bluesky thought hard, reflecting on his time with Treeflower and the others. He looked up at Nightwind. "They were nice to me. They let me watch them, and they let me ask questions. But ... I don't think they want to be my friends."

"Why not?"

"I'm ugly. No one wants to be friends with a one-legged bird." Bluesky looked down with a forlorn expression.

"Did they say that?"

"No, but all the Mockingbirds say that. And most of the Sparrows stayed away from me. I saw them staring at me because of my missing leg."

"However, a few talked with you."

"I don't want to meet any more birds. I don't see how this journey is helping me. I just want to be left alone. I'll live with the Doves the rest of my life." Bluesky sighed with a deep sadness.

"Don't give up, Bluesky. Not yet -- you've only

just started." Nightwind smiled benevolently at him. "You did well, you really did. And soon, sooner than you think, you will find a friend."

Bluesky thought this statement over a moment.

He hopped closer to the Owl.

"Ol' Gray Mama and her flock want to help me. Those four Sparrows also want to help me, so that I can find a friend." Bluesky paused. "They want to help me find a Mockingbird who will become my friend like Treehopper."

Nightwind slowly shook his head. "Your journey is only begun, little Mockingbird. Let me emphasize the other goal from my original request, something that will help you to find a friend."

"Okay," Bluesky said, though his voice was full of doubt.

Nightwind smiled kindly before he spoke. "Tomorrow, go to other birds as you did with the Doves and Sparrows. But this time, you decide which birds to approach -- approach any you want. This time, not only observe what makes each family of bird beautiful, but also what makes the individual you find beautiful."

"Won't that particular bird look like all the others in its family? I don't get it."

Nightwind nodded with understanding. "Don't just look for what makes them beautiful on the outside, when you converse with a bird -- discover the 'beauty on the inside.'"

Bluesky remembered a famous bird proverb -- 'There's good in every bird.'

"How can I see inside a bird?"

"You can't just look at a bird's feathers on this

journey of discovery; you must also look inside their heart. That is even more important."

"How can I do that?"

Nightwind laughed. "Although each type of bird wears the same color of feathers that distinguish them from other kinds of birds, we all possesses inner qualities that make us unique individuals. These inner qualities of the heart become apparent in our words and actions."

"Oh." Bluesky nodded with a puzzled expression.

"Listen carefully to what they talk about. Note how they treat other birds ... and how they treat you."

"Then I will see what's inside their heart?"

"You will discern their inner qualities. You will be able to tell if they have a happy outlook or a negative outlook ... if they are modest and kind ... or if they are cruel and arrogant. Listen and observe and learn."

Bluesky thought a moment, remembering the different birds he'd met yesterday.

"Treeflower was very kind ... and very nice to me. She treated every bird the same way, always nice to them," Bluesky said.

"Good -- you noticed some of her inner qualities."

"I still don't know how this will help me find a friend!" Bluesky said with an exasperated tone.

"If you look for the good in others, you'll always find it."

"Okay ..."

"If you look for the bad in others, you'll always

find it."

Bluesky felt his mind spinning again, which seemed to happen a lot when he talked with Nightwind. He shook his head in confusion. "I don't get it."

"I could explain it to you." Nightwind smiled with a knowing twinkle in his large brown eyes. "But it will benefit you more if you learn what it means."

"How can I learn the meaning?"

"I will give you two hints," Nightwind said mysteriously.

Bluesky waited eagerly.

"If you fly with wise birds, then you will become wise. And if you fly with stupid birds, trouble will soon follow."

Bluesky's eyes grew wide with appreciation. He repeated the words over and over inside his mind. He earnestly sought out their hidden truth.

"My other hint is about you yourself." Nightwind paused to allow his words to sink into Bluesky's mind. "You have some fine qualities, young Mockingbird. You are kind and caring. You exhibit a powerful love of life, and you have a sharp and inquisitive mind -- all fine qualities of the heart -- inner qualities that make you ... you!"

"This will help me make friends?" Bluesky asked with a puzzled tone.

"My words today are meant to help you in choosing a friend -- and to identify the more important beauty of a bird. As you said, when most birds meet you all they see is that you only have one leg. But there is more to any bird than simply their outward appearance -- much more. And that is the most important part."

"I am so confused, wise Owl. All I want to do is find a Mockingbird who would like to be my friend. You make it sound so hard and mysterious!"

"You must continue your journey!" Nightwind said with urgency.

Bluesky frowned a moment, thinking over everything Nightwind had told him. "You want me to observe what makes them each beautiful, and also ... look for the good inside them?"

"After you have done that, then come tell me what you've learned about each bird you've met. In addition, try to get to know them better, which will take more than one meeting and one conversation."

Bluesky stared at Nightwind a few moments with a blank look on his face. Suddenly, another memory came to his mind.

"I did find something good about a cat."

"What?" Nightwind said in obvious surprise. The Owl opened his eyes wide and suddenly hopped excitedly up and down on the branch in a good imitation of Bluesky.

Bluesky laughed. He had finally said something that surprised the wise Owl. As quickly as he could, he related the incident with the cats and how two of them had saved his life from the dreaded Tiger.

Nightwind listened to the entire story in amazement. Bluesky added at the end how KC asked him a favor -- to fly for him and also to talk with him again.

The Owl was silent a long time, meditating deeply on what Bluesky had shared. The shadows around them grew deeper and darker, and the sun finally settled below the distant trees.

Finally, Nightwind spoke. "This is something totally unexpected!"

"It took me by surprise too, in more ways than one!" Bluesky laughed.

"Do you think you'll talk with this cat again?" Nightwind asked, his tone a mixture of puzzlement and excitement.

"I think so." Bluesky paused. "I hope I do."

"Then, not only tell me about the other birds you meet, but tell me more about KC when you meet her again. I am very intrigued by this. In fact, I am at a loss to know what to think of it!"

"I am too. Do you think she will try to kill me next time?"

"Hmmm, perhaps you should be careful. Yes, use care and don't approach her too close, not unless you have a way of escape available."

"What if she wants me to ride on her back again?"

Nightwind blinked rapidly in thought. "I don't know. You'll have to make that decision."

Bluesky turned to leave.

"And, Bluesky -- you are not ugly," Nightwind said with the greatest kindness.

Bluesky smiled happily.

Nightwind gave him a friendly wink.

Chapter Eight

Bluesky flew back to the trees near the house where KC lived. Ol' Gray Mama and her Doves roosted in a tree just outside the fence. In the gathering darkness, Bluesky looked for the cat, but there was no movement anywhere in the yard.

It grew late, so Bluesky found Ol' Gray Mama and perched next to her. She was fast asleep, but her eyes fluttered open when Bluesky settled against her. She smiled at him.

His mind slowed down more and more until sleepy dreaminess filled it like a cloud. Inside his heart, he once again felt a deep contentment. It felt so good to perch here with the Doves. It almost felt as good as when he'd perched with his own mama so long ago.

Almost ...

He awoke the next morning and realized that most of the soreness was gone from his right wing. He took to the air before the others awoke and flew joyously through the air far above the green canopy of trees.

The air felt so clean and so good!

He beat his wings faster and flew even higher into the sky. Up above, the clear and cloudless sky seemed to stretch forever in every direction. A cherished memory from his childhood came back, and he smiled with inner joy.

Yes, one day when the warm air returned and the great mountains of clouds sailed low in the sky, each cloud growing higher and bigger by the second, he would fly up to them. Yes, he would fly up to the clouds and see what was inside those great mountains of billowy, white softness.

He figured he could easily land on that white softness and rest and sail along with the cloud as long as he wanted. Bluesky imagined himself sitting on the white softness watching the world slowly passing by below.

The dream from his childhood made him feel good inside.

Bluesky flew through the wide open sky a long time, simply enjoying himself.

After the sun had risen fairly high in the sky, he slowed and flew down toward a tree in the neighborhood that he had never visited before. After he settled on a branch, he discovered three Brown Thrashers sitting on the tree with him.

He looked at them while they eyed him silently.

"Hello!" Bluesky said cheerfully. "Hello, cousins!"

The three Brown Thrashers continued to watch him without the slightest movement.

The brown birds were shaped like Mockingbirds but on a slightly larger scale with slender, curved beaks and long, graceful tails. They were covered by brown feathers except for their chest and belly, which were streaked brown and white.

And most distinctive, their eyes had a bright yellow iris that added to their piercing expression.

The three Thrashers stared unblinking at Bluesky. One of them lowered himself to stare at Bluesky's leg. He turned and whispered to the other two.

112

Bluesky felt the familiar sadness fill his heart again. He wanted to speak, to ask them a question about their kind and find out the beauty in them, but first he smiled again, hoping against hope they would smile back.

They didn't.

"You're that one-legged Mockingbird, aren't you?" the largest asked, staring harshly at the emptiness of Bluesky's missing leg.

"Um, well ..."

"Our cousins have told us about you," another added quickly.

Bluesky sighed deeply. "I wanted to ask you a question, if that's all right ..."

But in a flurry of feathers, the three Thrashers flew off without another word. As they flew away, each looked over their shoulder and cried back at him, "Go away, one-legged bird. We don't want to talk with you!"

Bluesky felt so sad inside. They hadn't even given him a chance to speak, much less get to know him. They'd simply stared at his leg and flown off.

How was he supposed to get know the beauty in other birds, the good inside them, when they didn't even give him a chance to speak?

He shrugged off their rejection and took wing again.

This time, however, he wouldn't fly up to a group of birds. This time he would look for a solitary bird, and he'd look for a bird that smiled a lot and seemed friendly like Treeflower.

Bluesky flew around the trees and houses searching for a bird sitting alone. But most of the time, birds were either in pairs or in small groups. He noticed two Cardinals at a seed-nest and soon afterward five Goldfinches sitting near each other in a tree. Everywhere he searched, he found birds, but none of them alone like him.

Finally, he spotted a Bluebird perched on a telephone line above a street. Bluesky settled in a nearby tree to observe the bird a moment before he approached.

In the distance, he noticed three other Bluebirds playing and eating, but none of them flew near the one sitting on the wire all alone. After a few more minutes passed, Bluesky flew down and lighted on the wire near the solitary Bluebird.

The Bluebird glanced over at him a brief moment, smiled briefly, and then shook himself nonchalantly and looked away without speaking.

Bluesky crouched lower on the wire, hoping to hide the emptiness of his missing leg and to keep his balance more easily. He didn't want this bird to fly away because he was different. He decided he'd just sit there quietly for a bit. After all, the Bluebird seemed quite content sitting there in his peaceful repose.

Bluesky watched him closely and thought the Bluebird seemed a little nervous, almost as nervous as Bluesky himself felt.

Bluesky realized when he felt nervous, he just needed some time until the feeling passed. Perhaps this bird needed that as well? He decided to sit quietly. Almost ten minutes passed by in a kind of awkward silence.

Finally, Bluesky decided it was time. "Hello.

My name is Bluesky."

And then the worst thing that could happen did happen -- Bluesky lost his balance.

He fluttered his wings as he started to fall on his side. With his face burning with embarrassment, he struggled and fluttered his wings more. Finally, he settled in a comfortable crouch again.

"D-d-did I make you nervous?" the Bluebird asked with a slight stutter of surprise.

"Um ..." Bluesky struggled to think of what to say.

"I-I'm sorry if I did."

"Um ... I'm all right. No need to worry."

The Bluebird looked at him hard. He carefully looked Bluesky over a second time, as if confirming something. Then he took a long, deep breath, gathered up his courage, and spoke. "W-why are you talking to me? Are you a Mockingbird?"

"Yes, I am. I'm on a journey -- that's why I'm speaking with you."

The Bluebird looked at him with surprise now. "W-what kind of journey?"

"A journey to discover the beauty of other birds."

"Oh." He paused a moment while he considered Bluesky's words. "That sounds fun."

The awkward silence returned.

Bluesky wasn't sure if the bird was bothered by his presence or not. He seemed very quiet, much quieter than any bird he'd ever met -- almost as if he preferred silence.

Bluesky decided to sit and observe him for a while.

His first impression was the sheer beauty of a Bluebird -- the dark blue feathers seemed to glow in the bright sunshine and contrasted sharply with his red breast feathers and the white feathers on his belly. Bluesky quickly realized he had never met such a colorful bird ever before.

"I-I think Bluebirds are the most beautiful birds I've ever met," Bluesky said tentatively, afraid he might offend this bird somehow and make it fly off.

"Oh, really? Have you met many birds?"

"I-I have met a few. Well, some Doves and Sparrows. I hope to meet more birds soon."

The Bluebird now seemed puzzled. He scooted himself away from Bluesky a little, seemed to think better of it, and pushed himself back to his original position on the wire.

It appeared to Bluesky that this bird felt uncomfortable, and his old sadness returned. He felt that what had happened with the Brown Thrashers was about to happen here. When they noticed his missing leg, it had made them feel uncomfortable and they flew off. He expected that at any moment this Bluebird would fly away too.

"My name is Dancingleaves."

Bluesky's beak fell open in surprise.

"You seem like a beautiful, er, well, not exactly beautiful. Well, I guess in your own way you are, maybe ..." He shook his head as if confused. "I'm sorry -- I'm not good with words. What I mean, well, you seem like a nice bird yourself."

"Thanks," Bluesky replied with relief.

The awkward silence returned. Bluesky wondered what he should say next. He decided to ask another question. "What is unique about Bluebirds?"

The briefest of smiles graced Dancingleaves' face. "We can catch bugs in mid-air as we fly! Let me show you."

Dancingleaves seemed relieved as he took wing.

In a flash of blue feathers, Dancingleaves began to fly back and forth hunting for bugs. He soared low to the ground in his searching and when he found none he flew up higher. Finally, he frightened a moth into flight skimming over a bush.

He circled back quickly.

With short, powerful strokes of his wings, he tracked down the moth. The moth now flew erratically in an attempt to flee, but Dancingleaves kept up with his every move. The Bluebird flapped his wings faster and then slower as he approached for the kill.

Suddenly, it seemed as if Dancingleaves froze in mid-air. He fanned out his wings to maintain his position for just the briefest of moments, jabbing at the bug with his beak.

But the bug evaded capture and darted off in another direction.

With acrobatic ease, Dancingleaves swooped down to gain speed and with a quick burst rose again until he was right next to his intended prey. Once again with wings spread wide, he seemed to pause in mid-air as he lunged with his beak.

Just as quickly the moth changed direction and escaped again.

Finally, the persistent Bluebird flew on a quick intercept course but purposely overshot his prey.

Now right in the moth's path, Dancingleaves executed a quick turnaround followed by another momentary holding position. With a strong downstroke of his wings, he raised his wings and held them out for a fraction of a second to hold himself directly in the moth's path.

Dancingleaves snapped his beak shut right on the moth.

With a triumphal dive followed by a graceful circle around his engrossed audience, he finally flew back and perched beside Bluesky with a happy smile.

He bent over and quickly wiped each side of his beak on the wire.

"That was great!" Bluesky laughed. "You really performed some precise maneuvers. And that last move, intercepting him in mid-air -- that was awesome!"

"Can Mockingbirds catch bugs in the air?"

"We usually hunt bugs on the ground, but if they try to fly away, we can catch them as they're trying to fly away."

"Oh." Dancingleaves frowned with disappointment.

"But we don't hunt them in the air like you. Nothing as acrobatic as Bluebirds."

Dancingleaves smiled proudly. Then, once again, he grew silent.

"Am I bothering you?" Bluesky finally asked with a sense of foreboding.

"I, well ... not really." Dancingleaves shrugged. "It's not you. I get nervous around any bird I meet. Actually, I get kind of scared."

"Why?"

"I was the only baby to hatch this season. My parents were upset that the other eggs didn't hatch -- they think it was the unseen poison that ruined the other eggs -- and so they were very protective of me. They wouldn't let me play with other birds. Now that I can fly off on my own, well, I just can't bring myself to fly up to other birds. Most of the time when another bird flies up to me, like you did, I panic and fly away before they can speak." Dancingleaves hung his head down sadly.

He suddenly straightened. "It's okay though. I like being alone -- it's not all that bad. I do lots of fun things."

"Are you nervous around me?" Bluesky asked cautiously.

"A little. But, you were very quiet when you first flew up. I think that's why I didn't get scared and fly away."

Bluesky nodded.

The awkward silence continued, but this time Bluesky decided to sit alongside Dancingleaves and remain quiet. After a few minutes, Dancingleaves spoke.

"I love to look up at the sky. Did you know that the sky and the clouds are different each day?" His tone grew more excited. "The sky is so beautiful. It changes and moves -- well, the sky changes color, and the clouds move -- but very slowly, almost without your realizing it ... almost like it's alive ... And if you really look at the clouds, you'll realize that no two clouds are exactly alike."

Bluesky looked up at the sky with a new

appreciation.

He observed the sky and the clouds and contemplated its vastness sitting alongside Dancingleaves for several minutes in a comfortable and peaceful silence.

"It never struck me that every cloud is different. You're right; the sky does change -- if you keep watching. The clouds way up high move so slowly ..."

"I love to watch clouds."

"You know what I want to do one day?" Bluesky said excitedly.

"What?" Dancingleaves peered at him with open interest.

"I want to fly up to a cloud and perch on it and float on it and watch the world far below passing by."

"Wow! Can you do that?"

"I'm going to try one day."

"Can -- can I go with you?"

"Sure. The clouds are lower and bigger in the summer. I plan to try it then."

In his excitement, Bluesky had raised himself up with his beak pointed at the clouds.

Dancingleaves stared at the emptiness of Bluesky's missing leg.

Bluesky felt a touch of sadness inside his heart.

"Did it hurt when you lost your leg?"

"No, I was born like this."

"Oh."

"Does my missing leg bother you?"

"Uh, no. It's just different. You know, I think it makes me feel less nervous being around you."

120

His words made Bluesky feel good for some reason, although he wasn't sure why.

"Does it seem like everyone else is having more fun that you are?" Dancingleaves asked.

Dancingleaves' question caught him off-guard.

"What do you mean?"

"When I sit here alone, I see the other birds playing and singing all around, and it seems they're all having so much fun. It makes me sad, and it makes me wish I could have fun like them."

"I feel like that ... in a different way."

"What do you mean?"

Bluesky felt the familiar sadness creep into his heart. He thought of all the times he wished he could play with the other Mockingbirds. Even now, although he was meeting birds of different families, he still felt he was an outsider.

"How do you feel?" Dancingleaves prompted him again.

"I feel like I'm on the outside looking in."

"Oh." Dancingleaves frowned while he thought deeply on Bluesky's words. Finally, he spoke. "I don't understand."

Bluesky started to speak but held up a moment as his mind raced. Actually, now that he was asked to put this feeling into words, he grew unsure. He pictured himself with other birds, especially meeting Treeflower and the other Sparrows. He thought of Ol' Gray Mama and the Doves as well as Nightwind.

"I feel that even when I'm with other birds that -- that I just don't fit in. I feel separate from others, even when I talk with them, as if there is some invisible barrier between us."

"I don't understand," Dancingleaves repeated.

Bluesky closed his eyes and concentrated, willing himself to put this feeling into words. He had to transform this strange, familiar sadness into words now, so that not only could Dancingleaves understand it, but that he could too.

"Even when I'm with other birds, I still feel alone."

Dancingleaves' eyes widened with surprised. "I think I understand that."

"Really?" Bluesky asked hopefully.

"Yes."

This made him feel good somehow, knowing that someone else understood how he felt. And now, he wanted to help Dancingleaves feel good.

"Maybe if you go up and meet the other birds, maybe they'll like you and want to play with you?" Bluesky smiled enthusiastically.

Dancingleaves shivered with fear at Bluesky's suggestion.

Bluesky felt bad, for it seemed he had caused the opposite reaction than he had intended. He was so surprised a bird as beautiful as Dancingleaves would be afraid of meeting other birds.

He could understand why other birds didn't want to play with him -- he was ugly. Still, he wanted Dancingleaves to feel comfortable around him. He thought a moment, trying to come up with something to please the shy Bluebird.

"Don't you have fun watching the clouds?" Bluesky asked.

"Yes, but I wish I could have as much fun as the

other birds. I want to do fun things like them."

"Me too," Bluesky said with a hint of sadness.

"They seem so happy when I watch them."

"Yeah, I know."

"I wish sometimes I could play with them and that I wouldn't feel so scared when they fly near me or sing out to me asking me to sing with them."

"What do you tell them?"

"I tell them ... that I'm busy ..."

"Do I make you nervous?" Bluesky stretched his wings.

Dancingleaves smiled shyly at him. "When you first sat on the wire, I noticed you only had one leg. I saw that you tried to hide it from me by sitting real low on the wire. After you sat there quiet for a long time, I think my fear kind of faded away, and then I started thinking what it must be like to have only one leg ..." Dancingleaves looked hard at Bluesky. "I hope I'm not hurting your feelings now?"

"No, please go on."

"Well, I guess I started thinking about that so much -- about how it must feel to have one leg -- that I forgot to be nervous."

Bluesky didn't know how to respond. Dancingleaves' words didn't make him feel sad, so maybe that was all right?

He finally shrugged with a puzzled expression. "I'm glad I don't make you nervous. Do you want to play a flying game?"

"I'm not sure ..." Dancingleaves replied hesitantly.

"Why don't we just sing together? We can just sit here on the wire and sing together."

"S-sure."

Bluesky sang out a short snippet. Dancingleaves answered with a series of brief whistles.

They smiled at each other.

For a while they sang out to each other and almost started playing the 'Singing Game', but Bluesky didn't push it as far as a real game -- he didn't want to intimidate this shy bird in any way. Dancingleaves still seemed somewhat nervous every now and then as they sang together, but at other times he whistled happily.

Bluesky noticed the sun starting to set. "I've got to go now."

"Are you going back to your parents?"

Bluesky felt a stab of pain in his heart, but he knew Dancingleaves didn't know anything about his family.

"No, I live with some Doves."

"Really? That's interesting."

"Um, could I come back and see you again?" Bluesky asked, his heart suddenly pounding in anticipation of rejection.

"Yes, that's fine. I do want to fly up to the clouds with you one day." Dancingleaves waggled his tail happily.

The feeling in Bluesky's heart switched to joy instantly.

"I've got to continue my journey, but I want to come back and talk with you and learn more about you -- that's part of my journey. Maybe we could play a little then? If you want to."

"You know, you're the first bird other than my parents that I've ever sung songs with. Yes, I would like to play next time." Dancingleaves smiled at him.

"I'm glad we sang together too," Bluesky said.

Bluesky felt a stirring inside his heart. He quickly went over in his mind what he had learned about this new bird so he could share it with Nightwind.

He decided that this Bluebird had a shy kindness about him and that this quality was his inner goodness. He also had a special way of noticing the subtle wonders of the world, and it seemed Dancingleaves needed someone too, just like he did.

Bluesky looked forward to playing with Dancingleaves on his next visit and learning more about him.

Chapter Nine

Bluesky awoke to the sound of Robins laughing.

He sat there perched next to the sleeping form of Ol' Gray Mama and listened quietly as the fog of sleep slowly dissipated from his mind.

Robins loved to laugh.

While he enjoyed the sweet sound of their chirping laughter echoing in the crisp morning air, it occurred to him that Robins must be some of the happiest birds in the world.

He also realized this was something obviously good about these birds -- the fact that they laughed so much.

Hopping quietly away from the sleeping Dove in order not to awaken her, he took wing and flew toward the happy sounds.

He sailed over the houses and trees of the subdivision until he found a small group of Robins hunting bugs in the short grass of a newly mown lawn. Bluesky alighted on the branch of a small tree.

Remembering Nightwind's admonition, he silently observed them a moment from afar.

About the same size as Mockingbirds, Robins were much stouter birds adorned with a plump red breast. The rest of their body was covered with black feathers except for their throats, which were speckled white and black.

Bluesky especially liked their bright, yellow beaks, but he decided that their most distinguishing feature was their red breast. Yes, their red feathers were the most beautiful thing about these birds.

He noticed a particular pair of Robins, most probably mates by their close cooperation. They hunted in spurts of synchronized motion. From time to time, especially after a successful jab of their beak netted them a juicy bug, they would both cackle out in a joyous round of laughter.

Across the lawn, several other Robins would answer them until the morning air filled with laughter.

It made Bluesky feel good inside to hear birds laughing so freely and easily.

He flew down to the grass and landed a few feet away from the pair.

To his delight, one of his favorite bugs jumped up, and Bluesky nabbed him with a quick strike. While he gobbled down the tasty morsel, he glanced over at the Robins.

Both were eyeing him carefully. They seemed a little nervous that another bird had joined them.

Bluesky smiled at them, remembering how Treeflower's smile put birds at ease.

The male Robin laughed joyfully back at him, and then he and his mate retuned to their breakfast.

Bluesky hopped closer to them since they seemed so friendly, but each time he hopped towards them, they would scurry away, always keeping the same distance from him. After a few cycles of this game, Bluesky decided they didn't desire company.

He looked across the yard and took wing toward the other Robins over there. Bluesky landed at the edge of a group of three. The largest looked up at him and checked him out a moment.

"C'mon, girls, it's time to go."

Bluesky felt his heart sink.

"I-I didn't mean to disturb you," Bluesky said with a hint of sadness.

"Naw, no problem. It's just that we like to stay with our kind, you know," the male Robin whistled in a matter-of-fact way. "Birds of a feather flock together, as the saying goes."

In a flash of black wings, they flew away.

Bluesky hung his head. He had so hoped these laughing birds would be friendlier to him. At least, he decided, it hadn't been his missing leg this time. It just seemed like these birds preferred the company of their own kind.

Turning to fly away, he noticed a Robin off to himself in the corner of the yard.

He was a really hearty fellow. It looked to Bluesky as if his red belly was double the size of the others. When he looked closer, it seemed this Robin was in some kind of trouble!

Again and again this overly plump Robin bent over and put his beak right into the ground and shook his entire body. It appeared to Bluesky that the bird tried to raise his head up several times, but something prevented it.

He wondered if something had hold of its beak.

Curiosity got the better of Bluesky. He leapt up and with a few wing strokes landed near the struggling Robin.

A moment later, he realized it was the Robin who had a hold on something -- a fat, juicy worm.

The worm, though, had most of his long body

deep inside the moist ground; the Robin gripped only the very end of the worm in his slender, yellow beak.

As Bluesky watched with wide eyes, the bird and worm engaged in an enthusiastic game of tug-of-war.

Of course, the worm had more incentive to win this game -- otherwise he would become breakfast. Every time the Robin pulled some of the worm out, the worm yanked back down until the tip of the Robin's beak was buried into the dirt.

Again and again, pulling up and yanking down, yanking up and pulling down, the bird and worm went at it with all their might.

Bluesky laughed out loud at the sight.

"Mmmmphhhhh," the Robin muttered.

Bluesky paused.

"Mmmmmphhhhhh!"

"What was that? I couldn't quite make it out."

With a dull thump, the Robin's beak banged into the dirt after the worm yanked down hard again. Setting his legs far apart for extra leverage, the Robin grunted and jerked his head back up with a mighty pull.

The worm's body grew thinner as the Robin stretched him further and further. Suddenly, the Robin's head began to shudder with its great effort.

"I-I think you've got him now," Bluesky said.

"Mmmmphhh, mmmmphh. Mmmmmmmmph!

"Say what?" Bluesky gasped. "I can't understand a word you're saying!"

Bluesky's eyes widened as he watched the contest. It seemed something had to give any second

-- either the rest of the worm was going to come flying up out of the ground, or the bird would finally have to let go.

And something did happen!

The Robin slowly twisted his head toward Bluesky. But he loosened his grip around the worm just a little, which allowed the worm to *push* instead of pull.

Suddenly, a brown stream shot out the end of the worm.

The Robin's eyes widened with shock. He cocked his head first one way and then another in a frantic effort to avoid the brown stream, but the stream swirled all around in the air until some of it finally hit the bird right on its face.

The effect was instantaneous -- the bird let go.

With a snap like a taut rubber band, the worm slapped onto the ground. In the blink of an eye, it disappeared into the safety of the hole.

In the same instant, the bird bounced backward and with a 'thud' landed on his tail feathers.

Bluesky stared in shock.

He looked at the Robin and noticed that right down the middle of its head some of the brown, sticky substance slowly oozed toward his yellow beak.

"Wha-what happened?" Bluesky asked hesitantly, afraid the Robin might be hurt.

The Robin burst into laughter.

Bluesky hopped a half-step closer and sniffed the air. He detected an odd smell.

"What is that stuff the worm shot out?"

The Robin laughed even louder.

130

"C'mon, tell me. What is it?"

His chirping laughter finally slowed down to a comical chuckling until that gave way to just a wide smile of his yellow beak. He sat there a moment, took a huge breath, and replied. "Worm poop!"

"Yuck!" Bluesky exclaimed.

"I guess I must be quite a sight -- a right plump Robin sitting flat on his tail feathers with worm poop dripping between my eyes, eh?" His eyes twinkled with mirth, and he laughed softly.

It struck Bluesky that this bird was actually laughing at himself. Such a concept seemed most strange indeed. In his mind, he remembered all the times that other birds had laughed at him. Most of all, he remembered how their laughter had hurt.

This bird laughed at himself!

When Bluesky realized he wasn't hurt, the Robin's situation did take on a humorous note. Actually, it was hilarious.

Almost against his will, Bluesky started chuckling.

The Robin smiled up at Bluesky and suddenly fell completely over on his back. He let out another round of chirping laughter.

His laughter was so contagious it caused Bluesky to laugh even harder.

Bluesky's sides began to ache he laughed so hard. The Robin finally rolled onto his side, wiped his head on the grass to get the poop off, and got up on his feet.

"Yeah, well, that worm got away all right. But ..." The Robin's eyes twinkled again. "I think he must've lost weight with everything he shot out!"

They both burst out in another round of laughter.

"That was hilarious!" Bluesky added as their laughter finally slowed down again.

"Well, you know us Robins -- we love a good laugh."

"I've noticed that," Bluesky said with a smile. "Almost every morning, I hear Robins laughing merrily."

"Yes, sort our trademark, you know." He fluffed out his feathers and shook himself a moment in case any dirt or grass clung to his feathers. "No other bird laughs quite like a Robin."

"I agree." Bluesky smiled. "It's kind of a chirping laugh -- a happy sound. I love to hear it."

"That's nice of you say." He looked closely at Bluesky a moment.

Bluesky waited pensively when the Robin glanced down at the emptiness where his other leg should be. He felt his heart beating rapidly. He knew this bird would now make a decision: either he would leave, or he would continue their conversation in spite of Bluesky's missing leg.

The silence grew longer, and the Robin now began preening himself.

Bluesky's heart sank as the silence continued. After a few more moments, he turned to leave.

"Hello -- where are you going? I haven't even introduced myself."

Bluesky turned with surprise. "I thought you wanted to be by yourself ... you ..."

"Oh no, sorry. I figured I ought to clean myself up a bit since I tumbled on the ground like that." He flapped his wings vigorously a moment and completed his preening. Satisfied, he scurried closer to Bluesky.

"Hello, my name is Tootight."

"Hello, Tootight. I'm Bluesky."

"Ah, a name of distinction. How nice."

Bluesky explained his journey. He told Tootight of some of the other birds he'd met, how he had learned what beauty they added to the world, and how he also tried to discern what 'goodness' he could find about each individual he met.

"Well, I'm not sure how beautiful a bird we Robins are -- you'll have to be the judge of that."

"I like your plump red breast and belly the best, I think."

Tootight laughed jovially. "Well, that's why my parents named me Tootight!"

"What do you mean?"

"When I was in the nest, sometimes I would eat so much that my belly would bulge out really full!" Tootight's eyes twinkled. "My mom said if I ate any more, I might explode, because my belly was 'too tight!'"

Bluesky and Tootight laughed together.

"I think Robins like to laugh more than most birds. That is another beautiful thing about you," Bluesky said with a chuckle.

"So true. Especially a big, happy fellow like me." The rotund robin laughed so hard he fell back on his rump, which made him laugh even harder.

After a few moments, Bluesky and Tootight took deep breaths and quieted down, although both still smiled like they might break out in laughter again any second.

"Ah, yes. Well, there's only one thing we Robins like better than laughing -- and that's eating! And I'm sure you can tell that I like eating a little more than most, eh!" Tootight chuckled heartily.

Again, Bluesky was amazed this bird could laugh at himself so easily. It was true; he was a big bird. In fact, some might call him fat. Although he didn't want to laugh, he found himself chuckling along with Tootight again.

"Yeah, you're a big bird all right."

"I know. I keep telling myself I need to go on a bit of a diet. But every time I decide to try, well, another juicy bug comes walking by, and I just can't help myself!"

"You have a happy heart, and you like to laugh," Bluesky said. "I think that is what is good about you."

"Thanks. I think you'll find when you meet other Robins that we all like a good laugh."

"You seem a bit happier than most. I'm glad I met you and not just any other Robin."

"I'm glad I met you too. I've heard about you, you know."

Bluesky felt a flutter of emotions stir inside his heart. He didn't know what to say.

Tootight noted his puzzled expression and continued. "Oh, don't worry. I don't listen to gossip. Sure, some birds will talk trash because you only have one leg and all. But see here, I kind of hoped I'd meet you."

"Why?"

"I just thought if I ever met you, well, I heard

how the other Mockingbirds had cast you and your family off, and I felt it wasn't right. So, I figured if I ever met you, I'd treat you nice, like any bird I meet. I don't mind that you only have one leg. I mean, you're still a bird." Tootight smiled widely.

"That's a very nice thing to say." Bluesky cocked his head to one side. "I sure could use a good laugh every now and then, and I've only spent a few minutes with you and laughed more than I usually do in an entire week!"

"We try to laugh every day. That's why we start every day with a good chuckle."

"I'd like to get to know you better, Tootight, and maybe you can tell me more about Robins so I can share it with Nightwind."

"Sure -- come around any time. I usually like to hunt bugs in the front yards away from the seed-eating birds around here." He paused a moment in thought. "I will tell you something we say about ourselves. You can share it with Nightwind."

"Great!"

"It's been said, because we like to laugh more than most birds," -- Tootight's smile grew even bigger -- "'*Robins are born laughing.*'"

Bluesky and Tootight spent the morning together talking and laughing. At times, they did more laughing than talking, but that was even better. And for the first time in his life, Bluesky did something he had never done before.

Right as he lunged at a bug, he lost his balance and fell flat on his face, but instead of feeling embarrassment, as he lay there on the ground he started laughing.

Tootight laughed along with him.

Too his surprise Bluesky didn't mind at all. The important thing was Tootight laughed with Bluesky, not at him.

Because he had met Tootight, Bluesky had learned he could laugh at himself.

They parted ways later that morning, and Bluesky promised to find Tootight again and spend time with him, especially when he needed a good laugh.

Chapter Ten

Bluesky spent a couple of hours flying happily around the small stands of trees that grew around the houses of the subdivision. From his perspective each housetop seemed like a rectangular island amid the leafless trees of winter.

He soon spotted two young Mockingbirds sitting in a tree. Bluesky slowed and circled near them. They were two young females, each about his age.

He kept circling them, his curiosity piqued. After all, he hadn't seen much less talked with another Mockingbird for several days. Still, he hesitated, afraid of rejection again even though his heart burned for the company of his own family of birds.

Finally, he landed on a branch in the same tree. They seemingly ignored his presence while he eyed them carefully, trying to determine if they would be friendly or not.

He didn't mind that neither was a male, although his utmost desire was to find a Mockingbird who might become his friend like Treehopper had been a friend to Cloudsky.

Actually, he felt intrigued by their presence. After all, the only young female Mockingbird he had ever known was his sister, Songjoy.

Deep inside his heart, Bluesky felt a new emotion stirring. Something about these pretty birds made him just want to sing!

Impelled by this strange and exotic stirring, he

hopped down onto the same branch with them and sang out. He crouched low to hide the emptiness of missing leg.

He sang out with a clear and melodic voice, and the females looked at him in surprise. Bluesky even surprised himself, because here he was singing to some lovely Mockingbirds like it was the most natural thing in the world. The more he noticed their glances, the more his heart fluttered with joy.

He sang louder. He sang every song he knew with great bravado.

They watched and listened intently to his display while enthusiastically wagging their long tails.

He sang a series of short but elaborate songs to impress them, although he still wasn't quite sure what impelled him to do this. Still, it made him feel good inside when he noticed their interest in his singing.

Finally, he could bear it no longer. He hopped up beside one of them and spoke. "Hello! My name is Bluesky."

The expression on her face changed instantly when she stared down at his solitary leg.

"Oh, Morningsun! It's that *deformed* Mockingbird I was telling you about yesterday!"

"Ewwww!"

The two looked at each other with frightened expressions, and in the next instant, they both flew off.

Bluesky's heart filled with sadness.

He sighed with a forlorn intake of breath and sat there a long time. He didn't understand why his own kind wouldn't even talk with him. The sun sank lower in the pale blue winter sky while he sat alone with his troubled thoughts.

He soon felt hungry, but it wasn't for bugs. No, he desired something different; he just wasn't sure what he craved. He flew on the fresh afternoon breeze and soon spotted a bush full of ripe, red berries.

Yes! Berries would do nicely for a snack.

He dipped his wing, sailed down, and landed on a thick branch laden with berries. He took a quick bite and enjoyed the tartness immensely. For long minutes, he enjoyed himself in the solitude of this exotic meal.

Without warning, the bush was suddenly alive with dozens and dozens of birds. On every branch around him, birds were either gorging themselves or crying out excitedly.

Bluesky almost bolted back into the sky he was so surprised by this unexpected onslaught.

He sat frozen in the middle of their frenzied movements and the cacophony of lisping whistles of this flock of birds that surrounded him. Soon his initial fear turned into amazement.

He'd never seen such a large number of birds in one place!

One of the cinnamon-brown birds with black masks hopped right next to him, smiled momentarily, and then cried out with excitement after he spotted a berry and gobbled it down.

Before Bluesky could speak, the bird flew to the next branch, where he cried out again with glee as he found several berries in a cluster and gobbled them up one after the other.

And when one bird cried with excitement, this stirred all the others to cry out in return.

Bluesky watched with awe as all the berries disappeared in less than five minutes. The bush, at first laden with hundreds of berries, was now almost completely devoid of its fruit.

While these strange and wondrous birds searched deeper and deeper into the bush for any remaining berries, their rapid movements finally slowed.

Another of the birds lighted on the branch next to him.

"H-hello, my names is Bluesky."

"Did you eat any berries? I hope you ate some -- they were delicious! But I'm afraid we've almost eaten them all now." He smiled at Bluesky.

"Yes, I ate a few."

"Good, good, good," he whistled breathlessly.

"Um, what kind of bird are you?" Bluesky smiled.

"Oh, us! We're Cedar Waxwings." He turned to display his right wing to Bluesky. "See my red spots? They're our pride and joy, you know."

"No, I didn't know."

"Yes, yes. We all look almost identical, right? Except we each have different numbers of red spots on our wings. Some have three on their left wing and four on their right, or two on their right wing and five on their left, or you know -- something different altogether!"

Bluesky glanced at several Waxwings preening themselves after their frantic meal. Each bird did seem almost identical except for the number of red waxy deposits on their wings, although he noted that their black masks were also slightly different, some having more white edges than others.

He also noticed how they were about half his size but seemed to have twice his energy.

"You are handsome birds," Bluesky said with appreciation. "I think your sporty crests and your black masks are the unique beauty you add to the world."

The Waxwing hopped excitedly up and down. "What a nice thing to say. I've always admired the way you Mockingbirds imitate any bird you meet!"

"Thanks," Bluesky said with a hint of embarrassment.

"My name is Rainday, by the way. Pleased to meet you."

"I'm glad you and your flock joined me here."

"Ah yes. I hope we didn't frighten you too much. When we storm a bush all together, it can be startling."

"You did startle me," Bluesky admitted with a laugh.

"Yes, we can be a bit overwhelming. We do everything together, you see."

"Everything?"

"Oh yes, we do everything together. We're never apart. In fact, we hate the very thought of being alone." Rainday turned to the others. "Hey, everyone, meet Bluesky!"

"Hi, I'm Cloudday."

"Hello, I'm Sunday."

"Hi, I'm Warmday."

"I'm Windday."

"I'm Hotday."

Bluesky turned from one masked Waxwing to another as every bird whistled out his name from every corner of the bush. Before they finished, Bluesky felt woozy.

"You're all named day?"

"Yes, we're the Day Flock."

"Cool."

Suddenly, one of the Waxwings took wing and left.

Bluesky shouted in surprise when every Waxwing opened their wings and took off after him. "Hey! Where are you going?"

Rainday circled back. "Not sure yet, but when one of us goes, we all go! C'mon!"

Bluesky dodged a couple of stragglers as they flew past him, and he too leapt up and flew after the flock. In the clear air, the flock of Waxwings flew almost as one. He observed how at times the flock would nearly disperse when some birds flew outward, but suddenly they would all change directions and the individual birds would close together until it seemed they must collide!

One of the lead birds cried out louder, his voice piercing through the cacophony of soft, whistling trills.

The flock dove toward another bush. Even from the air, Bluesky could see it was heavy with berries.

But not for long!

The Waxwings descended on the bush like a brown swarm. In seconds, the bush appeared to have as many birds as berries because of the continuous movement of birds hopping from one branch to another. It made it seem there were three times as many birds as there really were.

Bluesky laughed at their frenzied antics. He managed to eat a few berries himself before the ravenous appetites of the Waxwings once again stripped the bush in a matter of minutes.

"That was good, good, good!" Rainday whistled happily.

"Good, good, good!" the flock whistled in reply.

Rainday hopped up to Bluesky. "Is your leg hurt? Why don't you use both legs?"

"Well, um." Bluesky swallowed nervously. "I only have one leg."

"Oh."

Bluesky watched as Rainday paused in silence to contemplate deeply.

Bluesky felt this couldn't be a good sign; he'd never seen any of the others do this before.

Finally, Rainday spoke. "I've never heard of a one-legged bird before. That is, not unless it was hurt or attacked by a cat or something." He leaned closer. "Did you lose your leg in an attack?"

"Uh, no. I was born with only one leg."

"Dear, dear, dear," Rainday whistled. "Never heard of that. Must've been hard for you to leave the nest and all, learning how to balance."

"Uh, yes. But my parents helped me a lot."

"Good, good, good. Good of your parents to do that."

Bluesky smiled in amazement while Rainday hopped from branch to branch and spread the news to the others. It seemed that their endless whistling became more energetic as Rainday hopped from bird to bird.

Sitting there and watching their frenzied movements, he decided he would share with Nightwind the beauty of their stylish crests and their cinnamon-brown feathers -- the characteristics he'd noted before. He felt the internal goodness of these particular birds was their gregarious nature, the way they did everything together, and how they made sure each and every individual was cared for and part of the family group. Yes, they seemed to thrive as a group, almost as if the group itself were a living entity.

Suddenly he looked around and realized with surprise that every Waxwing was standing on one leg.

His heart quivered with emotion -- he wasn't quite sure if it was fear or shock or what!

Rainday hopped up next to him using only one leg, his other leg drawn up tightly against his belly. As Bluesky glanced quickly from one Waxwing to another, he confirmed it. The entire Day flock now hopped from branch to branch on one leg while continuing to gobble down berries as quickly as possible.

Bluesky watched in shock when one and then another almost lost their balance and fell. In fact, several lost their balance so much they were forced to take wing and fly to another part of the large bush.

But once there, they perched again on only one leg.

"Hey, Windday! You're using the wrong leg!"

144

Cloudday shouted.

In a heartbeat, Windday put down his right leg and lifted up his left leg, chuckling at himself.

"Sorry about that. Thanks!" he shouted back before gobbling down a berry.

Bluesky's eyes widened with surprise. His heart beat rapidly as he tried to understand what this phenomena meant.

Rainday smiled at Bluesky.

"Are you making fun of me?" Bluesky asked with a mixture of fear and sadness.

"No, no, no!" Rainday whistled. "You must understand -- Waxwings do everything as one. If one of us is sad, we are all sad. If one of us is happy, we are all happy. We are very sensitive to each others' feelings, you know."

Sunday hopped down beside Rainday and added, "We're very *empathetic* birds."

"I don't get it." Bluesky shook his head.

"Have you heard stories about Canada Geese when they fly south for the winter?"

"Yes," Bluesky said.

"If an individual in the flock gets hurt and cannot keep up, a few will slow down and help him while the rest continue. The few healthy Geese will stay with the hurt one and assist him the rest of the way. They will fly slowly and stay close to him in order to support him."

"Okay, I get that. But why are you all standing on one leg?" Bluesky asked.

"We like you. We want to understand how you feel. So, we all agreed to hop about on one leg while you are with us."

"Now I understand." Bluesky nodded and broke out in a smile. "I like you birds. It's cool how you do everything together!"

For the rest of the afternoon, Bluesky and the entire Day flock flew from bush to bush and hopped around on one leg.

It was quite a sight to see.

Other birds stopped in flight, cried out in surprise, and flew down for a closer look. Never in the entire history of birds had such a sight been seen before -- an entire flock of one-legged birds!

Word of this surprising spectacle spread to all the nearby families of birds.

Chapter Eleven

Bluesky searched for KC the next day. He had searched yesterday amid all his other adventures, but the black and white cat had been nowhere to be seen.

Bluesky came back to the yard again in hopes of finding the friendly feline.

Surveying the yard, he noticed Ol' Gray Mama searching for seed among a small group of Sparrows. He recognized Littleclouds and Treesinger and three others whom he did not know by name.

He was beginning to wonder what happened to KC. Perhaps she had been hurt more seriously than she let on after her fight with Tiger?

Bluesky decided to hop closer to the birds on the ground, hoping KC might spot him among them. After all, she'd said she liked watching birds from inside the house. Perhaps if he saw him, she would come out.

He flew over and landed close to Ol' Gray Mama.

"Hello! I'm so glad to see you, Bluesky," she said with kindness in her eyes.

"Good to see you too, Ol' Gray Mama."

"We heard all the excitement about you yesterday," she said.

Bluesky smiled patiently. Of course, they had already talked about his meeting with the Waxwing flock the previous evening, but Ol' Gray Mama, like the other older birds of her little flock, tended to forget easily.

Bluesky didn't mind talking about it again. He enjoyed hearing them tell their favorite stories again and again too.

For a few minutes, Bluesky relived his happy time with the Day flock while Ol' Gray Mama laughed as if she were hearing it for the first time.

After that, they all returned to breakfast.

She bobbed her head up and down as she sauntered around looking for seed. She seemed more content just knowing that her young charge was near.

He now looked over at the Sparrows, but they seemingly ignored him and continued with their urgent search for seed. He started to call out to Littleclouds and Treesinger, but they kept their eyes averted from him.

He waited for them to notice him so he could greet them; he hated to interrupt their focus. However, they hopped farther and farther away.

Bluesky felt his heart sink. Perhaps they no longer wished his company?

A soft, diminutive chirp came from above his head, from the direction of the seed-nest. He looked up.

It was Treeflower!

"Hi, Bluesky!" she whistled cheerily, flashing a happy smile at him.

Bluesky's heart leapt with joy. He smiled back. It seemed she was almost glad to see him.

The Song Sparrow flew down beside him. "How is your journey going?" She asked with keen interest.

Bluesky proceeded to relate his meetings with Dancingleaves, Tootight, and Rainday and the Day flock. He didn't mention the other birds that turned their backs on him. He decided to only talk about his happy encounters -- it made him feel better.

He decided it was best not to dwell on the negative.

"I'm glad you've met some nice birds," she said after he finished.

"I liked all of them too. They were fun -- each in their own way."

"Have you met any Mockingbirds?"

Bluesky frowned.

"You will. I'm sure of it, Bluesky."

"I hope so."

"Hey, I learned something new today. Do you want to know what it is?" she chirped excitedly.

"Sure, what is it?"

"I learned about a new seed-nest. It's over where the humans gather to feed."

"Really?"

She tried to explain to him how humans gathered at buildings built specifically to provided food and that many times in their haste food fell on the ground for birds to eat. Sometimes, a special, small seed-nest with some of the human food fell to the ground. It was small enough for a bird to carry away.

Bluesky tried to picture this strange seed-nest in his mind, but all he could see with his mind was the seed-nest on top of the metal pole.

She tried to explain this seed-nest was different, almost like a leaf, and inside, it was filled with tasty human food that even a bird could eat.

Try as he might, though, Bluesky couldn't picture that at all.

"I'll show you!"

The two birds flew high above the trees and houses. Bluesky followed Treeflower, who flew faster and faster. Soon, the familiar houses and streets were behind Bluesky, and still the Song Sparrow flew on.

Bluesky looked down nervously as he kept pace. They passed the last street of the subdivision and quickly crossed the main road into the shopping center beyond.

Treeflower flew straight for the fast food restaurant surrounded by cars and people.

After they drew near, Treeflower held her wings out straight and glided down to the parking lot to land at the edge of the line of parked cars. Bluesky landed next to her. Three House Sparrows glanced over at them and then watched the cars patiently.

Bluesky noted their black bibs and gray crowns, which distinguished them as House Sparrows. Like their cousins, their backs and wings were covered with brown and black feathers.

"What is this place?" Bluesky asked.

"The place where humans feed."

"Where's the seed-nest?"

"Watch."

Bluesky observed several people as they left the car and walked inside, though none of them were eating. Then Treeflower directed his attention to a car with the windows down and people eating inside. Yes, these people were eating; he could see that plain enough.

While he watched, a child in the back seat put his face outside the opened window and looked down looked at the birds on the ground.

Two of the House Sparrows hopped forward eagerly.

The small child laughed and threw a small yellow stick onto the ground.

The two Sparrows chirped excitedly and leapt for it.

One of them snapped it up with his beak and flew quickly away while the other looked up expectantly at the child.

The child threw another yellow stick, and the Sparrow caught it in mid-air and flew off.

"What is that?"

"Food. It's not seed, but it's quite tasty. Watch now ..."

Bluesky almost flew into the air when the man started the engine of the car. The sound startled him, but he held still, seeing that Treeflower was not in the least concerned. As he watched in awe, the car moved backward.

It stopped its motion, and the child suddenly threw out a square, white object.

"That's it!" Treeflower shouted, leaping into the air simultaneously with the remaining House Sparrow.

"Get it, Treeflower! Get it!" Bluesky shouted when he realized she was in a race.

Treeflower flapped her wings until they were a blur. She managed to reach the white object barely ahead of the other bird. She reached down with both her claws, snatched the white paper object, and flew up with the House Sparrow in hot pursuit.

Bluesky took off after them.

"Drop it -- it's mine! I was here first!" the House Sparrow shouted.

"You'll have to catch me!" Treeflower laughed over her shoulder as she flew even faster.

Bluesky was soon right behind the House Sparrow, who had closed the gap and was reaching for the white object with his beak.

Bluesky shouted at the bird as he closed from behind.

The startled House Sparrow darted away without a glance behind.

Bluesky laughed when the other bird sped away as if some fearsome Hawk were right on its tail.

It took them almost ten minutes to make the return trip back since the bag slowed Treeflower down considerably. To Bluesky's relief, he soon recognized trees and houses and knew they were almost back at their starting point.

They landed in the backyard a little distance from the other birds, and Bluesky gazed in wonder at the white bag held in Treeflower's claws.

"Let me see," Bluesky prompted.

Treeflower set the bag down on the ground. She quickly hopped all around it, her beak probing the bag until she found the opening.

Bluesky watched in shock when Treeflower's head disappeared inside the white bag. He started to shout out a warning, but even as he opened his beak, she reappeared with a small yellow object clenched in her beak.

"Mmmm," she said, chewing it appreciatively.

Bluesky hopped forward tentatively and looked inside the opening. Sure enough, down at the far end were more of the yellow crumbs. A pungent odor filled his senses, and he paused a moment. Finally, he poked his head inside and nabbed one of the crumbs.

He ate the tiny piece of french fry with a puzzled expression on his face. After he swallowed, his mouth filled with the taste of salt.

"Wow! That is an interesting food," Bluesky said, smacking his beak together several times with relish.

"Did you notice how the seed-nest carries the food?" Treeflower chirped happily.

Bluesky hopped all around the white bag. He could see that only one end was open; the rest was built sort of like a nest with sides and a bottom.

"But it's not really a seed-nest," Bluesky countered. "I'd call it a food-nest."

"I guess you're right." Treeflower laughed. "I'm just so familiar with a seed-nest, I call anything that carries food inside it a seed-nest."

Within minutes, the two ate every last crumb left inside.

After that, Treeflower flew back to the other birds eating seed.

Bluesky again looked for KC, but the cat was still nowhere to be seen.

Bluesky decided to fly over the house and into the front yard. He hoped he'd find KC over there.

Chapter Twelve

Bluesky flew over the green roof and found a tall ornamental pear tree. He landed on a branch and quickly noticed a flash of brilliant red above him. Peering through the maze of naked branches, he saw a Cardinal sitting on the highest point of the tree.

The Cardinal raised his crest upright and lowered his tail. He opened his thick, orange beak and broke out in a joyous song.

Bluesky felt a chill as a series of gorgeous melodies filled the air. After the last note faded on the wind, another bird sang out from the top of a nearby telephone pole. The jet-black feathers of the Towhee contrasted with the red feathers of his sides and the pure white of his belly.

Bluesky gazed intently at this bird, the first of its kind he had encountered. He became fascinated by the Towhee's startling, red eyes.

The Towhee opened his black beak and sang out two short notes followed by a melodic twinkling.

The Cardinal answered joyously with a series of brilliant 'cheers.'

Bluesky could tell that they weren't trying to out-sing each other. It seemed to him that both birds were simply singing together for the sheer joy of it. This amazed him, for usually birds of the same family sang together or answered each other across the trees. And yet, here were a Cardinal and a Towhee sharing songs together.

While he sat there, first the Cardinal would sing out, and after a polite pause, the Towhee would answer with his own distinctive song. After a few moments of this beautiful and moving duet, Bluesky's heart filled with such joy that he felt compelled to join. When the two singers paused, he sang out to them.

Bluesky uttered a series of chirps and warbles as a kind of tribute to both birds, doing his utmost to blend the Cardinal's beautiful song with that of the Towhee. In so doing, Bluesky composed his first unique song without even realizing it.

Up to this point, Bluesky had either repeated songs his parents had taught him or sang in direct imitation of other birds he had heard. But now, in the passion of the moment, he had created a brand new song.

After he sang the last note, this wonderful realization hit him.

He looked over at the Towhee and smiled.

The Towhee smiled back and shouted, "Well done!"

Bluesky looked up at the Cardinal and smiled.

"Bravo!" the Cardinal chirped brightly. "Let's sing another round!"

The air filled with their three distinct voices. In the trees around them, the other birds grew silent in admiration of the special concert being performed.

It amazed Bluesky every time the three completed a round. Neither of them was singing out of a sense of competition nor bravado. And especially not because one bird felt he was superior to the other.

They all sang simply for the joy of singing!

Each time Bluesky's turn came, he sang louder

and stronger only to add to the beauty of the moment. Sensing it themselves, the Towhee and the Cardinal also sang out with all their might until the air echoed with song and emotion.

Suddenly, the magic of the moment was interrupted by the ugliest whistling Bluesky had ever heard. Looking down, he decided the bird must be sick or dying to sing as badly as that.

He searched everywhere along the ground, and finally he saw the answer -- it was a man!

And he was trying to sing along with birds.

How dare he?

Bluesky sang out with angry urgency. He burst forth with an endless stream of whistles and warbles as he chastised the pretender below. After his indignation reached a climax, he spread his wings and leapt into the air just above the branch, all the while singing non-stop. He performed a slow loop with his tail feathers spread wide, singing out his displeasure at the man.

He felt certain the man below had been humbled by his magnificent display and would now walk away in disgrace.

Bluesky paused and looked down at him with a triumphant glint in his eye.

Incredibly, the man tried to sing again! An awful torrent of harsh whistles and toneless warbles gushed out of his untaught mouth.

Bluesky hopped excitedly from one end of the branch and back again. He peered intently at the silly creature below -- first with his left eye, and then with a quick turn he peered down at him with his right eye.

Did this man have no dignity? Did he not realize he was trying to sing with a Mockingbird?

Even more incredible, it seemed he was daring to challenge a Mockingbird to the 'Singing Game'!

Didn't he realize his place in the world? How could any non-bird hope to out-sing a Mockingbird? Why, no bird in the entire world could hope to hold his own with a Mockingbird, except maybe another Mockingbird!

Raising his head high, he allowed his tail to droop and sang forth with his entire being in order to teach this man a lesson he'd never forget.

He repeated the cheerful song he had just created with the Cardinal and Towhee, but this time he added a couple of melodic flourishes and ended it with a long, soulful trill just for good measure.

Bluesky paused expectantly.

The man whistled back in a sad attempt to mimic Bluesky's sumptuous song, but his notes were out-of-tune and poorly whistled. His pitiful attempt at a trill at the end was completely laughable.

Bluesky stared at him with open beak.

He wondered if the man considered that a song at all! It was more like noise!

Even though the outcome of this 'Singing Games' was a foregone conclusion to Bluesky, he sang out again with a beautiful voice and clear notes. This time, he ended with a double trill!

Bluesky eyed the man carefully, waiting ...

Surely the man would give up and not disgrace himself any further.

As he watched, the man stared back up at him.

Bluesky could see his eyes fixed on him. It seemed he even stared at the emptiness of his missing leg. Bluesky peered back down at him, matching the intensity of his gaze, and then he sang out another challenge.

The man laughed with joy.

Flabbergasted, Bluesky sang out again, embellishing his song even more. Down below, the man laughed even harder as he placed his hands on his hips. This only spurred Bluesky to further efforts to overwhelm him and win the game.

After a few moments more, the man turned and walked inside the house.

Bluesky cried out with chiding calls while the man retreated in shame, "See, you didn't stand a chance against me -- I am a Mockingbird. You can't play the 'Singing-Game' with me! Keep on walking!"

Hearing a noise on the branch beside him, he stopped chastising the man and turned to find the Cardinal perched next to him.

"He wasn't trying to out-sing you, you know."

Bluesky frowned in puzzlement. "The man kept trying to imitate my song, although they were feeble and pitiful attempts, and anyone who tries to imitate a Mockingbird is issuing a challenge to play the "Singing Game.' Every bird knows that!"

"Mockingbirds shouldn't be so quick to jump to conclusions." The Cardinal raised his crest upright.

A flurry of feathers signaled the arrival of the Towhee. Bluesky opened his eyes wide in surprise when the Towhee landed right next to the Cardinal. Even more astonishing, both birds bowed their heads to each other in greeting and smiled.

"Wow, that was awesome!" the Towhee chirped excitedly.

"It really was. The three of us singing from the treetops, and especially how the Mockingbird created a song that was part yours and part mine and part his! That was totally cool!" The Cardinal laughed.

"Yeah, it was great." The Towhee smiled, but the smile disappeared as he looked at Bluesky. "Well, it was great until you 'went off' on that poor man."

"He was challenging me," Bluesky said with indignation

The Towhee and Cardinal looked at each other, and then both broke out in happy laughter. It seemed to Bluesky that these two birds, although completely different kinds, acted like close friends.

"No, he just wanted to join in our fun. He loves birds." The Cardinal fluttered his wings and smiled confidently.

"Now, how do you know that?" Bluesky's puzzlement increased.

"He keeps the seed-nests full of seed for us, and he spreads them on the ground for birds that prefer to eat them there, like me," the Towhee said.

"I visit his seed-nest several times every day. It's winter, and food is scarce." The Cardinal raised his crest erect. "But pardon me. We haven't properly introduced ourselves."

The Towhee and Cardinal bowed their heads in unison.

Bluesky was doubly amazed; he had never

experienced such a formal greeting from any bird before, and these two seemed to relish doing it.

"My name is Daymoon," the Cardinal chirped in a crystal-clear voice. "I am most pleased to meet you."

"And I am Bushhopper." The Towhee hopped twice for emphasis.

"My name is Bluesky," Bluesky responded, in somewhat of a daze. The Towhee's name echoed inside his mind.

After Bluesky's silence continued, Daymoon spoke. "We're glad you joined us. I especially liked your song. I felt you honored us, mixing parts of our two songs with yours."

"Daymoon is right. For just a few moments, the three of us sang in perfect harmony. It was awesome." Bushhopper closed his eyes and sighed in delight over the recent memory.

Bluesky kept staring at the Towhee. His heart beat rapidly with excitement. The Towhee's name reminded Bluesky of his great desire to find a Mockingbird friend.

"I like your name, Bushhopper," Bluesky said tentatively.

"Ah, it's a common enough name among the Towhee family. We love the bushes. We nest among them. We feed among them. The bushes are our home." Bushhopper flapped his wings a couple of times for emphasis.

"It's too bad you're not a Mockingbird." Bluesky sighed.

"What do you mean?" Bushhopper laughed.

"I've always wanted a friend like Treehopper.

You know, from the Song-Tale."

"Why does your friend have to be a Mockingbird?"

Bluesky's mind reeled. He wondered why Bushhopper would ask such a thing. Everyone knew that birds stayed among their own kind. Their family, their friends, and their mate were always of the same family of birds.

"Birds of a feather flock together," Bluesky said simply.

Bushhopper looked at Bluesky with a puzzled expression. A strange silence settled around the three birds.

Finally, Daymoon spoke. "I think the only birds who loves bushes as much as a Towhee are the Catbirds."

"Yes, we rub wings with Catbirds a lot. They're good birds mostly."

"I've met a Catbird once." Bluesky thought back many weeks to his chance encounter. "He was a friendly bird."

"I'm glad to hear you reached out to a bird of another feather. It expands one's mind, you know." Bushhopper paused a moment in thought. "It helps us to see things from another's perspective. It builds understanding ..."

"I'm on a journey to meet other birds," Bluesky said with pride.

"That is a noble undertaking. I am doubly pleased we met you now." Daymoon glanced a brief moment down at Bluesky's solitary leg.

Before Bluesky felt the slightest embarrassment or sadness, Daymoon quickly looked back up at him and smiled.

"I had heard there was a one-legged Mockingbird living nearby."

"Er, yes. That's me." Bluesky looked down at the branch between his toes, unwilling to meet their gaze now. "I-I hope that doesn't bother you, does it?"

"Not in the least. We don't judge birds solely by their feathers," Bushhopper said. He hopped right next to Daymoon and put one wing around him. "What they are inside is more important to us. In fact, Daymoon and I think all this talk about 'birds of a feather' is over-rated actually."

"Yes, my friend is correct. Too much emphasis on what a bird is on the outside -- how gorgeous his plumage or colorful his feathers. And if they only make friends within their own kind, think of how much they miss out."

Bluesky was utterly surprised at both Bushhopper's and now Daymoon's statements. He lifted himself erect and gazed from the Cardinal to the Towhee and back again.

"You two are friends?" Bluesky asked. "That's incredible. You're two completely different kinds of birds."

"If you look at our feathers, we are a Cardinal and a Towhee," Daymoon said with a glint in his eyes. He glanced over at Bushhopper.

"If you could look inside our hearts, you'd see we are as close as brothers born in the same nest!" Bushhopper added with a laugh.

"And think about this." Daymoon's tone took on a mysterious air. "Even if our feathers mark us as a

Towhee or a Cardinal or a Mockingbird ... inside, we're all birds, right?"

"We all have wings, eyes, tail feathers -- and we all fly!" Bushhopper shouted with glee.

"I've never heard of two birds from different families being friends -- ever." Bluesky shook his head.

"It's not common, but it should be. As the wise saying goes, 'There's good in every bird,'" Daymoon sang out joyfully.

"What about your family? Your mom and dad?" Bluesky asked.

"Nothing can replace your parents or your brothers and sisters," Bushhopper said. "But if birds only make friends with others of their own kind, that's when they miss out."

"I never thought of it like that."

"Daymoon and I are alike -- we're brothers of the heart."

"How?" Bluesky asked. Suddenly, Nightwind's words echoed inside his mind.

"We both love to sing. We both love to fly to new places we've never been. And we both love to meet new birds -- of all kinds!" Bushhopper said excitedly.

"We love adventure too!" Daymoon chirped cheerily. "We like to keep things fun. We'd rather laugh than cry. We'd rather sing with others than argue or fight."

"Don't forget our personal motto!" Bushhopper said with a sparkle in his red eyes.

Daymoon let out a series of chirps like a trumpet fanfare. After he finished, the two friends readied themselves and shouted out together, *"Do something fun every day!"*

Bluesky stared at them in absolute amazement. They were each so different on the outside. Each was beautiful in his own way, but still, they were different kinds ...

"We're different on the outside," Daymoon said, almost as if he had just read Bluesky's very thoughts.

"But we're the same inside -- in spirit," Bushhopper chirped happily.

"Have you never heard this before?" Daymoon paused a moment. "'The ties that bind *brothers of the heart* are stronger than those which bind *brothers of the feather*.'"

"No, I've never heard that one before." Bluesky's mind whirled with this new concept.

"It's an adventure to meet birds of all kinds," Daymoon added.

"My journey is kind of like that!" Bluesky whistled.

"Tell us more," Daymoon said.

Bluesky explained how all the Mockingbirds had ostracized him and forced his family away. With pain in his heart, he told them how he met Ol' Gray Mama and how it was her suggestion she talk to Nightwind.

He filled in the details about his conversations with the wise Owl and especially how Nightwind directed him to seek out birds of all kinds, and the two listened even more intently. When he explained the goal of his journey was to learn what was good and beautiful about each bird individually and as a

164

kind, Bluesky could sense the excitement growing in both Daymoon and Bushhopper.

He told them of the birds he had already met. He told them what he learned about each one, the beauty their species added to the world, and also about the good of each one that he discerned by observing them closely and talking with them.

"Is Nightwind your friend?" Bushhopper asked earnestly.

"I-I don't know. I never thought about it that way." Bluesky's mind whirled with activity, but he focused his mind back on his journey.

It seemed obvious the outward beauty of this Cardinal was his brilliant scarlet feathers and contrasting black mask. As for the Towhee, his jet black feathers contrasted with the rufous-red of his sides and white of his belly, but Bluesky felt especially drawn to his red eyes.

However, the outward beauty of both paled in comparison to their joyful spirit and adventurous outlook. Somehow he knew these were two birds Nightwind would love to meet. Most important, he felt a special joy simply being in their company -- their joyous spirit was contagious!

"I'd like to meet Nightwind," Daymoon said. "He sounds like a 'brother of the heart' to me." He glanced over at Bushhopper.

"Absolutely." Bushhopper laughed. "He's obviously a very wise bird, and we've not met an Owl yet, have we?"

"I think we will, and perhaps before the sun sets this very day." Daymoon lifted his crest with keen interest.

"Let's go find him!" Bluesky leapt into the air with Bushhopper and Daymoon right behind.

The sun had set low through the leafless branches when Bluesky finally found the tree he sought. He landed on the familiar branch and peered up and down the tree in search of Nightwind. A movement caught his eye right beside the trunk two limbs up.

A mysterious HOO HOO HOO pierced the air.

"It's me, Nightwind! And I've brought two birds I just met. I think you'll like them very much." Bluesky flew up to the branch.

Nightwind slowly blinked his large yellow eyes and smiled. "I am glad to see you again, my young Mockingbird." He turned his head until he faced directly over his right shoulder and peered intently at the Cardinal and Towhee. "And WHOO are you?"

"I am Daymoon, Mister Owl. Bluesky has told me many good things about you."

"Nightwind, please." The Owl smiled benevolently.

"I am Bushhopper," the Towhee whistled.

Nightwind chuckled knowingly. He turned his head effortlessly back to face Bluesky. "I imagine you like his name a lot!"

"I do!" Bluesky agreed.

Bluesky proceeded to tell Nightwind about his journey and the birds he'd met since the last time they'd talked.

He started with Treeflower and the food-nest. Nightwind found this quite intriguing and asked Bluesky a number of questions, but Bluesky felt the most important thing was how glad he felt that the Song Sparrow had treated him with such friendliness and kindness again. She had almost seemed as glad to see him as he did to see her!

Next, he told of meeting the funny Robin and the laughs they'd shared. He mentioned he felt the inner goodness of Robins was their merry attitude on life and that Tootight in particular displayed this wonderful trait. He told Nightwind it was the most he had ever laughed with another bird in all his life. Bluesky looked forward to looking up Tootight again and having another good laugh.

Finally, he talked of meeting Daymoon and Bushhopper.

"I've never met two birds more different on the outside but who seem like brothers on the inside!" Bluesky said excitedly.

"I see you've had a wonderful time, Bluesky." Nightwind turned to the others. "And I'm particularly glad he met you two."

"We're glad we met Bluesky too!" Daymoon chirped with a clear voice. "In fact, we'd like to accompany him on his journey."

"I'd like to meet this Tootight for sure," Bushhopper said eagerly. "I love a good laugh."

Nightwind smiled at them. He turned back to Bluesky. "I'm glad your journey is bearing fruit. In fact, I think it's time to take it to another level."

"Whoa," Daymoon whistled.

"You believe that there is good in every bird, correct?" Nightwind asked them all.

"Yes!" Bluesky, Daymoon, and Bushhopper said simultaneously.

"I want you to continue to meet other birds, just as you have, but there are two birds in particular I want you to seek out."

The Mockingbird, Cardinal, and Towhee held their breath as the Owl paused for a long moment.

"I want you to seek out the Crow."

"The Crow?" all three shouted in disbelief.

"I thought you felt there is good in every bird?" Nightwind asked with a hint of humor.

"We -- we do," Bushhopper said without conviction. "But a Crow?"

"Yes, even a Crow brings a unique beauty to this world. And even more important is what he is on the inside."

"But everyone knows a Crow is a harbinger of evil!" Daymoon protested.

"A myth. A tale. Not a bit of truth to it. It's a label given these large black birds all through history." Nightwind blinked slowly.

Bluesky thought for a moment of all the birds he'd met, thinking of each in turn and how he had been so glad he had met each of them.

"I'll do it." Bluesky looked over at Daymoon and Bushhopper, who dropped their beaks in surprise.

"All right -- we'll join you," Daymoon said after a pause.

"Me too." Bushhopper fluffed out his feathers.

"There is one other bird I want you to seek out, but with this bird you cannot simply fly up to him and meet. You'll have to be careful -- *very careful*." Nightwind closed his eyes and waited for the obvious question.

168

Bluesky felt a sudden chill in his heart, almost as if he knew what bird Nightwind meant.

"What bird is that?" Bushhopper asked breathlessly.

"The Hawk."

"The Hawk!" Once again, the three shouted their total disbelief in unison.

"But, he'll eat us!" Daymoon exclaimed.

"I certainly hope not. That could put a damper on your journey." Nightwind smiled mischievously.

"What?" Bluesky shouted in complete shock.

Nightwind lifted his left wing and preened his feathers nonchalantly while the other three stared at him with open beaks.

"What kind of answer is that?" Bluesky cried out.

"You'll need to learn how to approach a Hawk first. There is a way a bird might approach a raptor safely." Nightwind's tone was matter of fact.

"And just how can we learn such a skill?" Daymoon laughed nervously.

"Why don't you ask a Crow?" Nightwind raised his right wing and continued his meticulous preening.

"Huh?" Daymoon and Bushhopper said at the same time.

"This is impossible!" Bluesky said with emotion. "Besides that, what can be good about a bird which eats other birds!"

"Agreed," Daymoon said.

Bushhopper remained silent, obviously in deep thought.

Nightwind continued his preening as if they

were no longer there. He continued with the feathers of his belly. Finally, he sighed and spoke earnestly so they could hear his conviction. *"There's good in every bird."*

After repeating that familiar saying, he closed his eyes and grew still with a contented pose.

For the first time since his journey began, Bluesky felt real fear.

It did seem an impossible task. One of the first things any bird learned from its parents after it learned to fly was to always keep a sharp eye on the sky -- for the Hawk was the most feared predator of all -- silent and lightning-quick in its attack.

Bluesky shivered.

"A Hawk is a bird too," Bushhopper finally said.

Daymoon looked at his friend in shock, but after a moment, he nodded agreement. "Yes, but I don't know how in the world we can ever get close enough to talk with one and find out!"

"I guess we'll ask a Crow," Bluesky said with a questioning glance at the Owl.

"Yes," Nightwind said with his eyes still closed. "Ask the Crow. I know just the one you should seek."

"What's his name?" Bluesky asked.

"Blackfeather."

Chapter Thirteen

Mark glanced at his watch after he pulled into the driveway.

It was almost six thirty. He'd gotten home later than normal this Friday evening, but traffic was always worse on Fridays in Atlanta. At least he had a better commute than most -- for the last ten years he had commuted via Camp Creek to an office building within sight of the runways of the airport.

He got out and grabbed his laptop case.

Strolling up to his front door, he paused a moment as the joyful whistling of a bird filled the evening air. Mark looked up, hoping to spot him.

A familiar series of clear and powerful whistles came from the ornamental pear trees in his front yard. He looked up toward the top of the leafless branches and quickly spotted the red feathers of a cardinal.

Far above, the cardinal raised his scarlet crest straight up as he cocked his head and looked down at Mark. The bird opened its orange beak and sang three bright and clear chirps in quick succession.

Mark and the bird eyed one another for a moment, and then the cardinal sang to him again.

"Daddy! What are you doing?"

Mark glanced at the opened front door where Katie stood.

"I'm watching a cardinal serenade me."

"Oh," Katie said with a knowing tone. "Well, Mom says that supper's almost done."

Mark nodded and chuckled before he replied.

"Tell Mom I'm on the way in now."

He strolled up as Katie shouted into the house and repeated Mark's message to Jane. From the kitchen, he heard Jane cry back, "Good!"

He placed the strap of his laptop case across his shoulder to free up his right hand so he could pick Katie up when she ran up to him. He held her close a moment, and they embraced happily.

"I'm glad you're home, Daddy."

"Me too, Katie."

He carried her up to the front door. Above him the cardinal renewed its happy chirping while an unseen catbird burst forth with its own happy song.

As he opened the door, a third bird suddenly gave voice from the small stand of trees next to his home. It was a two-part snippet -- two whistles followed by a flute-like twinkling.

"Do you hear that bird, Katie?"

"Which one, Daddy? I hear lots of them."

"The one over there, the one singing like this." Mark performed a passable imitation of the bird. Right as he finished, the bird sang out again as if on cue.

"I hear it, Daddy! What is it?"

"It's a towhee. I hear them a lot around our house. I think there are several of them living right around us."

"I like him." Katie laughed with childish glee.

"I do too. They're nice birds -- and pretty."

Katie giggled.

"Let's sit on the front porch and listen to them a minute before we go in." Mark set down his laptop bag. He placed Katie gently on his lap after he sat down on the wicker chair on the front porch. Together, they listened to the cardinal and towhee singing their cheerful refrains over and over again.

"Why do they sing like that?" Katie asked inquisitively.

"Maybe because they're real happy. Or maybe they're real lonely."

Katie giggled with a lilting, innocent tone.

Suddenly, a third bird joined the chorus.

Mark sat up. "Hear that bird, honey?"

"Yes, Daddy."

"That's a mockingbird. Listen close-- he's imitating their songs and mixing them with his own song."

"He's a good bird," Katie said with a smile.

"He's a *real singer*."

They listened to the three birds for several minutes, mesmerized by the joyful, happy singers.

"Watch this." Mark sat Katie down and walked back into the front yard until he was beneath the trees in which the birds sang. He looked up, glancing from one bird to another as they continued their round-robin sing-along.

Finally, after timing each bird's song, he pursed his lips and whistled out right after the mockingbird finished, doing his best to imitate a bit of the mockingbird's song. When he finished whistling, he looked up into the tree and noticed a mockingbird staring sternly back down at him.

He chuckled as the mockingbird hopped around in rising agitation, all the while peering directly at him as if daring him to whistle again.

Mark whistled out again.

The mockingbird launched into a forceful and ultra-melodic reply almost at once.

Mark put his hands on his hips and laughed at the bird's antics.

"Daddy, is that bird mad at you?" Katie called out.

Right at that moment, as Mark stared up at the mockingbird hopping about and scolding him, he noticed that the bird only used one leg.

He felt a strong sense of déjà-vu fill his heart.

Yes, he'd seen this one-legged bird before ... back in the spring when it had first left the nest. He'd guessed then it had hurt its leg. But now that it was grown, he realized it only had one leg.

In a pang of emotion, Mark realized this particular bird must have had a tough life. Somehow he knew it, though he wasn't exactly sure how he knew.

He stared up at the mockingbird while it continued to scold him with a myriad of twitters, whistles, and trills.

The bird became so worked up that he leapt off the branch and flew in a slow circle, still singing away. When he finished his 'singing circle,' he landed back on the same spot he had started.

Mark watched the bird with a mixture of awe and sadness.

"Mark! Katie! Supper's on the table. Come on!"

Katie ran inside to her mother.

Without a sound, Mark walked toward the front porch. He grabbed the shoulder strap of the laptop case and opened the door.

He glanced back at the one-legged mockingbird

one more time. The bird scolded him again, leaping back into the air.

Mark chuckled to himself while he walked inside his home. He set his laptop case down and walked into the kitchen.

Jane smiled at him as she placed a bowl of steaming rice on the table alongside the other food.

He walked up and kissed her.

He always kissed his wife when he left for work and when he first arrived home. He also hugged Philip and Katie before he left for work and when he got home, but kissing his wife was special. Every morning, the last thing he did before leaving for work was to kiss Jane.

Now they sat down and ate supper together as a family -- their normal routine.

After supper, Jane started clearing the table while Mark and the kids retired to the den. Katie turned on the TV to watch a favorite show while Mark walked across to the desk and the PC. He wanted to check the news and sports and then check his personal email.

While he read an email from his good friend Sam in South Carolina, Katie suddenly appeared beside him with a big smile and a twinkle in her eyes.

"Can I get a new toy?"

"Hmm, well, what kind of toy is it?" Mark closed down his email to give Katie his full attention.

"A doll."

"A doll? Why, you've got dozens of dolls already. Why do you want another one?" Mark asked.

"She talks."

"You have plenty of dolls that talk, honey."

Katie's cherubic face turned into the most exaggerated expression of seriousness that a five-year-old could manage.

Mark laughed out loud.

"Daddy! I only want a toy."

Mark put his arm around her and pulled her close, though she neither uncrossed her arms to hug him back nor changed her childish, serious expression.

"Baby, tell me why you really want another doll."

"Because ... she will make me happy."

"Happy?" Mark said in surprise. "How is that?"

"Because ... the kids on TV are happy when they play with it."

Mark nodded his head with understanding. "Honey, that's a TV advertisement. They make it seem like the things they want to sell you will make you happy. Or make you pretty. Or --"

"But they're all smiling and laughing when they play with the doll." Katie pouted with an expression of the greatest disappointment.

"Baby, *things* don't make us happy."

"Mama says your new car makes you happy."

Mark sat back in his chair, contemplating her words -- or the words of her mother. He sighed. "Sometimes we confuse fun with happiness."

"Oh!" Katie looked at him questioningly.

"My car doesn't make me happy. You make me happy!" He wrapped his arms around Katie and picked her up in a warm embrace.

Katie giggled and laughed with childish glee while Mark held her close.

"How do you know the new doll won't make me happy?" she asked.

"Well, things are nice, things are fun. And things can make life enjoyable, like my new car. But they don't make us happy." Mark looked down at his little daughter's lovely face and smiled. "If I didn't have that car and if I didn't have my HDTV, even if I didn't have this house, I'd still be happy."

"Why?" Katie asked with a look of surprise.

"Because you and Philip and your mom would still be with me, no matter where I lived or what kind of car I drove."

Katie hugged him tight.

"I love you and Mommy!" she exclaimed.

Her embrace tightened. Finally, she released her bear-hold on his neck and leaned back with a questioning expression. "Can I still have the new doll?" Katie asked

Mark chuckled at his daughter's persistence. "I think your mother and I assigned you some chores around the house, right?" Katie nodded. "We asked you to put up your toys each night and put your dirty clothes in the hamper, to help your mother keep the house clean?"

"Yes ..." Katie's tone changed to doubt. "I think I forgot to do that yesterday."

"Yes, your mom told me." Mark paused. "Let's see if you can remember to clean up your toys and put away your clothes for a whole week. If you can do that, maybe ... maybe I might buy you that new doll."

"Oh, Daddy!"

"Remember, a doll doesn't make you happy -- that's TV trying to make you think that."

"But I'll have fun playing with her."

"Yes, it will probably be fun." Mark smiled broadly. "And Saturday, we're going over to Mrs. Williamson's house and help her around the house. That is something that will make us all happy -- 'there's more happiness in giving than there is in receiving.'"

"Can Philip and I play with her dog, Bounce?" Katie asked.

"After I rake up the leaves and your mother helps her clean up inside the house."

"Will she bake us a pecan pie?"

Mark grinned and rubbed his belly with keen anticipation. "I sure hope so! She usually does that as a way of thanking us."

"That will make me happy!" Katie laughed with glee.

"Doing nice things for other people can make us happy, especially those less fortunate than us."

"Is Mrs. Williamson ... less fortoo ..." But Katie couldn't quite pronounce it.

"Fortunate. Yes, in a way. She has everything she needs money-wise -- her husband provided well for her -- but her children live far away, and after her husband died, she now lives all alone."

"I like visiting her. She always gives me a big hug and tells me about when she was a little girl."

"See, people make us happy. Our relationships with others are what truly bring us happiness -- not

178

things. I want you to always remember this, okay?" Katie nodded enthusiastically.

Katie hugged him and slipped down to go back and watch TV. Mark got up from the desk and started to walk upstairs to join his wife, who was probably reading.

When he passed the front door, KC looked longingly up at him.

"Who's the pretty kitty?"

"Mrrrrowwww."

He reached down, caressed the top of her head, and gently rubbed her left ear.

"Do you want to go out, KC?"

KC looked up expectantly at the doorknob.

"Now, now, you know you can't go outside. We don't want you and Buddy getting into any more fights with that bad yellow cat. Maybe you can go out in a week or two."

"Mrrrrroww. Meooowww," KC complained.

Mark leaned down and stroked her affectionately. KC purred and then walked toward the kitchen.

Mark trudged up the steps to the second floor and walked into the master bedroom. Jane lay across the bed reading a novel. He took off his shoes and sat on the bed next to her. He reached over to his nightstand and picked up his novel and opened it at the bookmark.

After he began to read, Jane spoke. "Have you heard any more about the EPA testing?"

Mark's thoughts rushed in a sudden flurry of activity as he focused. The memories came flooding back.

"Yes, our group has gone over them in detail, those made public."

"What did the EPA testing of the air indicate?" Jane set her book down.

"Well, first, you've got to remember we live in a suburb of Atlanta and Atlanta is a city of cars. The air pollution is worse around here than out in the countryside. In fact, the normal air quality is so bad it's like a person smoking a pack of cigarettes every day."

"That's pretty sad!" Jane exclaimed.

"Sad, but true."

"But did anything show up that might be causing these miscarriages? And the rise in deformities in babies?"

"The sub-divisions where most of the incidents originate, well, they tested the air, and they tested soil extensively as well as the water table underneath." He sighed. "You know, to make sure no one accidentally built on top of some kind of toxic landfill like they did back at Love Canal in New York."

"I remember that, all those people got sick -- some kind of rare cancer. And many of them died." Jane's eyes filled with tears.

"Well, they eliminated that possibility -- all the soil tested clean. That included our sub-division, so we know our homes weren't built right on top of something toxic. And the water is clean and healthy."

Jane leaned over and hugged Mark tightly a moment. Mark sensed that she sought comfort, so he simply held her as she rested her head against his shoulder.

Finally, she raised her head and smiled. "Well, at least that's two worries off our minds -- the soil and water."

"Yes, they're concentrating on more testing of the air in the affected areas, but the initial results are inconclusive."

"They won't stop testing will they?"

"No, they'll keep on."

"Mark, they might take months and months to act. What will happen to all these expectant mothers and their babies? And what about our children? They could be at risk!"

"Now, now, honey."

"Mark! I just feel ... I just feel we have to do something!"

"Well, our group is doing something." Mark caressed his wife's hand. "A few weeks back, we asked for reports on any businesses that operated in Douglas County the last twenty years that had anything to do with chemicals."

"What kind of chemicals?"

"Any kind -- swimming pool chemicals, pesticides, paints, fertilizer, any kind. We figured that big plants are probably regulated and monitored, so we asked for any smaller companies that obtained licenses to operate with any kind of chemicals. We got quite a list and have been looking into them ever since."

"That sounds like a good idea. But what are you looking for?" Jane's blue eyes echoed her plea.

We go out in pairs and ask them if they've had any spills the last few months. We also look around for any spills or leaks or anything suspicious. If we find something, we report it to the proper agency so they can check into it more."

"Have you found anything?"

Mark reflected a moment.

In reality, the EPA had listed a half-dozen incidents of accidental chemical releases over the years, including ones by Charles Marcion and his company. Most had been due to truck accidents and subsequent spills of their cargo. In each case, the official response and clean-up had been swift and efficient. And in several incidents, including the incident with Marcion's company, the chemicals had been safely contained and transported to an approved landfill according to regulations.

Still, something about the crazy old man and the way he acted just didn't add up. Mark felt a growing suspicion that Marcion hadn't told him everything ...

"Mark?"

"Well, we've found a few reports of actual chemical spills," Mark said as he focused again, "but all of them were cleaned up and then disposed properly. Most businesses operate in a responsible way. And that's good!"

"Mark, do you think this is really helping?" Jane's worried expression did not change.

"Well, it might. I mean, I feel like we've got to do something. These government agencies move so slowly. And well, bad things keep happening."

"Someone has to find out what's killing these unborn babies." Jane stifled a sob.

"We'll keep trying."

"Mark!" Jane exclaimed with tears in her eyes.

"I-I haven't told you the bad news."

Mark felt a chill in his heart.

"I found out today at the grocery store, when I ran into Helen." Jane wiped her eyes. "Helen lost her baby -- she was so distraught. She had a miscarriage two weeks ago and was in the hospital an entire week with complications."

Mark shook his head sadly.

"Don't you realize what this means?"

Mark paused, trying to fathom her meaning, but he drew a blank.

"Mark, she lives on the same street that we do!" Jane sobbed.

***

Our Feathered Friends of the Southeast
A. C. Wages

Ruby-throated Hummingbird
Latin: *Archilochus colubris*

(excerpts)

Hummingbirds are a special breed of bird -- Dorothy E. Wages

Ruby-throated hummingbirds 'hum' because they can beat their wings *fifty-three times a second* in normal flight!

Now, think a moment about that single, amazing fact -- *fifty-three times a second*. That's a lot of motion. Doing anything fifty-three times a second is simply mind-boggling!

No wonder their wings are a blur of motion when you watch one of these 'flying jewels' visit your feeder. You'll normally hear the humming of their wings right before they show up. They usually hover with a humming drone while they feed, their bodies arched while they voraciously drink the liquid.

If they notice you are watching, at intervals they'll stop feeding and fly backwards, squeaking excitedly as they ensure you haven't come an inch closer since their last check. If everything checks out fine, they'll dart forward and hover again for a drink before their next spot check.

The ruby-throated hummingbird is the only one of its species that breeds in the southeast and the entire eastern section of the United States. These fascinating birds migrate north from Central America and cross the Gulf of Mexico in order to spend the entire summer feeding on flowers and feeders here.

They are about three inches in size and are covered with iridescent green feathers over their back and head. The male sports red iridescent feathers on his throat (called a gorget) bordered with a white collar of feathers. He also has white feathers on his belly.

The female is slightly larger with feathers the same color as the male, with the exception that she wears plain white feathers across her throat. One other difference is that the lower edges of her tail feathers are edged in white.

In normal light, the male's gorget may appear

black, but when direct sunlight strikes at just the right angle, the ruby-red feathers sparkle like glowing jewels.

Although their wings are fast and powerful, the ruby-throated hummingbird's legs are so short that they walk awkwardly at best and have even more trouble attempting to hop.

Hummingbirds live only in the Western Hemisphere; they can be found throughout the Americas as well as the islands of the Caribbean.

They are the only bird capable of hovering in one place. In fact, the ruby-throated hummingbird can not only hover motionless as it feeds, but it can fly backwards and even upside down!

In normal flight, they can travel at speeds of twenty-five miles an hour. In a power dive, they can reach speeds of nearly fifty miles per hour.

These small birds are indeed bundles of energy. Their normal heart rate is six hundred and fifteen beats per minute -- wow!

No wonder we love to set out our hummingbird feeders every spring and sit in awe as these amazing birds come and go in rapid succession, filling the air with continuous squeaks of joy.

The Cherokee word for hummingbird is *walela*. We must assume it is specifically meant for the ruby-throated hummingbird, since it is the only one of its species that migrates and breeds in the eastern United States.

Both the Cherokee and the Creek tell a similar myth entitled "The Race Between the Crane and the Hummingbird." The gist of the story is that both a hummingbird and a crane fall in love with a beautiful maiden. She is attracted to the *walela* more than the crane, and yet she must choose between them. She finally devises a solution -- a race around the world.

Whoever wins the race will marry her.

She imagined her favorite bird, the speedy hummingbird, would win such a race easily. However, in the Cherokee version, the maiden did not realize a hummingbird only flies during the day while a crane will fly day and night.

In the Creek version, the crane wins because the hummingbird flies in zigzag patterns while the crane flies in a straight line. In both versions, the crane easily wins the mythical race and marries the beautiful maiden.

The first person to mention these birds in writing was none other than Captain John Smith, the man who founded Jamestown Colony. In his written description back to Europe in 1608, he described this bird as '*Scarce so big as a wren and less than a kinglet.*'

The first written reference that included its present-day name was written by William Wood during the 1630s -- '*For colour Shee is glorious as the Rainebowe, as shee flies shee makes a little humming noise like a humble bee; wherefore shee is called Humbird.*'

The ruby-throated hummingbird was one of the first native birds of the Americas to become both famous and beloved by people all around the world.

Even more shocking than the oversight of the Eastern Towhee, not a single state has chosen this wonderfully unique bird as its own state bird.

Chapter Fourteen

The cold of winter quickly evaporated under the warming rays of the southern sun as the spring equinox approached. Every day grew longer and warmer.

Bluesky visited regularly with Dancingleaves, Treeflower, Daymoon, Bushhopper, and Tootight. In fact, not a week would pass without him talking and playing with each in turn.

Treeflower was easy to locate, since she regularly visited the seed-nest near where Bluesky lived along with Ol' Gray Mama and the other Doves. Dancingleaves was also easy to find, since he was shy and stayed close to his parents. Bluesky would usually visit the Bluebird during the early evening and watch his aerial acrobatics as he caught bugs in mid-air.

Tootight was harder to locate, since he was always on the wing searching for food and a good laugh. Since all American Robins loved to laugh, it was hard for Bluesky to distinguish his individual laugh from that of another Robin. Eventually however, Bluesky learned that where one Robin laughed, Tootight was never far away.

Above all, Bluesky earnestly sought out the company of Daymoon and his friend Bushhopper during those final days of winter. He loved to hear them tell of their adventures and of their own journey to meet birds of all kinds. It was because they liked to fly farther afield in order to visit new places and new birds that they were so hard to find.

And yet, the times Bluesky spent singing and visiting with the Cardinal and Towhee were very special, and he cherished those times deep inside his heart.

Bluesky also visited with Nightwind at least once each week. He'd tell the Owl more wonderful things he'd learned about each of these birds as well as any new birds he'd met.

During all this time, Bluesky continued to search for KC, but she was nowhere to be seen in the yard or the woods around the house.

Finally, he remembered her telling him that when she was inside the house, she would sit by the window and watch birds outside. With that realization, he returned and immediately spotted her watching intently from inside the house. Bluesky was ecstatic.

He flew up and sat next to the window on the edge of the picnic table.

KC quickly explained through the screen of the open window that her dad had been very upset with her and Buddy for getting into a fight with Tiger. In fact, their dad had to take Buddy to the veterinarian the next day because his wounds became infected.

Their human parents had kept them both inside the house all this time. But now Buddy was fully healed, and they sensed that their discipline was coming to an end. In fact, KC had been allowed outside for a short time yesterday. Both cats hoped they would soon be able to come outside for longer periods during the day.

KC mentioned that she had seen Bluesky several times through the window, but he had been so intent on finding her out in the yard that he had never looked toward the house.

Bluesky was very excited to meet KC again.

Resting next to the window, Bluesky related a brief summary of his recent adventures.

He had met many other birds besides Treeflower, Dancingleaves, Tootight, Daymoon, and Bushhopper. However, these particular birds were the ones he liked the best, so he sought out their company again and again. Of all the birds he'd met, these few always welcomed him back again with a smile and open wings.

He did not mention the next goal Nightwind had given him.

He'd put it off all this time, though he wasn't quite sure why. Well, he knew why he hesitated to meet the Hawk -- he was afraid.

Nightwind had advised him to 'learn' how to approach this hunter. That was the reason why he needed to seek out the Crow first.

Crows were a mystery to Bluesky. They were always around. He heard their raucous cries, and sometimes he caught a glimpse of their jet-black forms flying above the trees as if on some urgent errand.

He could have sought out a Crow at any time.

But still he hesitated.

Crows were so *different*. They had an aura about them -- a strangeness.

Some birds spoke about them only in hushed tones while others mentioned them with outright distaste and distrust. Even more surprising, some thought they were the smartest birds of all.

Bluesky didn't know what to think.

However, he knew the day would come when he would need to force himself to meet one, and he knew he would have to seek out the great leader of the Crows -- Blackfeather. Bluesky's only consolation was that Nightwind was personally acquainted with this particular Crow. He hoped that fact would help him when he finally brought himself to seek the Crow out.

On the other wing, why should he finish the journey? After all, he still hadn't found a friend like Treehopper. In fact, not a single Mockingbird had even approached him in a friendly manner. Perhaps this journey had been a waste of time after all.

KC asked Bluesky to come back the next day when the sun was at its highest point in the sky. Her dad would allow her outside at that time. She wanted to talk more, and, most of all, she wanted to visit face-to-face with Bluesky.

The next day couldn't come fast enough for Bluesky.

"You've met some interesting birds," KC said.

"I sure have, but I think you're the most interesting creature of all, KC."

"Get up on my back. Let's give the birds another show," KC purred mischievously

Bluesky stood on KC's back just behind her shoulders, balancing himself as the cat slowly ambled across the backyard. He constantly flicked his long tail up and down as well as right and left in order to maintain his balance in rhythm with the cat's movements. Every second or two, when he sensed his center of balance shifting too much to one side, Bluesky also fluttered his wings. If KC took a longer step than normal, he'd sometimes have to fully unfold his wings to balance himself.

It took concentration, but Bluesky loved the ride.

He heard the excited chirps of Chickadees in the trees above as well as the fussing cries of the Titmice while they all watched in surprise -- and Bluesky knew he and KC were quite a spectacle.

He stood proudly on KC so all the birds could stare at them in amazement.

After all, who had ever heard of a bird riding on the back of a cat?

And that's what most of the birds were chattering about excitedly:

"Look there, what a sight!"

"A bird is actually riding on a cat!"

"What's next?"

Bluesky chuckled to himself.

"You doing all right up there?" KC asked. "I feel your little claws gripping my fur, but sometimes it feels like you're slipping."

"I'm all right. When you keep a steady pace, though, it's easier for me to balance."

"I'll do that. Hey, we're putting on quite a show, aren't we?" KC purred contentedly.

"Yeah, it's kind of fun knowing every bird in the neighborhood is watching us."

Indeed, as the Mockingbird stood on the cat while she continued to slowly walk around the yard, more and more birds flew up into the trees for a gander at the unthinkable.

"Why do you think the wise Owl wants you to

meet all these different kinds of birds, Bluesky? And why seek out what is beautiful and good in each one?" KC half-purred and half-meowed.

"I'm not too sure, but Nightwind said when I finished my journey that I would find a best friend." Bluesky paused in puzzlement. "But if another Mockingbird never talks to me ever again, I don't know how that will be possible."

"Perhaps Nightwind has another purpose?" KC said with a tone of mystery.

"I hope not," Bluesky squawked. "I'm going to a lot of trouble to meet other birds and find out good things about them. I'm doing it so I can get a best friend."

"I didn't mean it quite like that," KC said. "I meant, perhaps there's more to this mysterious journey than the obvious goal. But I do believe it will help you find a friend in the end."

"I don't know what you mean."

"It's been said -- 'we are a part of all that we meet ... '"

"What does that mean?" Bluesky chirped.

"It means that for everyone we meet, something about them rubs off on us."

"You mean their feathers rub off on us?"

"No!" KC laughed.

Bluesky listened while KC laughed a few moments. She was starting to sound like Nightwind a little bit. And as he crouched on her back, the familiar sadness filled his heart. Once again, he yearned for a best friend, a friend like Treehopper.

"I don't know if there are other reasons for my journey. I only know I'm lonely." Bluesky hung his head sadly. "And at this rate, I'll never find a best friend."

"Do you consider the birds you've met in your journey to be your friends?"

Bluesky recalled Bushhopper's words when he asked him -- 'Is Nightwind your friend?' He had thought that over many times.

He realized that he had come to respect the wise Owl. He enjoyed the times he'd spent with Nightwind and the wonderful things they talked about.

But they didn't play together. Not like best friends should.

"I don't know. I mean, I like them, and I think they like me. We laugh together and talk. We fly and sing together sometimes. But I don't see any of them every day. And it seems like I'm an outsider, really."

"What do you mean?"

"I come to find them, but they never seek me out in return."

"Have you told them how to find you?"

"Uh, no. But they also never invite me to come play ..."

"Have you told them you'd like an invitation?"

"No. I just figure if they've never invited me, they probably don't want to."

"That's what you assume."

"Yes."

"Have you ever invited them to play with you?"

"Well, no. I just sought them out as part of my journey."

"Perhaps it's time to push beyond your journey?

Maybe next time, you should simply go to play with them? Or invite them to play with you?" KC asked with a smile.

"But we're not the same kind of bird! I'm a Mockingbird and ... and they're all different kinds of birds."

"Does that really matter? After all, you and I are having fun right now. I love to watch you fly, and you seem to like 'showing off' for me. And I enjoy simply being with you."

Bluesky's mind whirled with thought as he tried to digest KC's words.

"I always thought that 'birds of a feather flock together' and that's who our friends should be."

"But Daymoon and Bushhopper are best friends, and one is a Cardinal and one is a Towhee. You told me yourself how you admired them for that, because they were best friends even though they are different kinds of birds."

"I-I do," Bluesky said hesitantly. "I just always wanted my best friend to be another Mockingbird, like me."

"But if you like them, although they are different ... and you enjoy their company ..."

"I don't know."

"They may tell their other friends, their friends of a feather, about you. And they may tell them that you are indeed a friend of theirs, although you are a Mockingbird!"

Bluesky shook his head in disagreement, which caused him to get off balance a moment. He gripped KC's fur tighter, fluttering his wings wildly until he regained his equilibrium.

"All their friends are birds of their own kind, their own family." Bluesky protested.

"Not Daymoon and Bushhopper!"

"They're different."

"You can be different too."

"I'll have to think about this some more."

"I want to give you something else to think about." KC's green eyes twinkled.

Bluesky waited expectantly.

"*I want to be your friend*," KC said with an earnest tone.

Bluesky became so dizzy the entire world seemed to wobble.

KC purred so loudly and so strongly that Bluesky suddenly lost his balance and fell over toward the ground. At the last second, he flapped his wings and just missed hitting the ground flat on his beak.

He beat his wings rapidly and flew several feet away. Then he swooped around and came back to land directly in front of KC.

"We can't be friends!" Bluesky said in disbelief.

"Why not?"

"Why, why ... because you're a cat and I'm a bird!"

"That's what I like about you -- you're so observant." KC chuckled gleefully.

"But it's impossible," Bluesky protested.

"I like you. I've always liked birds."

"All cats like birds -- they like to kill them!"

"I don't. I like to watch them."

"A cat and a bird can't be friends," Bluesky protested.

KC smiled and licked her forepaw. She then wiped her forepaw against her cheek and purred. She paused a moment and peered at the Mockingbird.

"Give me a real reason why you and I can't be friends."

"It's just not done -- we're different. In fact, not only are we different, we're *really* different. You have four legs and fur. I've got two wings and feathers and -- "

"We're alike inside. Remember what Daymoon said about him and Bushhopper being 'brothers of the heart.'"

"You're a girl cat!"

"You really are observant!" KC chuckled. "Regardless, why don't we just be friends, Bluesky?"

"But why me?"

"You're the first bird to ever talk with me, for one thing, or else I might have tried to make friends before. Most birds are so afraid they fly away before I can talk with them. So, maybe it's because we were kind of thrown together." KC smiled.

"You did save my life," Bluesky gasped, "and I'll always be grateful to you for that!"

"And I like you. I really like you -- for who you are." KC purred loudly. She then resumed her meticulous cleaning by licking her left foreleg and using it to wash her face.

"You like me?"

"Sure. I enjoy being with you. I like talking with you." She paused again in her cleaning. "So, we should be friends."

"I ... I ... just don't know."

KC laughed. After a moment, she leaned her head forward and peered intently at Bluesky with her green eyes. Then, she spoke words that shocked Bluesky for the second time that day.

"I want to invite you to come back and play with me tomorrow."

"What?" Bluesky's beak fell open in total shock.

"Sure -- you can ride on my back again. I like it. I enjoy how the birds all squawk and cry out in shock as they watch us. You can do some more aerial acrobatics for me and make me laugh. And we can talk about things."

"What things?"

"Whatever friends talk about."

"What do friends talk about?" Bluesky asked.

"We'll find out tomorrow."

Chapter Fifteen

Bluesky told all the other birds about his new friend, KC the kitty cat.

Their responses ranged from mild disbelief to outright incredulity. More than one looked at Bluesky as if he'd lost his mind. After all, how could a bird and a cat be friends? Even Daymoon and Bushhopper were shocked to hear Bluesky's news.

Daymoon explained it was one thing to make friends with birds of other kinds, but it was an entirely different thing for a bird to make friends with a cat!

After all, cats had been terrible enemies of birds since times untold. Such a friendship was impossible. It just wasn't done!

Without a doubt, one day KC would kill and eat Bluesky.

It's just how cats were!

He shivered at the thought whenever a bird whispered those words to him -- whether it was a Dove or a Sparrow or a Cardinal. Yes, they all agreed that instinct would take over one day. It was bound to happen -- it was inevitable.

Birds and cats could never, ever be friends.

Despite all the words to the contrary, Bluesky accepted KC's invitation and came back to play the next day.

Bluesky performed more aerial acrobatics while KC watched and purred contentedly.

After his aerial displays, Bluesky once again sat

on KC's back, flicking his tail like a piston as he balanced himself, tall and proud. While they marched around the backyard, they chatted about anything they pleased, any subject that came to the mind, whatever fancied them at that moment.

They talked and laughed and thoroughly enjoyed themselves.

KC invited Bluesky back another time. And again ... and again.

The one-legged Mockingbird soon found out that friends talked about whatever they liked -- and they simply enjoyed being in each other's company.

Each time Bluesky returned to visit KC, their friendship grew stronger.

March came in like a lion with strong winds and heavy downpours. The month ended with a steady breeze and gentle rain. The following month was welcomed with a profusion of colorful flowers blooming in flowerbeds around homes as well as wildflowers springing up along the roadside. Surprisingly, the strong winds continued throughout the beautiful month of April.

One particularly beautiful spring day while Bluesky visited with his friend KC, he met an entirely different kind of bird.

Bluesky perched on a chair on the back porch while KC sat upright on the seat of another chair across from him. As they paused to enjoy the invisible caress of the wind, Bluesky noticed an unusual 'humming' noise zip past his head.

"What was that?" He quickly looked all around, but there wasn't a bird in sight.

"It was a tiny bird." KC yawned, showing off

her fangs.

"There's not a bird here that I can see," Bluesky protested.

"It's gone now. You didn't look fast enough."

"What?"

"See that red thing hanging there?" KC swished her tail while nodding in the direction behind Bluesky's shoulder.

He turned and for the first time noticed a strange red object filled with red liquid.

"What's that?"

"My dad puts them out for the tiny birds when the weather grows warm again." KC stood up, leaned forward on her front paws, and then stretched luxuriantly.

Suddenly, the humming sound returned, but this time it seemed to stay in one place.

Bluesky turned and spotted it.

The tiniest bird he'd ever seen hovered in the air watching him closely -- but what really astounded Bluesky was the fact that this bird had no wings!

"How can you fly when you don't have any wings?" Bluesky shouted in surprise.

"Oh, I have wings." With an amazing burst of speed, the tiny bird flew up to Bluesky and hovered right before his eyes. It happened so fast, Bluesky almost flew away in fright.

The humming sound filled Bluesky's ears as he stared dumbfounded. Now that the diminutive bird was so close, he could see a blur of the bird's wings. In a flash of understanding, he realized this bird was flapping his wings so fast they were practically invisible!

"What kind of bird are you?" Bluesky's voice filled with awe.

"I'm a Zoomer. I come from a long line of Zoomers."

And to demonstrate that fact, the bird flew backwards a few inches and with a blinding burst of speed zoomed across the yard and was out of sight in mere seconds.

Bluesky's beak fell open in surprise.

On the wind, the faint humming sound returned. While Bluesky watched, he saw a small dot growing larger and larger until the teeny bird suddenly hovered right before his eyes again.

"How do you do that?" Bluesky asked, his voice almost a shout.

"I have a need for speed, baby. I can't go anywhere slow. No, absolutely not! I've got to zoom. It's either zoom or doom, and there's no in between!" The little bird's voice was a rapid-fire series of squeaks.

"You talk as fast as you fly!" Bluesky said with a laugh.

"It's the water-flower."

"The what?"

With a sparkling flash of the green feathers on its back, the bird whisked away in a blur of motion.

Bluesky turned. He saw the tiny bird sticking his long, slender beak into the object filled with the red liquid.

Again and again the tiny bird stuck his entire beak into the object. After a quick sip he would fly backwards and hover a moment as if waiting for something. Then he would suddenly fly back up to the red object and stick his beak in for another sip.

Bluesky discerned the bird was feeding. And at that very moment, he noticed a few bubbles boil up within the red liquid.

Before he could blink his eyes, the little bird zoomed back and hovered right before his face again.

"Those water-flowers give me energy -- especially the one here. It's here every season, and it's the best one around. It's shocking good!"

"Shocking good?" Bluesky asked in wonder.

"You know, something can be good. But when it's better, it's really good. When it's the best, then it's shocking good!"

"W-why?" Bluesky stammered.

"Sugar. Lots of sugar. There are nutrients too. I know -- they energize me whenever I drink from it. But this water-flower is so-o-o-o sweet it makes me want to zoom and zoom and zoom and zoom some more!"

The little bird zipped forward with a flash of green and a sparkle of red. Bluesky sat in total astonishment as the humming sound disappeared into the distance.

Just as quickly, the sound returned.

"What kind of bird are you?" Bluesky asked again.

"Technically, we're Ruby-throated Hummingbirds. But we like Zoomers for short. It explains what we're all about really, in a single word. Simple -- to the point -- and fast. Just like we are."

While Bluesky watched the bird hover in one

place in mid-air, he noticed how the sunlight caused the feathers on his back to sparkle. The hummingbird's belly was covered with white feathers like lots of other kinds of birds, but as Bluesky observed intently, he noticed what at first appeared to be black feathers on his throat suddenly flash ruby-red.

"Your feathers -- they sparkle in the light!" Bluesky gasped.

"They're iridescent. If the light catches them just right, they sparkle!"

"Why don't you ask our new friend his name?" KC purred.

The hummingbird zoomed in a tight circle and hovered about ten inches in front of KC's face.

"You're a cat."

"I see that hummingbirds are quite observant," KC snickered.

"My name is Bluesky. My friend's name is KC." Bluesky hopped excitedly when he realized that KC had referred to this bird as their new friend.

"You're friends with a cat? Wow, that's a good one. My name is Coolbreeze. You want to know why?"

"Sure," KC and Bluesky said together.

"Let me show you."

Coolbreeze zipped around Bluesky's head in a blur of motion. Again and again the hummingbird zoomed so fast Bluesky could hardly turn his head quickly enough to keep him in view.

With a renewed burst of speed, Coolbreeze flew off into the distance once again, his body growing smaller and smaller until he disappeared among the distant trees.

"That's the fastest bird I've ever seen!" Bluesky shouted excitedly.

Bluesky and KC continued to look at the trees into which Coolbreeze had disappeared, any moment expecting to see a tiny dot reappear to indicate his return.

But as they stared, nothing happened.

The seconds dragged on, but still no Hummer returned.

Without warning, a loud humming sound came from behind them, but even before they could turn their heads to look, the sound whipped past them.

Bluesky felt his feathers rustle in the wake of Coolbreeze's flight. He smiled widely, amazed at how fast this pint-sized creature could fly!

Coolbreeze quickly disappeared into the distance once again.

Just as he was about to enter into the trees far away, his tiny form turned and now grew larger with each passing moment.

In another second, Coolbreeze hovered effortlessly right before them with a big smile.

"See what I mean! Now, do you know why my name is Coooolbreeeeeeze?" Coolbreeze said with emphasis.

"Uh, you're as fast as the wind?" Bluesky asked half-heartedly.

"No!" Coolbreeze said emphatically.

"You're as fast as the breeze," KC meowed with confidence.

"Wrong again. Give up?"

"Yes," they both replied.

"I fly so fast, you'll think it was just a cool breeze blowing by!" he squeaked happily.

"I get it!" Bluesky chirped excitedly.

KC chuckled with bemusement as she nonchalantly licked her right paw.

"Yeah, I like your name a lot. It really fits you!" Bluesky said, quite impressed.

Bluesky remembered his journey.

"I see what's beautiful about you -- it's your iridescent feathers. And I know you're the fastest bird I've ever seen. Can you tell me what is good about you personally?"

"Something good about me?" Coolbreeze asked.

"Yes, a good quality about you." Bluesky replied.

"Oh, I'm fast!"

"No, something distinct about you. What's good about Coolbreeze?" Bluesky smiled.

"I'm super-fast!" he squeaked rapidly.

"My friend, Bluesky," KC began, "he wants to know if you're a happy bird or maybe a brave bird or a kind bird. What quality of the heart permeates your spirit?" KC methodically licked her forepaw while she waited for Coolbreeze's answer.

"Oh, I'm a brave bird. And I take care of my water-flower!"

Before Bluesky could ask, Coolbreeze zipped off toward the water-flower.

With Bluesky watching him intently, Coolbreeze stopped in mid-air and spread the feathers of his tail out until they looked like a fan. Coolbreeze squeaked valiantly as he flew forward with his tail fanned out to make his teeny form more imposing.

Bluesky looked closer and realized another Hummer was perched on the water-flower. This other Hummingbird pulled its long beak out and watched Coolbreeze fly closer.

In a blur of sudden motion, Coolbreeze closed and caused the other bird to lift off and zoom away in a hasty retreat.

Coolbreeze gave chase, scolding the other hummingbird with bursts of rapid-fire squeaks.

A few moments later, thoroughly satisfied the interloper had been taught a lesson and would never dare to return, he zipped back and perched on a branch from which he could keep a wary eye on his water-flower. From up on the branch, he squeaked down at Bluesky, "See, I'm brave and protect my territory from all comers!" He cast a quick glance back at the water-flower to ensure no one else dared to drink from it.

"You sure are," Bluesky agreed.

Several more times Coolbreeze launched himself in speedy pursuit when other Hummers dared to grab a quick drink from 'his' water-flower. Coolbreeze dove directly at them in a blur of motion with his wings humming like a turbo-charged engine. Each time he attacked, the other Hummer grabbed a final, quick sip and zoomed away just before Coolbreeze arrived.

But as many times as he chased them away, it seemed they always returned.

However, one particular female was very smart. She waited patiently and observed Coolbreeze's attacks. She quickly learned to dive in for a quick drink while he chased another Hummer away.

After Coolbreeze landed on his lookout branch, he'd instantly realize she had been drinking from his water-flower the entire time he had chased the other intruder away. In a burst of speed and squeaks, he would dive upon her.

She squeaked in laughter each time Coolbreeze chased her away, since she'd already gotten a good drink.

Bluesky and KC chuckled at her crafty successes again and again, although Coolbreeze always chased her away before she had too many free drinks.

Finally, Coolbreeze came over and hovered before them again.

"I could use some of your bravery," Bluesky said.

"Sure -- maybe I can help you?"

Bluesky felt his heart beat happily. He liked that his new friend was so eager to help him.

"Would you go with me to meet a Hawk?"

"Why sure. I can fly with you and zoom --"

Coolbreeze stopped squeaking in mid-sentence and stared at Bluesky a moment. "I must have heard you wrong. What did you say again?"

"I said, maybe you could accompany me to meet a Hawk."

"Huh -- that's what I thought you said." Coolbreeze zipped silently around the air a few moments. He came back and hovered right in front of Bluesky's beak. "You're not crazy, are you?"

"No, I don't think so." Bluesky smiled. "But you're right -- it does seem kind of crazy to want to go and meet a Hawk, doesn't it."

"Why would you want to?" Coolbreeze asked with wide eyes. "I mean, won't he eat us, er, I mean you?"

Bluesky explained to Coolbreeze about his journey and how he wanted to meet another Mockingbird who would become his best friend. He told him about Nightwind and all the wonderful birds he'd met. And last, he told him of Nightwind's directive to meet a Crow and a Hawk.

Coolbreeze hovered silently a long time. "Yes, I see you have one leg. I noticed it right away. I don't know why other birds are bugged about it."

"It doesn't matter to me," KC said.

"Me either -- you strike me a nice bird," Coolbreeze added.

"And you strike me as a fun kind of bird!" Bluesky said with a laugh.

"Well, if you're serious about meeting a Hawk, I'll go with you," Coolbreeze said confidently.

"Wow, thanks!"

"You need to meet a Crow first, remember," KC said. "Nightwind said that a Crow will know the secret on how to approach a Hawk without getting eaten."

"You're right. I guess I need to find this Blackfeather first."

"I'd like to meet some of these other birds you've met," Coolbreeze squeaked excitedly.

"Hmmm." Bluesky paused in thought. "Okay, I'll meet you here at the water-flower tomorrow after the sun rises over the treetops, and I'll take you to meet Dancingleaves first."

"That will be shocking good!" Coolbreeze squeaked with excitement.

The trio talked happily until the sunlight faded with the setting sun. Then Bluesky took his leave and flew off to find Ol' Gray Mama and tell her all about his new friend.

The Mourning Dove listened patiently while the darkness gathered around them. She opened her beak and smiled at Bluesky several times as he told her about Coolbreeze.

After he finished, she spoke. "What about all these other nice birds you've met? Aren't they your friends too?"

"I'm not sure. I mean, we talk and have fun, but they never said they were my friend -- not like KC."

"Tell them you want to be friends with them." She smiled.

"I'm kind of afraid."

"Pshaw! Afraid of what?"

"What if they don't want to be friends with me?"

"They enjoy your visits. You see them quite often now, almost every day. If they didn't like you, they'd fly away when you approached."

Bluesky hung his head in sadness, remembering all the birds that had done that very thing to him.

"Don't be sad," Ol' Gray Mama crooned.

"I'm not." Bluesky sighed. "I'm just afraid that if I do ... it might ruin everything. It's been so much fun visiting them on my journey."

"You have to tell others how you feel about them. Don't you see? How else will they know?"

"I-I guess." Bluesky glanced down with a sad look on his face.

"I'm your friend." Ol' Gray Mama's eyes twinkled. "Did you know that?"

Bluesky's face took on a look of utter surprise that was soon replaced with puzzlement.

"Well, I declare, I sure didn't expect that reaction. You act like you don't want to be my friend!" she exclaimed.

"Well, it's just that I feel different about you," Bluesky said shyly.

"How do you feel about me?" Ol' Gray Mama peered at him questioningly.

Bluesky hesitated.

"Come on then -- you've got my curiosity now. Tell me straight."

"I think of you more like my ... my ... *second mother*."

Ol' Gray Mama sat back on the branch a moment in profound silence. She smiled at Bluesky with a twinkle in her old eyes and moved closer until her feathers pressed against Bluesky's. Then she wrapped her wing around him.

"That's about the nicest thing any bird ever said to me. I'm glad you feel that way." She started laughing. After a few moments, she was laughing so hard that she shook the leaves on the branch.

"What's so funny?" Bluesky asked.

"Tomorrow, I'm going to tell the others that I have a new baby."

She hugged him tighter.

Her embrace made Bluesky feel good inside. He leaned against her and closed his eyes.

"Why didn't you tell me this before?" she asked.

"I didn't know if you'd like it or not."

210

"You've got to tell others how you feel, Bluesky. None of us are mind-readers."

Bluesky smiled shyly up at her.

"And tomorrow, you just go right ahead and tell those other birds that they're you're friends too."

"I will."

He paused a moment in thought.

"I'll tell Dancingleaves first that he's my friend. He'll be especially glad to know it, since he's such a shy bird and doesn't have many friends."

Bluesky closed his eyes and enjoyed the comforting warmth of Ol' Gray Mama's feathers.

"Tell me, what songs did your mother teach you?" Ol' Gray Mama asked.

"She ... she only taught me one song."

"I'd like to hear it."

"Um, I haven't sung it in a long time." He looked away. "Actually, I haven't sung it since the night my mama taught me. It even makes me sad when I hear other birds sing it."

"Why?"

"It reminds me of her."

"You need to remember her, Bluesky. Don't never forget your mama! Remember the good times, the fun times."

"I-I don't know how."

"Start by singing this song your mother taught you. And tomorrow, I'll teach you a new song."

Bluesky felt a new happiness begin to bloom inside his heart. "I'd really like that! For you to teaching me a song."

"Good," she said. "Now every time you sing it, I want you to think happy thoughts about me -- Ol'

Gray Mama."

"I will."

Bluesky straightened himself and lowered his tail, and for the first time since his mother died, he sang the song of Skysinger.

Chapter Sixteen

"Are we really friends?"

Bluesky sat beside Dancingleaves on the branch of a small magnolia tree. He noticed the look of utter surprise in the Bluebird's eyes.

"I've never really thought about it that way. I mean, I just thought you were a nice bird who came to visit me now and again." A puzzled expression filled Dancingleaves face.

"I ..." Bluesky paused, and a familiar fear rose inside his chest. He recognized it easily -- the terrible fear of rejection. He looked at Dancingleaves, afraid to say anything else.

"What were you going to say?" Dancingleaves asked. "Are you afraid of me? You don't have to be," he added with a reassuring tone.

"I ... I think of you as my friend." Bluesky hung his head, waiting for the rejection he knew would come next.

"Really?"

Bluesky jumped in surprise. Dancingleaves had uttered that word not in a tone of shock but in one of urgent hope!

"Uh, yes." Bluesky smiled shyly.

"Wow! This is kind of exciting for me, you know. I mean, you know, I don't have many friends. Well, I don't really have any friends. Except, I guess, that I do now!" Dancingleaves hopped excitedly on the branch until the leaves waved as if in a stormy wind.

"Are you glad you're my friend?" Bluesky

asked, still expecting a possible rejection.

"I just never thought of it like that. I thought a bird's friends were always from his own kind."

"I guess we can make friends with whomever we like," Bluesky said.

"What a concept!" Dancingleaves flew up with a cheerful song. Around and around he flew in the air, all the while singing out with a happy cry.

Bluesky just sat there, dumbfounded and amazed.

Dancingleaves returned and perched beside him, all the while singing joyfully. Bluesky continued to look at him with a mixture of shock and happiness.

"I'm glad we're friends," Bluesky finally said after Dancingleaves stopped for a breath.

"Me too! I can't wait to tell my parents. They'll be happy I finally have a friend."

Bluesky felt his heart sink again. "Do you think your parents will mind that your friend is a one-legged Mockingbird?"

"I think they'll be happy with any bird who calls me friend!"

Bluesky perked up. "Well, would you like another friend?"

"What? Another friend?" Dancingleaves looked around. Suddenly, his happiness turned to apprehension. "What kind of a bird is it? It's not a big bird is it? Or a ... a scary kind of bird?"

"No, not at all. In fact, he's the smallest bird I've ever met!"

"Really?"

Bluesky turned and called out with a strong, clear whistle. "Coolbreeze!"

Bluesky watched Dancingleaves closely as a distant humming sound, faint at first and stronger with each second, grew audible.

"What's that ..."

Dancingleaves jumped with surprise when Coolbreeze suddenly hovered directly before him.

"Hi, there! I'm a Zoomer! I come from a long line of Zoomers!"

"You scared the bejeebers out of me!" Dancingleaves laughed. He stared a moment at the Hummingbird. "How can you hover like that? And where are you wings?"

As he'd explained to Bluesky yesterday, Coolbreeze quickly reiterated how Hummingbirds flew. And especially how fast they flew. And how very brave he was. And all about why he was such a great little bird.

Dancingleaves listened in rapt attention to the endless squeaking chirps.

Coolbreeze went on to relate how he met Bluesky the day before and everything they discussed.

This took almost three minutes for Coolbreeze to complete.

"I like this ... Uh, what kind of bird are you again?"

"Well, technically, I'm a Ruby-throated Hummingbird. But since we're friends, you can call me a Zoomer."

"Ha!" Dancingleaves laughed. "I'll call you Coolbreeze. I like that name!"

"Yeah, it's a *cool* name." Bluesky laughed.

"Way cool!" Dancingleaves added.

Coolbreeze laughed along with them.

Suddenly, he zipped up above them and hovered, staring at the sky.

"The clouds are huge, floating islands today. See how slowly they float across the sky."

"Wow -- they are quite low today," Bluesky said with growing excitement.

"Yes, I like it when they are so low and float slowly by. I love to watch their shadows passing along on the ground ..." Dancingleaves looked at Bluesky with sudden realization. "Are you going to fly up to the clouds today?" he asked excitedly.

"Yes! Would you and Coolbreeze like to fly with me? We can all perch on one and watch the world slowly slide by below us."

"Yes!" Coolbreeze and Dancingleaves said simultaneously.

"Could I invite one more bird to join us?" Bluesky asked hesitantly.

"Another bird?" Dancingleaves said with shock. "Really?"

"Yes, he's a funny fellow. I mean, he's always laughing and happy. You'll both like him."

"That would be shocking good! The more the merrier, that's what I always say!" Coolbreeze squeaked rapidly.

"Tootight, fly on up here."

The plump American Robin flew over to them from a nearby tree.

They quickly exchanged pleasantries, and, of course, Tootight told a few jokes to break the ice and make everyone laugh.

While they continued to talk, first Bluesky and

then Dancingleaves glanced quickly up at the huge, billowy clouds floating above. However, each seemed too high or perhaps too small or didn't seem to have enough puffy slopes on which to perch.

Finally, a particularly large cloud crept into sight. It was bigger than every other cloud they'd seen. More important for their purposes, it was so low in the sky its flat bottom seemed to almost touch the treetops. Its apex, the four birds realized, rose thousands of feet high, like a great, white mountain in the sky.

Countless billowy shapes grew and sometimes erupted out of the whiteness as if the cloud were somehow alive. The shifting mass of glowing whiteness rose high above its flat base until it reached a grand, rounded pinnacle far, far above.

It was the perfect cloud.

"Let's fly to the clouds!" Bluesky shouted with burning enthusiasm.

"Let's fly to the clouds!" Coolbreeze, Tootight, and Dancingleaves shouted in unison.

Coolbreeze zoomed far out in front of the other three, who flapped their wings with a steady beat and rose up into the sky to meet the mountain-cloud.

Soon, the cloud seemed to melt together in a blinding whiteness, and the vast bottom filled their vision. As they flew closer, what they thought was a flat, white bottom was actually a series of rounded bumps that rolled and boiled and slowly changed shape just like the top.

Even more exciting, the cloud seemed to become more solid with each beat of their hearts.

"See, it is solid!" Bluesky shouted. "We'll have to fly around to the side so we can perch on it. Follow me!"

And yet, the closer they came, the more the air grew laden with moisture. Soon, tiny water droplets dampened their feathers.

"I wonder why no other birds have thought of this before?" Tootight asked, slightly out of breath.

"I wondered that myself," Coolbreeze squeaked rapidly. "I mean, clouds are always in the sky on most days. I've never heard a song or a tale of any other birds flying up to a cloud and sitting on one."

Dancingleaves flew faster until he was right beside Bluesky.

"It is strange that we've never heard of any other birds doing this before, don't you think?"

"Nah," Bluesky retorted. "We're just the first to try! We are bold and brave birds!"

"Oh, I guess we are." Dancingleaves said softly.

"Bold birds out for adventure -- that's us!" Tootight laughed out loud.

"Watch me -- I'm going to get there first." The motor-like hum of Coolbreeze's wings grew even louder as he zoomed ahead, his body growing smaller until it was a distant dot. A moment later, the small dot reached the side of the cloud and seemed to melt into the shining whiteness.

"Let's hurry -- he made it!" Bluesky shouted.

Bluesky flew faster, but a strange sensation quickly filled his heart. It almost felt like fear -- but not quite. He definitely felt a thrill of excitement right after a rush of adrenaline shot through his body. And yet, something didn't feel right ...

As they neared the cloud, the gargantuan mass of whiteness towered above them and blocked out the entire sky. Bluesky focused on a small, rounded peak and flew toward it.

The white magnificence of the cloud filled his vision like some massive white wall. Bluesky felt the air temperature drop suddenly as the cloud now blocked even the sun from their sight. The closer they flew toward the moving white wall, the colder the air felt.

Bluesky flew faster, yearning to perch on the cloud just like he'd dreamed so many times.

But now the strange feeling burning inside his heart grew stronger. In a flash of insight, he realized what was causing this storm of emotions: It seemed the closer they approached the white flanks of the massive cloud, the farther away it became ... so close ... and yet so far ...

As if he would never, ever quite reach his dream ...

He flew harder.

Suddenly, Bluesky realized everything had disappeared, including all of his friends. A shining whiteness completely surrounded him, and yet, the wall of the cloud still seemed to float before him in the distance -- still out of reach.

He glanced quickly around.

In every direction huge, luminous curtains of mist floated and twisted in slow motion as if they were alive. All around him huge ramparts of glowing whiteness towered higher and higher until all the sides merged into a pure whiteness.

A peaceful and complete stillness surrounded

him now -- a quietness he could almost feel.

Bluesky shivered.

The cold, refreshing air caressed him like a crisp, autumn morning. He also realized beads of water covered his feathers almost as if he'd flown through a rain storm.

He slowed his flight, gazing in awe. Dancingleaves and Tootight suddenly appeared out of a wall of whiteness and caught up to him. Together, they all gazed in silent appreciation at the beauty that enveloped them.

It was like they were flying inside a special place, a wondrous place with twisting veils of glowing mist hanging from a pure white ceiling.

He breathed deeply, and the cool air sent chills through him.

The air felt so good, so fresh, and so clean.

The soft, unbroken silence added a peaceful tranquility to the majestic beauty that totally engulfed them.

Bluesky spotted a white mound in the near distance.

"Let's go perch over there."

He shuddered, realizing his voice had pierced the undisturbed silence.

He quickly flew over to what appeared to be a landing spot, but just as he reached it, what appeared solid in the distance now turned into swirling veils of mist.

Undeterred, he flew onward.

He realized they had somehow entered the cloud without actually touching its side.

Or had they?

It was like being inside a huge mass of fog -- except the fog was all around them -- even below them.

"This is the coolest place. It's fantastic ... it's amazing ... it's ... shocking good!" Coolbreeze shouted after he zoomed up to them from out of the mist. "We're actually inside the cloud!"

"It's so ... otherworldly. I feel like I've flown to a completely new world." Tootight chuckled with awe.

"We're inside a cloud!" Dancingleaves shouted out with joy. "I never thought I'd ever fly inside a cloud! We've done it!"

"We are cloud conquerors!" Coolbreeze zipped around the Bluebird three times to emphasize his joy.

"It's ... it's really wet inside a cloud!" Tootight laughed.

Bluesky, however, felt consumed with disappointment. "I don't see a place where we can land. Every time I get close, what I thought was a good spot to land turns into mist." Bluesky's voice echoed his disillusionment.

"It doesn't matter -- I like it!" Coolbreeze shouted.

"It does matter. It's ... it's not what I expected," Bluesky said with disappointment

"What do you mean?"

"There's no place to perch, and I can't even see the ground below." Bluesky sighed, a terribly sad and forlorn exhalation. "It's not at all what I expected."

"That's all right, Bluesky. The main thing is that

221

we did it. We really did it!" Dancingleaves shouted with joy.

"Yes, yes, yes! We are inside this huge floating cloud, baby!" Coolbreeze squeaked.

"My feathers are wetter than if I were on the ground in a rainstorm. I would have never thought a cloud was so wet! But I don't mind it at all. It's so different, like we're inside a vast, white place that moves and changes every second. It's really ... fascinating, in a surreal, beautiful way." Tootight laughed.

But the wetness on his feathers made Bluesky feel heavy and miserable. He slowed down and watched while the others flew onward. They didn't seem to notice he was no longer with them.

It didn't matter.

He slowly dropped lower into the swirling mists below.

The others would never miss him. They were having a good time and didn't need him anymore. Besides, everything about this place was a disappointment to him.

He flew lower, and suddenly the swirling whiteness disappeared and the ground below became visible again.

Bluesky didn't recognize the islands of treetops mixed with the rectangular roofs of the houses.

He didn't care. He was wet and tired and just wanted his feathers to dry off in the warmth of the sun.

He spotted a tree that rose higher than the others and flew toward it. Bluesky figured if he landed near the top of this tall tree, he would dry out all the faster.

Bluesky landed on a branch filled with leaves that danced in the wind. He turned his back to the sun and extended his wings so his feathers would dry faster. The comforting warmth seeped through his feathers and down onto his skin. Slowly, the wetness disappeared. He closed his eyes to enjoy the magnificent feeling.

He never noticed when another Mockingbird flew up from below and landed on the same branch. While he soaked up the warmth of the sun, the other Mockingbird cocked her head and stared at him with wide eyes. Finally, she spoke. "Bluesky, is that you?"

Bluesky instantly recognized the voice of his sister. "Songjoy!"

He couldn't believe it! It was his sister!

"Bluesky, I'm so glad to see you."

Inside his chest, his heart fluttered with both happiness and sadness.

"I'm ... glad to see you too." But his words betrayed his mixed emotions.

Songjoy's smile faded a little. After a brief silence, she hopped closer. "I missed you so much, brother."

"Did you really?" he asked with a hint of doubt.

In answer, Songjoy hopped up to Bluesky and wrapped her wings around him in a big hug. She hopped back a few steps and smiled again. "Yes, I really missed you."

"I missed you too," Bluesky said sadly. He looked deep into her eyes, searching for the truth.

"I never wanted to leave you and Mom."

Songjoy's eyes glistened with tears.

Bluesky froze.

He saw his mother's smiling face clearly in his mind's eye for the first time since her death. A hurricane of emotions flooded his heart and filled his being.

"I asked Dad to turn back many times," Songjoy added. "I pleaded with him to go back."

"Why didn't he come back?"

"He said he wanted us to live a normal life. We flew and flew into the night toward the first light of the rising sun. Dad wanted to fly until we found some Mockingbirds who didn't know us. He wanted us to start over with a new group. He said we deserved a *fresh start*."

Bluesky understood -- almost.

He knew he was a pariah to his family. He had already understood he would need to fly away one day and leave them all. Still, his dad's sudden departure with Songjoy and Cloudshadow had devastated him emotionally.

And then his mother's death ...

"Will you forgive me?" Songjoy pleaded through her tears.

"I ... uh ... Of course."

"Good! I hope you'll come and see me now that you know where I live."

Bluesky closed his eyes, fighting back his own tears. He couldn't share his sister's joy until he asked her one question. "Where's Dad?"

Songjoy's countenance changed to surprise and then into sadness. She turned her head away as tears rolled down her feathered cheeks.

Bluesky felt his heart beating rapidly with fear.

"Is he ...?" Bluesky hesitated to finish.

"Yes, he stopped flying." Songjoy's voice shuddered with emotion. "He was never really happy after we left you and Mom. Oh, he tried. We met new Mockingbirds and laughed and played with them. But he was never really happy ..."

"How?" Bluesky choked with emotion, unable to finish the question.

"He didn't prepare for the winter like he should." Songjoy's eyes locked with Bluesky's eyes. "He urged us to feed and gain weight, but he seemed to lose interest ..."

"What night did he stop flying?" Bluesky's heart hammered inside his chest as he waited for Songjoy's reply.

Somehow, he knew what she was going to say.

"It was one of the coldest nights of last winter. It may have even been the coldest night -- I don't know. Cloudshadow and I were huddled on a branch, and Father was off by himself on another ..." Songjoy choked back a sob.

"And ..." Bluesky softly prompted.

"We fell asleep and never knew when it actually happened. It was bitter cold. All I can remember is trying to keep warm and dozing in and out of sleep. When Cloudshadow woke up, he cried out when he saw Father was gone."

"Did you find him?"

"Yes, we found him later ... on the ground. He was --"

"Don't say anymore."

Bluesky quickly told Songjoy how their mother

died. They both agreed it might have been the same cold night. Both also agreed that if only the family had stayed together, perhaps their mom and dad would have kept each other warm, helped each other, and everything might have been different ...

A deep sadness settled between them. They each looked off into the distance and remembered the happy times of their youth for a few, precious minutes.

Finally, Songjoy spoke. "I have a mate."

"Really?" Bluesky said excitedly, but his excitement quickly turned to a mixture of sadness and envy.

"Yes, I met him last week. He's a nice Mockingbird, and he's good to me. We've just today found the perfect place to build our first nest!"

Bluesky stared at her a moment. He smiled. "I'm glad for you, Songjoy."

"Would you like to meet him? He's off searching for nesting material. His name is Morningwind."

Even as she said it, Bluesky knew he shouldn't stay. He saw in her eyes how happy she was. He realized that not only was she in love with her mate, but more important, she had finally found a measure of happiness.

It was something he hoped he would find for himself one day.

He wouldn't spoil her happiness.

He knew all Mockingbirds still shunned him. He didn't want to take a chance that Morningwind might not only feel the same way, but that perhaps when he realized Songjoy's brother was the infamous one-legged bird, this new realization might taint their relationship.

These dark fears sent a chill though his heart.

No, he couldn't stay.

"What about Cloudshadow?" he asked, quickly changing the subject.

"When the warm weather arrived, he said he wanted to fly away -- far away. He said he wanted to find his own place in the world. It was ... difficult to see him leave." Songjoy looked down with sadness.

"But you have a mate now!"

Her smile returned, and her eyes sparkled. "Yes, I do."

"I will return, but I know you and your mate have a lot of work to do building your nest. And soon there will be eggs. And after that, babies to feed and train." Bluesky smiled joyfully.

"Yes, we will be busy," Songjoy agreed.

"I'll return in a few weeks, after the babies have left the nest. Things will be better then. I will not only meet your mate but my nephews and nieces too!"

Bluesky turned to go.

"You will come back, won't you?" Songjoy's voice pleaded. "Please ..."

Bluesky felt the love and sincerity in her words.

"Y-yes, I will. One day ..."

After they hugged each other one more time, he flew back toward his home.

As he flew, he wrestled with the thought of whether he should return or not. Perhaps it would be best if he left her alone with her new family. After

227

all, his presence might ruin things for her -- for her mate. Or maybe the hatchlings might shrink back in fear when they found out that their uncle was a deformed, one-legged Mockingbird.

He didn't know.

He'd have to decide later.

Deep inside his heart, a new determination took hold. Deep down inside, he knew he needed to take the next step on his journey.

It was time to seek out Blackfeather.

Chapter Seventeen

"Where did you go? We thought you were lost - - or worse!" Coolbreeze chastised him with a flurry of squeaks.

Bluesky's face burned with embarrassment. He slowly swallowed a bug and averted his eyes away from the Hummingbird.

"I-I don't know. The cloud just wasn't what I expected. And, well, all of you were having such a good time -- I didn't think you'd miss me when I left."

Coolbreeze suddenly zipped through the air to chase off another Hummingbird that was sneaking a quick drink from his water-flower. His fussing squeaks filled the air as he dove and chased the intruder away. He zoomed right back to Bluesky, still fussing the entire way.

"I don't know what those birds are thinking! I tell them again and again that this is my water-flower and no one else can drink from it. But do they listen to me? No!"

Bluesky couldn't keep himself from smiling, although his face still felt flushed from his embarrassment.

"Now, where were we?" Coolbreeze flew slowly backward, deep in thought. In an instant, he zipped right up to Bluesky until their beaks almost touched. "Yes, you left us without saying a word! Did you know that poor Dancingleaves started crying? No, I see by your reaction that you didn't know. Yes, the poor Bluebird just cried and cried because he thought you were lost and maybe hurt. Tootight and I flew everywhere looking for you. We were all worried sick."

Bluesky now felt really terrible inside. "I didn't mean for that to happen -- really. I saw all of you having so much fun inside the cloud and, well, I felt so disappointed ... I thought I'd spoil your fun if I hung around any longer."

"Hey, if you wanted to leave, that was fine by us, but you just disappeared without a peep! Dancingleaves feared you might even be dead. We spent the rest of the time looking for you."

"I guess I owe you an apology."

"Yes, you do."

"I-I'm sorry." Bluesky hung his head in shame.

"That's okay, no problem. Just next time, tell us when you're leaving."

"I will. I promise."

"You need to go apologize to Tootight -- and especially Dancingleaves. In fact, he's probably still worrying about you."

Coolbreeze and Bluesky flew into the cloudless sky and over the treetops and housetops. They heard Tootight's happy laughter long before they saw him. After Bluesky made his apologies, Tootight laughed even more loudly at how silly they'd been to worry so much. The plump Robin always seemed to find a happy side to everything.

Tootight continued his search for more bugs while Coolbreeze and Bluesky flew away to find Dancingleaves. This, of course, was always an easy thing to do since Dancingleaves never strayed far from his parents and his favorite perching places.

They found him sitting silently on the wire exactly like Bluesky had first found the shy Bluebird.

"Hi," Bluesky said meekly after he landed.

Dancingleaves looked over at him with sadness in his eyes. He only sighed softly in reply.

"I-I'm so sorry, Dancingleaves. I did wrong. I should have told you before I left yesterday."

The Bluebird looked away.

Bluesky felt a frantic fear grip his heart. He flew up and over until he landed on the other side of Dancingleaves. He looked into his eyes. "Oh, please, Dancingleaves. Please don't be mad with me. I'm really sorry. I didn't mean to worry you or the others. I just didn't want to spoil your fun."

"I thought you were hurt ... or dead. Suddenly, you weren't there any longer. It ... it scared me."

"I am so, so sorry." Bluesky put his wing around the shoulders of his friend.

Dancingleaves' eyes narrowed. "I thought friends were supposed to look out for each other -- and ... and confide in each other."

"You're right!" Bluesky said energetically. "I was so wrong. I was only thinking of myself, I guess. I was so disappointed, and you guys thought it all so beautiful and nice ... I just felt like I would spoil it for you if I didn't leave."

"I knew you were disappointed. I was trying to get you to see how nice it really was, even if we couldn't perch anywhere and watch the world float by below us. But you left before I could."

Bluesky felt a chill of amazement. It made him feel so good to realize Dancingleaves knew him well enough to sense his own bitter disappointment and then want to help him.

His amazement grew as he realized that Dancingleaves had just shared with him what he had actually been thinking yesterday. Bluesky understood the situation from their viewpoint and now realized how wrong he had been to simply vanish, although at the time he had felt it the best thing to do.

He liked this kind of sharing -- sharing each other's thoughts and feelings.

"I'm glad you wanted to make me feel better. And I see where I was wrong in leaving without telling you. I wish I had stayed now."

Bluesky spent some time with Dancingleaves just talking and flying around. Coolbreeze suddenly remembered his unprotected water-flower and zoomed off to defend it, but they continued their warm conversation and simply enjoyed being in each other's company.

Soon Bluesky felt hungry again, and after he said farewell and apologized one more time, he flew away to find some juicy bugs.

A little later, he found Daymoon and Bushhopper singing in the trees just like the first time he met them. He listened to them call out to each other with their familiar songs. Bluesky refrained from joining in, not wanting to interrupt their happy duet. After a while, Daymoon noticed him and flew down to join him.

"Where have you been? We haven't seen you in a while," Daymoon chirped happily.

"I've been around."

"How is Nightwind? I'd love to talk with him again."

"He's fine. I hope to see him tomorrow, after I meet Blackfeather." Bluesky smiled confidently.

"Oh! So, you're going to meet the Crow soon?"

"I am on my way to seek him out now," Bluesky said.

Bushhopper flew over and now sat down beside Daymoon. "Did I hear you right? Are you going to talk to a Crow today?"

"Yes, and I was hoping you two might want to go with me."

The two birds agreed enthusiastically.

"I hope you don't mind if another bird joins us?" Bluesky asked.

"Sure. Is it the Robin you told us about?" Daymoon raised his crest with interest.

Instead of answering, Bluesky whistled out a single name, loud and clear. "Coolbreeze!"

Daymoon and Bushhopper both cocked their heads to one side as a faint humming sound grew discernable. In a matter of seconds, the sound grew so loud they opened their beaks in shock.

"What is it?" Bushhopper gasped.

Suddenly, Coolbreeze zipped right by them in a blur of movement.

Daymoon and Bushhopper turned their heads, but all they saw was a dot growing smaller by the second.

"That's a bird?" Daymoon shook his head in wonder.

"He's just showing off. Hang on -- I think he'll come back and introduce himself now." Bluesky chuckled.

The humming sound that had been growing fainter now reversed and just as quickly grew in volume. Just as Daymoon and Bushhopper peered to catch a look, Coolbreeze zoomed up and hovered perfectly still right before their startled faces.

"I'm a Zoomer. I like to zoom!" Coolbreeze squeaked rapidly.

"We see that!" Bushhopper laughed.

"A Ruby-throated Hummingbird! Well, well, well, I've always wanted to meet a Zoomer! And now I have!" Daymoon's chirping laughter joined Bushhopper's.

"Well, well, well, I'm glad to oblige." Coolbreeze gently mocked the Cardinal in return. "Actually, I've heard all about you. Bluesky told me."

"The good stuff is all true!" Daymoon said with a smile.

They all laughed.

Introductions were quickly made, and soon the four feathered friends were off in search of Blackfeather.

While they flew, a fresh wind blew from the west and aided their efforts.

They landed in a small grove of pine trees that grew next to the subdivision. The four birds perched near the top of the tallest pine and waited expectantly.

"Why are we waiting here? Will we meet Blackfeather in this tree?" Daymoon asked after a silence.

"I followed three Crows earlier until they

landed. I asked them if they knew him. They did, and so I asked where I could find him. They said it would be better if Blackfeather found me." Bluesky raised his left wing and preened himself.

"That sounds a bit mysterious," Bushhopper said.

"I like mysteries," Coolbreeze squeaked.

"I'm still a little nervous about meeting a Crow," Daymoon said, his voice edged with tension.

"Why?" Bluesky stopped his cleaning.

"Well, you know what they say about Crows." Daymoon raised his jaunty crest and looked around cautiously.

"No, what do they say?"

"They're trouble," Daymoon whispered. "And worse, they'll steal eggs right out of a nest if you're not careful."

"Yuck!" Bluesky said with disgust.

"Bad as Blue Jays," Bushhopper agreed. "And even worse than Jays, they'll even take baby birds."

"That's terrible!" Bluesky whistled.

"You can't trust them, I've always heard," Coolbreeze added.

"Harbingers of evil," Daymoon said. "Regular birds avoid them."

"Kind of disgusting birds, if you ask me. I hear they eat dead things too ... smelly, stinking dead things," Bushhopper said in a loud voice.

"Shhhh! Keep quiet! They might hear us," Daymoon whispered urgently.

"How?" Bushhopper asked in surprise, looking around furtively.

"You can never be too careful with Crows. They

can be dangerous. You have to keep your eyes on them all the time," Daymoon said with a knowing tone. "That's why lots of birds will chase them away. In fact, I've seen many a Mockingbird chasing a Crow out of their territory."

"Yeah, they may be big, but they fly slow as slugs," Bushhopper added.

"Well, there must be some good in them and they must bring some beauty to the world, or else Nightwind wouldn't want me to seek them out," Bluesky replied in a matter-of-fact tone.

Without warning, the sound of movement came out of the shadows near the lowest branches of the tree in which they perched.

Bluesky jumped in surprise and almost took to the air.

Daymoon and Bushhopper both jumped as well, except they did fly off a short distance. Once they realized nothing was chasing them, they turned and quickly landed near Bluesky again.

Only Coolbreeze remained frozen in the same spot, though the diminutive bird looked around nervously for the source of the noise.

Suddenly, the air was filled with the haunting cries of Crows.

Chapter Eighteen

"CAW! CAW! CAW!"

Bluesky's heart pounded, and he desperately fought against an overwhelming urge to fly away. The unexpected nearness of the harsh cries sent a chill of fear throughout his being.

"Sooooo, we fly slooooow as a slug, do we?" a raspy voice said from the shadows.

Bluesky and the others strained their eyes trying to see the Crows hidden from their view.

"And, we're disgusting birds, eh?"

Bluesky was so scared he couldn't move. The scary voice was so close ...

But he couldn't see the Crow anywhere.

"CAW! CAW! CAW!"

Bluesky swallowed nervously and closed his eyes.

A fluttering of wings caused him to open them right away.

Five large, black Crows flew out from the shadows and landed all around the foursome. Their huge black beaks opened and closed ominously while they stared from him to his friends and back again. Each Crow seemed identical, each the same size, and each completely covered with jet black feathers.

Finally, Bluesky spoke. "We've come to meet Blackfeather. Are one of you --"

"I am Blackfeather!"

A black Crow jumped up from the branch below Bluesky and landed right next to him. The huge bird towered over him, over twice Bluesky's size.

The other Crows leapt up and quickly surrounded them. Indeed, as Bluesky looked around he realized all the Crows towered ominously over him and his friends.

Blackfeather slowly turned his head to one side, staring down at him with a single eye. Bluesky tried to stare back in order to show the bigger bird he wasn't afraid.

Deep inside, however, his heart fluttered with a potent mixture of fear and excitement.

Although he tried to look back into Blackfeather's unblinking eye, his gaze drifted; he noticed wrinkles under the feathers of the great black bird. Although Blackfeather stood as huge as his dark brethren, it quickly became obvious from his demeanor that he was a bird of great age. His dark eyes twinkled with insight.

Bluesky gulped nervously. Finally, he continued. "Nightwind sent me to meet you."

"Yes, I heard that you mentioned the Owl's name to my brethren and that he had sent you to seek me out. That's the only reason I decided to meet you." He turned his large head from side to side, observing Bluesky with an intense expression. "I don't usually waste my time with Mockingbirds. You're such a pesky bunch of birds."

"I-I only want to talk with you."

"Yes, so I heard. Well, what shall we talk about, my young, one-legged bird, eh? Shall we discuss how your kind shuns you?"

Bluesky felt a pang of sadness.

The big Crow shook his head and let out a

single 'caw.' After a moment of contemplation, he continued. "Yes, I see it still hurts. All right, we'll leave that subject. Now, why has my old friend Nightwind sent you to me? Yesssss, to seek me, of all the Crows?"

"He has sent me on a journey -- a journey to discover what is beautiful about every kind of bird. And ... and to find the good inside them."

"Ah, I see Nightwind has taken a liking to you." Blackfeather smiled mischievously.

"Uh, yes. I enjoy my talks with him very much"

"And well you should. So, what do you see beautiful about me, eh?" Blackfeather extended his neck and body and raised his wings forward. The jet-black feathers on his neck glowed dark as he turned to display himself. But everywhere Bluesky looked, he saw only the same black feathers. Then Blackfeather turned to face him again and opened his thick, black beak. The air resounded with the haunting sound of his kind.

"CAW! CAW! CAW!"

Bluesky felt like jumping out of his feathers. He stared at Blackfeather, trying to see what was beautiful about him and the other Crows, but all he could see was a jet-black bird with a huge black beak and black eyes.

The closeness of these huge Crows and the echoes of their haunting cries sent a shiver through him.

"No? Nothing beautiful about me, eh? Just a big, black, noisy bird?" Blackfeather chuckled knowingly. "No, we're not pretty birds like you. And we don't sing pretty songs like you either. So, my little one-legged bird, tell me, what's good and beautiful about a Crow?"

Bluesky gulped nervously. He couldn't see anything particularly beautiful. In fact, they all seemed rather frightening.

"CAW! CAW! CAW!!" Blackfeather shouted again.

The other Crows joined their voices, and the air echoed with their haunting cries.

Bluesky crouched in fear, readying himself to fly away from these fearsome birds.

Blackfeather noticed him shrinking back and grew silent. The Crow twisted his head to gaze at him again in deep thought. At just that moment, a beam of sunlight burst through the leaves and engulfed the Crow.

As Bluesky stared in wonder, a beam of sunshine glanced off Blackfeather's back. A deep purple sheen danced across his black feathers. Bluesky remembered the light dancing off the small patch of iridescent feathers of the Mourning Doves.

"C-Crows have iridescence in their feathers ... a purple shimmer when the sun hits you just so."

"Ahhhhhh, very good! Very good, indeed," Blackfeather crooned, his voice now full of interest. "You have learned to observe. Nightwind is teaching you well. Now then, what is good about me then? According to your friends here, Crows are despicable egg-stealers and eaters of baby birds. Why, we've even been known to pilfer our dinner out of garbage cans and consume fresh roadkill." He leaned closer until his huge beak almost touched Bluesky's. "Kind of disgusting, aren't we?"

Blackfeather waited a moment, but Bluesky was so frightened by the nearness of the Crow that all he could do was stare back at him.

Blackfeather finally turned and stared over at Bushhopper. "At least, that's what the Towhee said about us."

Bushhopper leaned back, looking fearfully from one Crow to the next while all of them stared ominously back at him.

"I ... I don't really think you're despicable. Kind of strange, maybe. But definitely not despicable."

"Let me ask you a question, eh?" Blackfeather turned back to Bluesky. "Don't you eat daddy bugs and mommy bugs? And don't you eat baby bugs? How do you think the bugs feel about you and your friends here, eh? They probably think you're a bit disgusting too, eh?"

Bluesky felt both surprise and shock. He'd never thought of bugs as, well, anything more than bugs.

"They're alive like you, right?" Blackfeather prompted him.

Bluesky remained silent.

"Well." Blackfeather raised his wing and preened himself a moment. After he cleaned his feathers a moment, he spoke again. "We only take eggs or hatchlings if necessary. If there's plenty of food, we eat berries and bugs and such, much like other birds. And it's true, we scavenge when we can ..."

Bluesky felt like throwing up, picturing these Crows eating a dead animal.

"Don't judge us solely by that."

"Then ... you tell me what's good about you,"

Bluesky said, surprising himself with his boldness.

Blackfeather quietly observed Bluesky a moment before he answered. "You're an interesting little bird, aren't you? Seeking out what is good about dirty old Crows. Perhaps there's nothing good about us?" Blackfeather smiled mysteriously.

"I think there is good in you," Bluesky replied.

"Good ... good!" Blackfeather turned to his black brethren, and they smiled in return.

Bluesky waited pensively.

"We see things, we observe things, *we understand things*," Blackfeather crooned with a cryptic tone.

Bluesky's eyes grew wide with surprise.

"We're crazy-smart. We are the *great tricksters*." He opened his large, shiny, black beak and laughed. "Crows are the great tricksters of the world, much like our cousins Raven and Magpie. Yes, yessss ... we live by our wits -- for we must."

Daymoon and Bushhopper gasped.

"Ah, surprised, are you?" Blackfeather laughed. "Well, don't be. We have to be smart. We can't get by on good looks and sweet songs like you pretty birds here. We have to live by our wits. Yes, yeeesssss ... Crows are the great tricksters."

Blackfeather leaned close to Bluesky again. He stared deeply into Bluesky's eyes, and then he opened his huge black beak and smiled.

"We are the smartest birds in the world," Blackfeather whispered urgently.

"What ... w-what do you mean?" Bluesky stuttered.

"Other birds fear us ... They misunderstand us ...

We use that to our advantage!"

Bluesky felt his mind spinning. Crows spoke in mysteries like the wise Owls, it seemed.

"That's an arrogant thing to say! The smartest birds in the entire world? What makes you think you're so smart?" Bushhopper asked, his tone challenging and demeaning.

"CAW! CAW! CAW!" Blackfeather shouted angrily at the Towhee. The old Crow had obviously been offended.

The four Crows hopped closer together, their feathers ruffled with their rising emotions.

In a flash of red feathers, Daymoon hopped beside his friend and stared with quiet determination back at the Crows crowding closer to the bold Towhee.

"Please, pardon my friend here. He means no disrespect, but it does seem a bold statement -- Crows being the smartest birds in the world. Give us an example so we can understand," Daymoon asked in a surprisingly respectful manner.

All the Crows unruffled their feathers almost at once in response to his calm and polite tone.

"You're a smart bird, Cardinal," Blackfeather said, obviously impressed.

"Why do you say that?" Daymoon asked with puzzlement.

"Your apology and calmness has erased the anger that was building. You rephrased the Towhee's question to make it reasonable too." Blackfeather smiled.

"Better to make new friends than make new enemies." Daymoon nodded respectfully at

Blackfeather.

"Good, good -- well said." Blackfeather and the other Crows relaxed. In fact, the tension in the air between the two groups of birds evaporated, and everyone seemed to relax.

"And your reply to my reasonable question?" Daymoon politely reminded Blackfeather.

Blackfeather nodded at Daymoon with a twinkle in his black eyes. "Only Crows know what men love -- the shiny metals. We steal them, we keep them, we play with them -- like men. Ah, we know other man-things too -- cunning we are."

"I don't believe Crows are so smart." Coolbreeze zoomed up and hovered right before Blackfeather.

"Ah, a tiny bird with a hum. And you don't think we're all that smart, eh?" Blackfeather crooned in a high-pitched tone.

"I'm not afraid of a big, slow bird like you!" Coolbreeze shouted in a series of squeaks.

Suddenly, Coolbreeze zipped right up to Blackfeather's beak. In a blur, he zipped around and around the huge bird's head, squeaking and taunting him.

"You can't catch me, slow bird! I'll fly circles around you!"

Blackfeather opened his beak and chuckled as he watched the tiny Hummingbird fly around and around his head. The first few revolutions around his head, Blackfeather twisted his head slightly to keep track of the little bird. It quickly became evident, however, that the Crow was not in the least impressed.

"It's true -- I could never catch a bird as fast as

you."

Blackfeather remained silent a moment longer.

Without warning, the Crow raised his left wing just as Coolbreeze came around again.

Coolbreeze slammed into the Crow's wing and bounced backward. He hovered in one spot, dazed and surprised at the unexpected move.

"See? I don't need to fly as fast as you. I only need to out-smart you." Blackfeather chuckled.

"What shiny things do men love?" Bluesky asked. "And what do you mean Crows are tricksters?"

"Ah, the shiny metals. Well, if you're a nice bird, I might just show you one of my stashes so you understand. Tricksters, we are. We know things most birds don't even understand."

"Like what?"

"We know how far a man's death-stick will reach into the sky so as to kill a bird."

"Death-stick?" Bluesky asked fearfully.

"You've never seen one, eh?" Blackfeather's voice changed back to a hushed whisper. "Men use them to kill. They make a sound like thunder. When a man points one at you and you hear the thunder, invisible death reaches out ..."

Bushhopper, Daymoon, Coolbreeze, and Bluesky trembled at the thought of the invisible death reaching out to them even when flying high up in the sky. After all, flying in the open sky was a bird's greatest protection -- and yet this death-stick could reach up and kill them even there?

"Yes, yes, there's a crazy man who lives nearby who has many, many death-sticks," Blackfeather whispered in a hush. "We know. We have raided his garden many times."

The four birds waited with tense expectation after Blackfeather paused.

"One of his death-sticks throws death out wide and deadly, but its reach is short. Another of his death-sticks will reach far, far up into the sky. We know each death-stick by sight. We know how far they reach. But this man is truly crazy. And the reason he kills is what makes him crazy."

"What reason is that?" Daymoon asked fearfully.

"Birds and animals kill for food. We also kill to defend our territory and our young. This man, he kills simply for the thrill of killing. He is consumed with a bloodlust," Blackfeather whispered in a dark and mysterious tone.

"Where does this man live, so we will make sure to never fly near him?" Bluesky asked in a rush of words.

"Across the large man-path of black rock and past the next group of man houses and beyond a great field just before you come to the only lake in this region," Blackfeather said in a normal voice.

"Is it far?" Bluesky straightened up and craned his neck in the direction Blackfeather gazed.

"It is not far by wing. You will recognize him easily enough, because three huge dogs live with him. They are great, fearsome beasts who the crazed man has taught to be just like him."

"What do you mean?" Daymoon asked in surprise.

"The dogs have learned to kill for the same

reason -- they too have the blood-lust. Like the man, they will hunt down and kill any hapless animal or bird they find. They're dangerous, very dangerous. Only the smartest crows dare to raid his garden -- or the stupid or the hungry."

"Why do you go there?" Bushhopper flew over and stood right before the large Crow.

Blackfeather opened his shiny, black beak and smiled down at him. "I used to go there when I was young and bold. It was a great challenge. But I am older now, the eldest leader of the Crows who live in these parts. I fly there from time to time in the early morning or the end of the day. I perch on a tree at the far end of the field and call out to him."

"That doesn't sound like a very smart thing to do," Daymoon said.

"I perch far away from the reach of his death-sticks. I never fly closer than they can reach." Blackfeather looked from one bird to the other. Finally, his black eyes fixed on Bluesky.

"Stay far away from the crazy man and his monster dogs. We have learned over the seasons that only bad things happen if you fly too close."

"I don't ever plan to fly that way," Bluesky said confidently.

"Do you have a name for this crazy man?" Daymoon asked.

"Marcion." Blackfeather's eyes narrowed.

"Why that strange name?" Daymoon asked.

"It is the name he gives himself."

"We shall never fly close Marcion and his monster dogs. We have been warned," Bluesky said.

"Good, good. Now, is that all you wanted from

me? Blackfeather asked.

"No, I need to ask you an important question."
Bluesky gathered his courage and continued. "I
need to know how I can get close enough to a Hawk
in order to talk with him -- without him eating me!"

Chapter Nineteen

Little Katie fell deathly ill.

It came over her suddenly, after she came inside the house from playing in the yard. She coughed continuously and even struggled to breathe. Jane quickly gave her some cough syrup and put her to bed, but her symptoms grew worse by the minute.

Within an hour, she was sweating profusely and running a dangerously high fever. Worse, her breathing deteriorated to the point where her skin began turning blue.

Frantic with worry, Mark and Jane rushed her to the hospital.

They spent an agonizing amount of time together in the waiting room, waiting for word from the doctors treating their precious daughter. A nurse finally came and sat with them. She explained the doctors were running tests in order to determine the cause of Katie's illness. The nurse did report that they had managed to stabilize their daughter's fever and she was breathing fine with the aid of a machine.

After the nurse left, they waited again for what seemed an eternity. Mark sat with an arm around Jane's shoulders while they tried to remain patient.

Both parents were devastated emotionally and physically. They felt helpless, overwhelmed. Most of all, they were just plain scared.

Finally, the doctor came and met with them.

After dozens of tests and hours and hours of waiting, nothing definitive had been learned, but although the tests were inconclusive, the doctor did have good news for them. The medical team had managed to lower Katie's temperature, and with oxygen tubes inserted into her nostrils, they had managed to get her breathing stabilized.

Then something totally unexpected had happened: Katie's condition had stabilized just as suddenly and mysteriously as it had all started. In fact, they had just removed the tubes, and she was now breathing normally on her own.

Mark and Jane stood up and hugged each other with relief. Mark turned and gratefully shook the doctor's hand while Jane put her hands to her face and took a deep, refreshing breath.

The doctor suspected some kind of severe allergic reaction that affected Katie's lungs -- but from what? Further tests would have to be run, though he wasn't sure if even those might identify the reason. Meanwhile, the doctor decided it prudent to keep Katie overnight in the hospital so they could observe her and make sure her condition remained stable.

Mark and Jane never left their daughter's side. Mark slept in a chair while Jane slept in a small cot the staff provided. Their sleep was interrupted at regular intervals all during the night as the nurses checked Katie's vital signs.

They were tired and still worried, but things seemed to be improving steadily. Jane's younger sister was at their house watching Philip, so at least they knew their son was fine.

Just over forty-eight hours after she first fell sick, Katie was released from the hospital.

It had all happened so fast ...

Mark carried Katie inside their house and up into her room, where he set her on her bed. After he turned out the lights and stepped out into the hallway to shut the door, Mark paused a moment and listened quietly.

From the darkness inside, he heard the rasping sound of her breathing. Each uneven breath felt like a knife cutting into Mark's very heart.

He gently closed the door.

In the darkness of the hallway, another sound grew audible and tore even harder at his heart. He heard his wife sobbing.

He figured that the worst had happened now -- one of their children had been affected by the mysterious illness.

In another second, he realized that the worst hadn't happened yet.

But what about next time?

Mark's mind raced back over the past months since the mysterious miscarriages had started. Now, even small children were being affected -- Katie had been affected!

During the past winter, the incidents had become less and less frequent. People had begun to think that perhaps the worst was over.

Spring had arrived. March and April had both been windy months, especially April. Everyone had hoped the breezy days and clean, cool air from up north would be healthy. And maybe, just maybe, the unseen sickness would go away with the wind.

Instead, as the winds picked up, so did the reports of new incidents. Now, something new was being reported.

Young children suddenly became ill with strange, flu-like symptoms. They had trouble breathing, loss of energy, and extreme vomiting. The doctor had told them that four children had been admitted to the hospital three days before Katie.

All of the children lived within two miles of their own home.

Mark didn't sleep that night. He tossed and turned restlessly. Jane dozed on the couch downstairs with the TV playing. Mark knew she was desperately worried when that was the only way she could sleep, hoping that the unceasing chatter would lull her frantic mind into restfulness and drown out her worries.

The next morning, they found Katie sitting up in bed seemingly as healthy as ever.

Mark and Jane cried tears of joy at the sight.

They all ate breakfast together along with a happy Phillip. Their entire family was back together again.

Mark volunteered to clean the table and the dishes while Jane took the children upstairs so she could be with them a while.

He quickly cleaned up, loaded the dishwasher, and turned it on. He then went into the living room and sat down in his favorite chair. Mark sat there a long time alone with his thoughts. Now more than ever, he felt an overpowering need to find the cause of this sickness -- especially before it hurt his family again.

After an hour passed in reflective silence, Mark

realized he'd heard no sound from anyone. He walked quietly upstairs and looked in Katie's room, but her rumpled bed was empty. He walked down to his bedroom and found the door shut.

He opened it and peeked inside.

Jane lay fast asleep with her arm around Katie, who lay nestled comfortably within her mother's embrace. Little Philip was fast asleep too, his tiny form snuggled up tight against Jane's back. All three rested peacefully.

Mark smiled and watched them a few moments. After quietly shutting the door, he went downstairs and called his best friend, Walter.

He met Walter at the end of Willow Hollow a few minutes later.

"How's Katie?" Walter peered at Mark with warmth and concern.

"She's much better."

"What was it?"

"The doctor's weren't sure. But I'm afraid it's related to this mysterious thing that's hurting unborn babies." Mark sighed.

"You mean it's affecting children now?" Walter's eyes grew wide.

"That's what I'm thinking, and I find it disturbing. That's why I want you go to with me."

Mark had his bird-watching binoculars around his neck. He handed another pair to Walter, and as they walked toward the rear entrance of the subdivision, he explained his plan.

They marched out onto Simpson Road fifteen minutes later and crossed it toward the new subdivision. After they walked down the main entrance, they continued to the far end, passed the last house, and entered a small forest. These trees formed a barrier between the houses and the land of Charlie Marcion. In fact, the forest stretched the rest of the way down Simpson Road all along the boundary of Marcion's land.

Mark reminded Walter that although the EPA ground tests had found no trace of poison or toxic materials, perhaps something just beyond the tested areas, just outside the directly affected areas, had escaped their notice.

"What exactly are we looking for?" Walter asked with a puzzled tone.

Mark held his small binoculars to his eyes and peered through the trees, slowly panning around. Finally, he spoke.

"I'm not sure. If there is something toxic getting into the air or water, it seems to be getting worse. If it's affecting more people, perhaps it's also affecting the wildlife. I'm looking for dead animals or dead birds. Perhaps they'll lead us to the source, to some kind of chemicals. If it's exposed, it could be getting mixed up in the wind and blowing toward our homes."

"I think there have been at least two searches in the last six months all up and down Simpson Road since this thing broke out."

"I know, but they might have missed something. Let's go deeper into the tree line."

Mark marched resolutely into the woods. Briars and vines tripped them up and impeded their progress, making it clear no one walked in this place except small animals. As they continued

254

deeper into the thick underbrush and trees, they came up to a rusted, barb-wire fence.

They realized this was the fence that protected Charlie Marcion's property.

The two men stared at the rusty barbed wire fence and glanced up and down its length. They soon spotted a faded sign nailed to a gnarled pine tree.

No Trespassing.

Mark walked up to the fence and leaned against it. He pushed aside a vine and turned his binoculars toward the overgrown fields of Charlie Marcion.

"Why don't we just walk on out into the field? We can't see much from here," Walter suggested.

Mark put his binoculars down and looked at Walter with a shocked expression. He shook his head. "We don't want to trespass on that guy's property, believe me. I just want to walk all the way down the length of this fence and take a good look inside there." Mark continued scanning with his binoculars.

"Yeah, I understand you tried to get the Commission to force an inspection of his property back in February," Walter said.

"They wouldn't do it. Not unless Marcion agreed voluntarily, which he didn't when he was called before the Commission. That was an ugly meeting." Mark tensed with the memory of the man's angry words directed at him and the entire group. It had taken an official summons delivered by a county sheriff just to get Charlie Marcion to show up in the first place.

It hadn't put him in a good mood.

All the government papers and court proceedings substantiated everything Marcion had told him the first time. After that meeting, Mark had lost the respect of the leaders of the Commission, since they had felt the brunt of Marcion's wrath.

Still, if Charlie Marcion was telling the truth as everything seemed to indicate, why did he act so suspiciously?

Maybe the Commission was right. They'd told Mark he had let his emotions get in the way and that was why the meeting had degraded into the foul cursing of the old man. In the end, the facts had supported Marcion.

If Mark did anything now, as far as dealing with Charlie Marcion, he'd have to do it on his own. The Commission, the EPA, and everyone had cleared Marcion of any suspicion and felt there was no need for a search of his land.

Still, if more children got sick, it seemed they'd have to change their mind, especially if the public outcry grew loud enough.

What frightened Mark was that the public outcry might come too late for his Katie.

He needed to act now.

They walked for over an hour, staying just outside the fence and stopping every fifty feet or so to carefully scan the fields beyond.

They stopped once again. About a hundred feet on the other side of the fence a small tree stood proud and alone in the field. It was a stunted, yellow pine tree. While they paused, a mourning dove coo'ed contentedly from the top of the small tree.

Mark smiled while the peaceful sound of the

dove soothed him and pushed his troubled thoughts aside..

Suddenly, a gunshot ripped through the air.

As he watched in total disbelief, the mourning dove disappeared in an explosion of feathers.

The thunderous report of the gun caused both Mark and Walter to jump in fear because it was so close and unexpected.

Charlie Marcion walked into view. He must have been standing just out of sight against the trees when he had fired. He spat on the ground and walked toward them.

"What'cha doin' next to my property?" Charlie Marcion growled as he lowered his shotgun, blue smoke swirling out the barrel.

King, Bear, and Jack growled menacingly, each dog standing around Charlie.

Walter stood frozen and speechless, staring at the wild-eyed old man and the three dogs baring their fangs at them.

Mark felt his own heart pounding inside his chest, but his fear was instantly replaced by anger.

"Why'd you kill that bird?" Mark asked angrily.

"Target practice." Marcion sneered heartlessly.

"That bird was a living creature. It had a right to live as much as you or I!"

"It was on my property. I kin do what I want here. So, I shot 'em."

"Don't you have any respect for life?" Mark shot back, his anger blazing, though in the next instant, a wise proverb came to his mind: *An answer, when mild, turns away rage, but a word causing pain makes anger to come up.*

Charlie Marcion walked toward him with rage in his reddened eyes. "I kin kill anything I want on my property. I shoot crows all the time and hang up the dead un's by their feet to scare the others away. That keeps 'em out of my garden."

Mark didn't reply right away. He concentrated on getting control of his emotions. He saw the rage in Marcion's eyes and noticed how the old man's hands shook with anger.

He wasn't there to start a fight. He was there trying to find the source of the sickness. Mark wanted to reason with Marcion, appeal to his feelings. He wanted all of them to talk calmly like adults. If he and Walter got angry in return, the whole situation could get out of control.

Besides, Marcion had a gun

"And me and my dawgs don't allow no cats on my land either." Marcion laughed as Mark's eyes widened with shock. "I see you don't like that either, eh meester."

"You shoot cats?" Mark asked in disbelief.

Charlie slapped his leg and howled out in laughter. The three dogs circled Charlie, each growing more excited by the old man's crazed laughter.

"No, no. I don't have to shoot 'em." Charlie reached down and patted the monstrous bulldog. "Jack will hunt down and kill any cat foolish enough to come on our land, right, boy?"

Long lines of drool dripped down both sides of Jack's mouth in happy response.

"Yep, that's how come I named him Jack."

"Jack? I don't get it." Mark's eyes narrowed.

"Jack rips cats to shreds. That's why I named him 'Jack the Ripper!'"

Mark stared at the bulldog with renewed disgust.

The dog panted proudly.

"I bet none of the homes on this end of that new subdivision has a single living cat now. Yep, those first few months those homes got sold, it seemed ol' Jack was draggin' up a dead cat every two days." Charlie laughed as he stroked the broad head of the bulldog again.

"You ought to have more respect for life, Charlie. Birds eat insects -- they have a niche in our world. Cats keep rodents away. You could train your dog not to --"

"I want him to kill cats!" Charlie screamed as he raised the shotgun upright and pumped it, sending a shell casing onto the ground.

Walter and Mark stared at him in a mixture of fear and disbelief.

Charlie raised the gun and aimed it above their heads.

Mark suddenly realized a bird was singing somewhere above his head. He recognized the fussing cries of either a chickadee or a titmouse.

"No!" Mark shouted right as Marcion fired.

Walter and Mark ducked when pieces of branches and leaves and other debris rained down on them.

"Are you crazy?" Walter shouted angrily.

Marcion laughed like a maniac and pumped the shotgun again, ejecting another spent shell.

"Stop shooting, Charlie. You're liable to injure

someone!" Mark stared at Marcion.

Charlie hefted the shotgun onto his shoulder with a flash of his yellow teeth. "I didn't like gettin' that summons from yore friends back in the winter. Besides, I'd already told you I'd properly disposed of all that fertilizer jest like the court ordered."

"That was twenty years ago, Charlie. What if one of those barrels is still on your land -- what if it got overlooked? What if that's what is killing these unborn babies and making our kids sick now?" Mark pleaded earnestly, "Don't you care enough to let us search your land just to make sure?"

Charlie reached in his shirt pocket and quickly lit up a cigarette. He took a long drag, staring silently at them.

"Please, let us search your land to confirm everything." Mark's voice grew calm as he tried to appeal to the Marcion's conscience.

"It ain't my concern!" Charlie spat.

"Yes, it is," Mark continued calmly. "We're all neighbors."

"It ain't my concern. I put mah hand on a Bible and swore before God and everyone that I would dispose of that stuff ... and I did. It cost me a lot of money, I nearly lost everything. But I still have my land and my home, and as long as I have my beer and cigarettes, that's all I need."

Mark groaned with frustration.

Charlie stared unflinching at them.

"You still swear that there aren't any toxic materials left on your land?" Mark asked with an even tone.

"By heaven above, there ain't nuthin toxic on

my land, accident or otherwise."

The silence returned.

"Now, next time I find you near my land, I just might make a mistake with my aim when I'm shootin' pesky birds. And I'd hate to see a man get hurt."

Mark and Walter froze at the man's blatant threat.

"We're going." Mark tapped Walter on the shoulder.

Mark and Walter turned and left.

"Are we going to let that old geezer get away with that?" Walter whispered after they had walked a prudent distance.

"No. We're going straight down to the sheriff's office and file a complaint." Mark said with conviction.

Mark returned home later that afternoon.

He walked into the house and found Jane cheerfully preparing supper while Katie and Philip played. She smiled at him and nodded at the children. He smiled in return.

He felt a sense of inner contentment as he watched his wife and heard her hum while the children laughed and giggled. He watched them happily for long while.

It made him feel good inside.

A soft scratching sound came to his ears. He turned and saw Buddy sitting outside the glass storm door. Buddy stood on his hind legs and pawed earnestly on the glass with both front paws. It was his way of 'knocking.'

"Do you want to come in, Buddy?"

"Meeeow, meowww."

Mark walked over and opened the door. Buddy hopped inside.

He reached down and stroked Buddy's back when the cat paused beside him. Buddy purred, turned around, and rubbed against Mark's other leg.

Mark gathered the tomcat up into his arms and held him against his chest with one arm while he slowly stroked him from the top of his head down the length of his back.

Buddy purred louder.

Mark rubbed the top of the cat's head in luxurious circles.

"You're a good boy," Mark whispered.

"Meeoow."

He stood there holding Buddy in his arms and petting him. Both he and Buddy stared out at the world through the glass door. Their attention suddenly turned to the hummingbird feeder hanging on the front porch. A female hummingbird zipped up to it, looked quickly around, and then took two fast drinks.

In a flash of movement, a male hummingbird dove on her.

The air filled with his urgent squeaks as he chased her away. While they watched, the ruby-throated hummingbird turned and took a quick drink from the feeder as a reward.

After he flew backward and hovered a second, the hummingbird noticed Mark and Buddy.

The tiny bird flashed his red gorget, first turning in one direction to hover a split second and then turning and hovering again. Suddenly, he flew right up to the glass door and squeaked non-stop at them.

Mark laughed, realizing the bird wanted to chase them away.

"Meooowww." Buddy put his nose against the glass for a closer look as Mark leaned forward.

"I think he wants us to leave," Mark whispered.

And he was right.

The hummingbird fussed even louder and zoomed right up to the glass door. He hovered directly before Mark, and they both locked eyes.

Mark laughed. He pursed his lips and tried to imitate the hummingbird's squeaking calls.

The overly courageous hummingbird squeaked back even louder.

Suddenly, both Mark and the male hummingbird realized another hummingbird was drinking from the feeder.

In a blur of movement, he was chasing after the intruder.

Mark laughed again.

"Honey, wash up. Supper's almost done," Jane called from the kitchen.

He stood a moment longer with Buddy in his arms, gazing at the little male hummingbird, who was now perched on a nearby branch and diligently guarding his feeder. While he watched, the tiny bird moved his head from side to side, both watching the feeder for interlopers and keeping a sharp eye on Mark and Buddy.

Mark smiled, slowly stroking Buddy in contemplation.

"You know, Buddy, sometimes I wish I could understand what birds are saying when they sing or squeak like our tiny friend out there."

"Meeeoow."

***

Our Feathered Friends of the Southeast
A. C. Wages

Red-shouldered Hawk
Latin: *Buteo lineatus*

The red-shouldered hawk is primarily found
only in the eastern part of the United States,
although a sizable population now lives in western
California.

A close inspection reveals the differences
between this hawk and his cousin, the red-tailed
hawk. The red-shouldered hawk is covered by
brown feathers on his upper parts and head while its
chest and belly are covered by a red-barred pattern
of feathers. The wings are striped with black and
white feathers with a red-brown patch on his
shoulders. The tail is also striped black and white,
although in a wider pattern than the wings.

Medium- to large-sized hawks, they can stand
twenty-four inches tall when full grown and have a
wingspan of forty-four inches. Although the male
and female are identical in coloration, the female is
much larger. They are impressive when gliding in
large, lazy circles with their wings spread wide and
their tail feathers fanned out.

Some observers might think the powerful wings
of the hawk are its greatest attribute. Others could

264

point to their strong talons with which they grasp their prey or their hooked beak that enables them to tear their prey. However, in this author's opinion, it is the hawk's keen eyes that are its greatest attribute. The hawk's eyesight enable it to survive and thrive at the top of the food chain -- it is, after all, where the age-old expressions 'eyes like a hawk' and 'hawkeye' originated. When a person is said to have 'eyes like a hawk', it means 'nothing escapes their notice' or 'they see everything.'

Hawks are highly territorial. Their native habitat is forested areas where they primarily hunt while perched silently in a tree. Once their prey is spotted, they will swoop down in total silence and kill the unsuspecting animal.

Like other bird species, the red-shouldered hawk has displayed a high degree of adaptability with the spread of civilization. These large hawks now live in urban centers, hunting among the steel and concrete skyscrapers as easily as they do in their native forests.

A couple of years back, this author was sitting at his window watching a mourning dove perched on a branch. The dove had been one of several eating seed on the ground. The other birds had become startled and flown off, but this one bird stayed close. This author expected to see it drop back down to the ground and start feeding again.

Suddenly, a blur of motion intersected with the dove, and feathers flew everywhere.

This author stared in shock through the window as the dove and another bird fell to the ground, locked in a tight embrace. It happened so fast, at first this author's mind did not comprehend what he was seeing. However, it quickly became apparent that a hawk had the dove in its talons and was trying to right itself. The author continued to watch in total surprise while the hawk spread his great wings and flew off with the limp form of the dove within its grasp.

This author had seen this same hawk earlier in the day in his next door neighbor's yard perched high in a tree with a clear view of the author's backyard. Now, its reason for doing so was clear. The hawk had noticed the activity of the birds feeding and had waited for the right moment.

Throughout history, hawks have always exerted a mystical presence on man. Perhaps it is the way they glide effortlessly on the currents of air with eyes searching far off in the distance.

Even today, directors add a mystical element to a movie scene simply by inserting a hawk's distant cry in the background. Listen closely, and you too might hear that distant 'kee-har' in the soundtrack of your favorite movie.

The western tribes of North American have many stories about the mythical thunderbirds. These thunderbirds were a kind of mighty hawk and were held in high esteem when mentioned in their fireside tales.

The Cherokee, Creek, Choctaw, and Chickasaw of the Southeast also saw the hawk as a mystical bird, and the mightiest hawks of all were the fearsome *tlanuwa*.

The *tlanuwa* were huge birds capable of carrying off small animals and even children as food. They were a mythical type of hawk like the thunderbirds of the western tribes.

The Cherokee told many tales that included the mighty *tlanuwa*. Perhaps the most famous tale is the one about the *tlanuwa* and the monster Uktena.

Uktena was the most formidable monster of all Cherokee myth. It was a huge serpent with wings on its back and great horns on its head.

Here is a summary of this famous tale:

A pair of *tlanuwa* had been terrorizing a small band of Cherokee camping near a great river. The people quickly discovered that their arrows bounced harmlessly off the strong feathers of the *tlanuwa*. Soon the Cherokee warriors discovered that all their weapons were useless in fighting the huge birds. No warrior's weapon could pierce the feathers and hurt them.

Mothers continued to cry out as they watched another of their children taken away in the mighty talons of the *tlanuwa*. Not even the greatest warrior of the tribe could stop them.

However, a greater monster terrorized the village.

No one dared cross the river because the great monster Uktena lurked under its waters. This terrible creature devoured any Cherokee foolish enough to try to swim across to the other side -- even the warriors did not try.

Many times the warriors fought with Uktena and shot at it with their arrows and spears from the edge of the great river, but as with the *tlanuwa*, their weapons were useless against the scaly hide of Uktena and bounced harmlessly off.

The months passed, and the tribe was in constant dread from the *tlanuwa*, afraid one of them would dive without warning and take another child. Even worse, the Uktena lurked under the water and sometimes crawled into the village at night to devour someone.

The brave Cherokee could fathom no way to rid themselves of these fearsome monsters. Soon, the leaders spoke of moving their camp far away in order to protect their people.

A young Cherokee hunter, however, quietly observed the *tlanuwa* as they flew fearlessly in the sky. He soon noticed the *tlanuwa* were feeding their young on a nest on top of the high mountain that overlooked the river.

He knew soon more *tlanuwa* would terrorize his people. What if Uktena also mated and laid eggs?

He meditated deeply in order to find a way to help his people. He realized that no Cherokee warrior could defeat either the *tlanuwa* or the monster of the river in battle. Both of these creatures were too strong and powerful.

The *tlanuwa* had talons like spears and wings strong enough to knock a warrior to the ground, and there was no way a warrior could sneak up and surprise them.

The mighty Uktena was more powerful still and had already killed many Cherokee warriors who had dared to face him. Uktena now grew bolder and regularly left the river at night in order to silently enter the tent of a sleeping family and take one of them for its food.

The enemies of his people were very strong, and

the weapons of the Cherokee warriors could not hurt either ...

While he meditated about the strengths of the monsters, something crystallized in his mind. He pictured both creatures, and the seed of a plan grew.

In his heart, he knew it was the only way.

The next day he prepared himself for death, for he realized it might be the price he would have to pay to make his plan work. He left the camp, alone and armed only with a knife.

He watched patiently from his hiding place until the great *tlanuwa* left the nest to go search for food. He knew they would be away for only a little while. He quickly climbed the huge mountain and found three hungry babies in the nest. He threw each down into the river far below, letting out a great war cry each time. His war cries echoed over the river, and he hoped all could hear for miles around.

It took only a moment for the first monster to appear.

He watched Uktena rise up from the dark waters. He shouted louder as he climbed back down. The scaly monster quickly spotted the three helpless birds struggling in the river and devoured the baby *tlanuwa* one by one.

The warrior shouted to the sky with his war cries while he watched Uktena devour the first two birds.

As Uktena swallowed the last one, the two *tlanuwa* parents dove like lightning from the sky. They had heard the warrior's cries and had rushed back to protect their young.

But too late!

The *tlanuwa* roared so loudly in anger that the mountain itself shook.

They swooped down upon mighty Uktena in revenge!

The battle of the monsters sent huge explosions of waves over the banks of the river. The entire camp fled deep into the forest in fear.

Alone, the Cherokee warrior watched from the base of the mountain as his plan unfolded.

The male *tlanuwa* stabbed Uktena with his talons, but Uktena flew up and bit the *tlanuwa* with his fearsome teeth again and again. The *tlanuwa* cried out in pain as his wounds dripped blood.

The male *tlanuwa* now grabbed Uktena by the head and flew high into the sky, calling out to his mate. Uktena hissed and tried to wrap its tail around the *tlanuwa* with a death grip.

The female dove and slashed Uktena again and again with her talons until the monster's blood fell like rain. Finally, she shredded the great serpent's wings. Wounded and weak, the male *tlanuwa* rose up close to the sun itself and released Uktena.

Uktena fell to its death on the rocks beside the river. The two *tlanuwa* dove down and shredded the monster's corpse.

In their great sadness, the *tlanuwa* flew far, far away, never to be seen again.

In this way, the young Cherokee warrior used his wisdom in order to rid his people of two of its greatest enemies in a single day.

Today, if you are observant, you may spot a red-shouldered hawk sitting in a tall tree silently seeking its next meal. More likely, you will hear its mystical 'kee-har' from high above. If you look quickly, you may see this mighty raptor with wings spread wide, gliding effortlessly on the invisible currents of wind ...

Chapter Twenty

Nightwind stretched his wings and yawned. With a quick shake of his head, he flapped his wings vigorously and prepared to sleep after a busy night.

"Hello!" Bluesky shouted happily as he landed on the branch next to the Owl.

"Hello, Bluesky. It's going to be a beautiful day today." Nightwind smiled at the young Mockingbird.

Bluesky paused a moment, surprised by the Owl's words, since the day was just beginning.

"How do you know it's going to such a wonderful day, Nightwind? I mean, the sun just rose above the treetops. It might rain later, or there could be a blustery wind."

Nightwind breathed deeply the fresh morning air. "It might, but that won't take away from it being a beautiful day. In fact, it would only add to it."

"You're such a funny bird!" Bluesky laughed.

Nightwind's eyes opened wide in surprise. "Now, what do you mean by that?"

"How can the rain make the day better?"

"The plants and trees need rain. Birds need rain to fill the streams and ponds so we can drink."

Bluesky digested this thought. "Okay, but how do you know that a day is going to be beautiful before it even happens?"

"Every day is beautiful, if you take the time to notice."

"Oh ..."

Nightwind smiled while Bluesky paused to contemplate his words.

"Did you meet Blackfeather yet?"

"Yes, I did." Bluesky's eyes twinkled.

"So, what did you think of that wily old bird? And Crows in general? What goodness did you perceive?"

"Well, they're smart. In fact, Blackfeather made the bold statement that Crows are the smartest birds in the world!"

"Even worse, they *know* that they are!" Nightwind chuckled. "That's also their greatest weakness."

"Yes, he made my head spin. It was sort of like talking with you," Bluesky said.

"Talking with Crows is stimulating. It exercises the mind and broadens your viewpoint."

Bluesky sat silent, recalling things Blackfeather had said to him. It had caused his mind to work at a feverish pace. In his mind, he relived the conversations with Blackfeather and the Crows. Again he heard Blackfeather tell him about the trickster Crows and some of their greatest ruses.

In the next instant, his mind traveled to the vast sea and he saw Pelicans flying in formation just like his uncle had described so vividly. His heart yearned to see this for himself and not simply with his mind's eye. He wanted to hear their cries, smell the salt in the air, stand on the sandy beaches, and experience it for himself.

In another instant, his mind swept far, far away to the distant islands where the Orange Doves lived, just like Ol' Gray Mama had told him. His heart pounded with excitement as he contemplated such an exotic place and such a beautiful bird. In his mind, he pictured an Orange Dove spreading its wings and calling out to him to fly and play.

Bluesky's mind swirled with distant places and birds he'd only heard about.

Time seemed to slow down.

"What are you thinking?"

The world inside his mind disappeared with Nightwind's calm voice.

"I perceive there are two worlds," Bluesky said reflectively.

"Oh?" Nightwind peered at Bluesky with inquisitive eyes. "Please explain."

"I see the world around me -- the world we live in."

"And what is the other world?" Nightwind asked with an eager whisper.

"There is another world inside my mind."

"Yes!" The Owl gasped.

Bluesky frowned. It seemed Nightwind knew exactly what he was going say, and it made him feel uneasy at times.

"What is the world-inside-your-mind like?"

"In some ways, it is like the 'real' world." Bluesky's eyes searched far off into the distance. "The birds I know are there. We talk. We play. We fly places, just like we really do."

"And ..." Nightwind prompted eagerly.

"We can do things in my mind that we cannot do here in the 'real' world. We fly to the great sea easily. I watch the Pelicans glide above the waves and meet other birds I've never really seen before, though I clearly see them in my mind from the descriptions of others."

"Go on! Is there more?"

"Um, yes. I can fly to the mountains too, though I've never really been there. But in my mind, I can. Everyone is my friend there too -- everything is wonderful."

"Good, good!"

"I've flown up to the clouds many times there. And in my mind, I can actually sit on a cloud -- they are so soft and so wonderful. I can watch the world sliding by below like a lazy river. Dancingleaves flies with me there. Other birds I've met are there too: Daymoon, Bushhopper, Coolbreeze, Treeflower, Ol' Gray Mama -- and you."

"This world that exists inside your mind -- is it also the place where you dream?"

"Yes. But then, the world-inside-my-mind is more puzzling. Things that I don't want to happen occur -- sometimes things that disturb me. I don't like that."

"No, none of us do," Nightwind said thoughtfully, "but at times, the most wondrous things happen inside our imagination!"

"Yes, sometimes when I dream, it is so wonderful that I want to go back to sleep right away and go back to the dream world!"

"There is a danger," Nightwind said in a low voice. "One must always know the difference between the two worlds."

"Danger?"

"One might confuse the fantasy world inside his mind with reality, blurring his perception between the two worlds. A bird under such a delusion could search to discover their fantasy in the real world only to be disillusioned when it is never found. And worse, such ones overlook the beauty of the reality around them in their vain attempts to find what exists only in their mind."

"I-I don't understand."

"Each world has its place. It is important to always know the difference."

"I will try. I think I've already confused the two a few times now..."

"Tell me, my young Mockingbird. Is the world-inside-your-mind a happier place than the world around us?" Nightwind paused a moment. "Or is it a sadder place?"

"Oh, it is happier." Bluesky looked slowly around at the trees and other birds flying around and then bowed his head. "The world-inside-my-mind is a much happier place."

"Good. That means you have the power to make the world around you a little happier. For what we feel inside, what we are inside, we can express to all whom we meet in the real world around us."

"It seems strange that there is an entire world inside of my mind," Bluesky said with a questioning tone.

"There is a world inside each of our individual minds," Nightwind whispered mysteriously. "A private fantasy world to each alone, unless we find a way to share it. And if we do find a way to share it with others, how beautiful it can be!"

Bluesky frowned at Nightwind with a puzzled expression.

276

"Now, did Blackfeather explain how you can meet a Hawk?"

"I made a deal with him!" Bluesky laughed.

"A deal?"

"He wanted me to share something new or exotic with him in exchange for his knowledge on how to meet a Hawk. I had a hard time trying to think of something that might be new to an old bird like him -- and then, it hit me!"

"What?"

"I told him that I have a cat for a friend! He couldn't believe it. He said he's never heard of such a thing. So, I told him I'd introduce him to KC, and he said he'd share with me the secret on how to meet a Hawk!"

"Bravo!" Nightwind cheered. "That wily old Blackfeather knows you can learn something from anyone, even from a young Mockingbird like yourself. And you proved it!"

Bluesky bid Nightwind a good sleep and flew through the branches, up and around some and under others, until he was above the island of treetops. Soon, he came to another row of houses. The cool air of the morning caressed his feathers as he sailed in the open air and over the yards.

When he arrived at his destination, the exhilaration of flying took over. As he flew around the yard singing happily, he noticed KC curled up in her favorite chair on the back patio. Her green eyes followed him while he sailed through the lower branches and around the trees, flying in circles around the yard again and again.

He also noticed Blackfeather and two other

Crows watching silently from the shadows of a small tree. In another tree, Daymoon, Bushhopper, and Coolbreeze waited in keen anticipation. After he flew over the yard a fourth time, he saw a small group of Sparrows eating seed on the ground across from KC. He heard Treeflower's familiar chirps.

"Hello, Treeflower!" Bluesky whistled.

"Hi, Bluesky!" she called back cheerfully.

Now he flew directly over KC, and he heard her 'meow' a greeting up to him, urging him to fly faster.

Bluesky flapped his wings harder until he soared through the air at top speed.

Near the side fence, he saw Tootight hopping eagerly after some bugs. Bluesky whistled a cheery greeting to the Robin, and Tootight called back to him with warbling laughter.

With each circuit around the yard, he flew closer and closer over KC until on the seventh circuit he slowed down while he approached the tuxedo cat. Bluesky landed on the arm of the chair right next to her.

"Hi, KC!"

"Good morning, Bluesky. I see we have some new birds visiting today." KC licked her forepaw and nodded in the direction of the Crows.

"Yes, that's Blackfeather and some of his friends. They couldn't believe that I am friends with a cat."

KC licked her forepaw and then gently rubbed it against the side of her face. She repeated her careful cleaning several times before she spoke.

"Well, shall we give them our usual show?" She

purred mischievously.

"How about we do this too ..." Bluesky bent close and whispered in KC's ear.

"Meowww! Are you sure?" KC asked.

Bluesky nodded enthusiastically.

KC hopped from the chair onto the ground and walked with a leisurely stroll toward the middle of the backyard. Bluesky flexed his wings a few times, just for show, and finally leapt into the air. With his wings spread wide, he swooped toward the unsuspecting feline.

He heard the intake of breath from the Crows as he glided right up to KC and, with a little upward motion, settled gently on her back. She continued walking without missing a beat, and Bluesky cocked his long tail proudly a moment before he started flexing it side to side in order to keep his balance.

"CAW CAW CAW!"

KC chuckled, and Bluesky broke into a wide smile at the chant of the Crows mixed with the normal chattering of excited birds watching the unbelievable spectacle.

"I can't believe it! And yet, I'm seeing it with my own eyes!" Blackfeather caw'ed. "A bird riding on a cat's back! A bird and a cat are friends!"

KC padded around a few trees and started back toward the patio. As they drew closer, KC meowed in a hushed voice so only Bluesky could hear, "Are you ready?"

"Yes!"

Without warning, KC jumped in the air and let out a loud "MEOW!"

Bluesky feigned surprise and fell off onto the ground. He lay there unmoving.

All the birds stared in horror! Silence filled the air as they waited in shocked suspense over what might happen next.

KC sniffed the still form of the Mockingbird. Without hesitation, KC then opened her mouth and picked him up.

Startled cries filled the air.

KC walked over to the patio and stood before the chair with the motionless bird in her mouth. Gently, she placed Bluesky on the chair, and then she sat back on her haunches and watched him carefully.

More and more birds chattered desperately for Bluesky to fly away to safety.

Bluesky bounced up with a flash of his wings and laughed.

KC picked up her right paw and licked it nonchalantly while Bluesky whistled and trilled at their merry joke. He sang out to the other birds that he and KC had staged the entire thing.

Some birds laughed while others chastised him.

The one-legged Mockingbird reached out and kissed KC on the top of her head.

"Thank you," KC purred.

Bluesky took wing and flew up to the branch where Blackfeather and the other Crows sat dumbfounded, their huge black beaks hanging open with astonishment.

"Kid, that's the craziest thing I've ever seen in my entire life," Blackfeather said, obviously impressed.

"Thanks! KC and I have fun together."

"I see you do!"

"Now, will you tell me how to meet a Hawk?" Bluesky peered inquisitively at Blackfeather.

"Actually, it's easier than you might imagine."

"Really?"

"Sure. Think about it a moment. Why are you afraid to meet a Hawk in the first place?" Blackfeather's black eyes twinkled with amusement.

"Because I'm afraid he might eat me," Bluesky said after a pause.

"Right. So, the best time to meet a Hawk is when he's *not hungry*."

Bluesky was struck by the simplicity of the answer. He thought about it a moment, before the next obvious question crystallized in his mind.

"How will I know when a Hawk is not hungry?"

"Ah! Very good. You've thought the problem through almost to completion, but I'll let you answer the question yourself by asking you another question." Blackfeather hopped closer to Bluesky until he towered over him. He leaned closer until his shiny black beak was next to Bluesky's ear. "When would you absolutely know a Hawk is not hungry?"

"Right after he's eaten," he said without hesitation.

"Good!" Blackfeather crooned. "So, you will need to carefully observe a Hawk -- from a safe distance, of course -- and wait until he has made a kill and finished eating it."

Bluesky felt his stomach churn with nervousness.

"Ugh, I don't know if I can do that!" Bluesky

protested.

"That is the only way I know for a small bird like you to talk with a Hawk. But perhaps you know a better way?" Blackfeather smiled knowingly at the other Crows, who chuckled in reply.

"No, I don't of any other way."

"Then, you will need to strengthen your heart, young Mockingbird. You will need to steel yourself while a Hawk makes a kill and then watch him eat it from a distance. Only then can you safely approach."

Bluesky swallowed uneasily.

Suddenly, a chorus of twittering cries filled the air.

"W-what is it?" Bluesky asked fearfully.

"Quiet!" Blackfeather whispered harshly, cocking his head to listen.

From all the trees around them, the chattering warning cries of the Chickadees resounded again and again. They called with more urgency with each passing second, causing birds everywhere to stop and listen.

"The Chickadees are warning of a grave danger!" Blackfeather hopped up and down with growing agitation.

Daymoon, Bushhopper, and Coolbreeze now hopped onto the branch with them. Another moment later and Tootight and Treeflower perched beside them too.

"What are they warning us about? Is something dangerous about to attack?" Bluesky asked.

"It's not the warning call for a cat," Treeflower said.

"It's not a warning for a Hawk or other bird of prey either," Daymoon concurred.

"I've never heard that warning call before!" Bushhopper whispered urgently.

"What are they saying?" Bluesky asked nervously.

"Listen closely," Blackfeather urged solemnly. "It's something far worse."

Bluesky and the others cocked their heads and listened intently to the chattering calls of danger until the meaning grew clear. In a flash of realization, he understood what the Chickadees were saying. And now, the dire warning throbbed with each beat of his fearful heart.

"Do you understand their cries now?" Blackfeather asked.

"They're saying the same four words over and over," Coolbreeze squeaked nervously.

"Yes!" Bluesky said with a hush.

All of them now heard the four words clearly.

"Death on the wind! Death on the wind! Death on the wind!"

Chapter Twenty-One

"Death on the wind!" Tootight repeated in a hushed tone.

"What does that mean?" Bluesky looked from one bird to the other with fear in his eyes.

"It means death flies on the wind!"

Every bird froze at Blackfeather's ominous words.

"How can we escape the wind?" Daymoon asked in shock. "The wind is everywhere!"

"Fly away! We've got to fly far away from here!" Blackfeather shouted urgently.

In a flurry of wings, the three Crows took wing with raucous cries.

"I must fly to my eggs!" Treeflower spread her wings.

"You have eggs?" Bluesky's eyes widened. "You're going to have babies soon?"

"Yes, my mate is sitting on them while I'm away eating. I've got to go!" The pretty Song Sparrow flew away in a frenzied rush.

Tootight turned to fly.

"Are you going to a safe place? Can I go with you?" Bluesky asked hopefully.

"I've got a nest and eggs to protect too."

"You have a mate?" Bluesky's asked with utter surprise.

"Of course!" Tootight flew away in a blur of feathers.

Bluesky watched him leave as if in a daze.

"Let's go!" Bushhopper shouted to the

remaining birds.

"Do you have a mate too?" Bluesky asked with a hint of sadness.

"No!" Bushhopper replied, his tone tense with fear. "But we've got to leave before the death comes closer!"

"He's right -- we've got to fly!" Daymoon flew away in a blur of scarlet feathers with Bushhopper right beside him.

KC jumped up and ran toward the back door of the house. She pawed urgently at the lowest pane of glass of the single French door, trying to get the attention of anyone inside.

"Where are you going to find safety?" Bluesky asked.

"I must get in the house. Katie got sick a few days ago after playing outside, but when they took her inside she got better. Now I remember, I heard warnings cries from the Chickadees that day too. I didn't know what they were saying then!"

KC pawed more urgently at the door.

"But how will going inside help? Doesn't the wind go inside there too?"

"Dad will know what to do. He's smart. And he takes care of all of us!"

KC's words struck a chord in Bluesky's heart. He realized that although it was a man and his family that lived inside the house with KC and Buddy, the cats viewed them as their family -- just like he viewed the Doves as his new family.

The twittering in the trees suddenly grew louder.

"Let's go, Bluesky!"

Coolbreeze's wings hummed like a revved-up

motor. In a blur of wings, he zoomed away. He looked back over his shoulder at Bluesky. "Come on, follow me!"

Bluesky realized he was the last bird still there. He took wing as a terrible dread seized his heart.

"Faster!" Coolbreeze squeaked, surging forward,

The Ruby-throated Hummingbird zipped between the tree trunks and lower branches. Bluesky kept him in sight, but there was no way he could match Coolbreeze's amazing speed. In a flash, he decided that, if he flew above the trees, he could fly faster.

He flew higher with each beat of his wings.

"Don't do that!"

Coolbreeze's voice startled him. He held his altitude near the upper branches as he dodged around them.

"Why not? I can fly faster above the trees!"

"The trees block the wind. If you fly above the trees, you may fly right into the death flying on the wind!"

Bluesky immediately dropped lower.

Coolbreeze flew effortlessly beside him, although Bluesky was panting and beating his wings as fast as he could.

"You're a smart bird, Coolbreeze."

"Thanks," he said. "I just figured it's safer to fly among the trees while we get away."

"I hope the others thought of that too!"

"I think they did -- they all flew away among the trees and not up over the treetops. I think that's why I figured it out."

"Okay, fly faster. I'll keep you in sight."

The hum of Coolbreeze's wings grew louder as the tiny bird surged forward.

Bluesky flapped his wings faster, but Coolbreeze kept growing smaller and smaller as he flew farther ahead. Just when it seemed the Hummingbird would disappear from his view, the tiny figure hovered to allow Bluesky to close the distance.

As soon as he came close, Coolbreeze turned and zoomed ahead again.

Bluesky felt like he was flying through mud compared with the ease with which Coolbreeze zoomed through the air.

He had no idea where they were going.

He just knew they were flying as fast as their wings would allow. Inside his chest, his heart pounded faster and harder.

Several times, he completely lost sight of Coolbreeze.

Because he was flying up and over tree branches and between tree trunks, the myriad of green leaves would block his vision momentarily, but when he flew into the clear air between houses or especially over a street, he would spot his friend again.

Bluesky now could barely make out even the blur of Coolbreeze's wings when the Hummingbird put on another burst of speed. He watched Coolbreeze surge ahead, his body growing so small that Bluesky now almost imagined he saw him.

Suddenly, he realized the twittering cries of danger from the Chickadees and Titmice had subsided. A strange and ominous silence replaced the calls of danger.

A small gust of wind lifted Bluesky higher into the sky.

"Stay down! Stay down!" Coolbreeze squeaked urgently.

He folded his wings and allowed the unseen force of gravity to pull him lower. After he reached his desired altitude, he spread his wings and flapped several times, surging forward and a little higher with each beat of his wings. Once again he folded his wings and fell forward through the air, now flying in the normal undulating flight of most birds.

Suddenly, he noticed Coolbreeze zoom over to a tree and perch on a branch overlooking an especially large man-road.

Bluesky flew over and within a minute perched near his tiny friend.

He looked around, panting to catch his breath. Everywhere he looked, he saw trees and bushes he did not recognize.

Below them, the man-road was different. The man-roads he knew were always lined with houses on each side. This one was not only wider, but on the side where he perched only trees grew. Behind him, the rows of familiar houses stretched.

On the other side of this man-road, an empty field of tall grass stretched to a stand of forest in the distance. When he looked to his left, he saw the same field stretching up to a small hill. Looking to his right, he saw the field filled with young pine trees; beyond them he saw the familiar rows of roofs of houses. He realized another sub-division with trees and yards existed there.

In his heart, he yearned to fly there and see what kind of birds lived there. And like the yearning he felt to travel to the distant sea and watch Pelicans flying in single-row formation, he felt the urge to travel there and meet new birds. Inside his heart, he wanted to travel like his uncle and really see these things with his eyes and not just his mind.

"I see we've flown in the same direction."

Bluesky jumped with surprise at the unexpected nearness of Blackfeather's baritone voice.

He looked up.

Four branches up, Blackfeather and two other Crows stared down at them with smiles on their shiny black beaks.

Blackfeather spread his large wings and fell forward until he landed on the same branch as Coolbreeze and himself.

"You flew low between the trees -- good, very good," Blackfeather crooned.

"Yes, I saw you and the others fly away between the trees. It struck me that the leaves and trees block the wind and might block the death on the wind," Coolbreeze squeaked proudly.

Blackfeather laughed as he towered over the tiny Hummingbird like a skyscraper over a house.

"Not all escaped."

Bluesky looked up at the two other Crows above, not sure which one had spoken.

They sat on the same branch, their necks craned forward with black eyes focused in the same direction. They peered solemnly.

He turned and looked toward the other side of the man-road and the distant rooftops.

As his gaze traveled along the road searching carefully, he stopped and felt his heart now miss a beat.

A new panic gripped his heart as it pounded back to life. Adrenaline filled his being, and he spread his wings to fly away again.

"They are dead."

Bluesky froze with his wings spread, staring at the bodies of three dead birds.

Silence, deep and somber, filled the air around them.

"What kind of birds?" Coolbreeze squeaked with fear.

"Two Robins ... the other is a Titmouse, he is much smaller and mouse-gray. I think I see the patch of rust on his side," Blackfeather said in a very low and serious tone.

"Why don't they move?" Coolbreeze asked in denial of the reality before him.

"They are dead, little Hummingbird. The dead do not move. Dead birds do not fly ..."

"Was it ...?" Bluesky asked, his voice cracking with emotion.

"I would assume it was the *death on the wind*, yes, but let's wait a while, and then we will fly closer and observe."

The five birds sat silently while the sun moved slowly across in the sky. Gradually, normal birdsongs and twittering calls grew in volume around them. From all directions and trees, birds slowly returned to their normal way of life.

But Bluesky and the others continued to stare silently at the dead birds.

"Let's fly along this side of the man-road and find a tree across from them. From there, we should be able to observe closer but still remain safe," Blackfeather said. He spread his wings and flew.

Bluesky and the others followed.

The broad-leafed trees gave way to a forest of pines. As they approached the dead birds, Blackfeather lighted on a branch of a tall pine directly across from them but higher than the branch they'd left.

Bluesky stared down at the two Robins. For a moment, his heart seized with panic. It seemed that one of them was Tootight lying there still and unmoving.

But no, in the next beat of his heart he realized this Robin had a different pattern of markings on his throat than his dear friend.

"I feel sadness inside my heart for those poor birds," Bluesky said. "It seems so unreal, so unnatural, to see birds lying so still."

"Do not be afraid of death," Blackfeather said. "Everything dies."

"Everything?" Bluesky asked in surprise.

"Everything of this world." Blackfeather peered a long time after he spoke. Several times he breathed deeply, sometimes twisting his head first in one direction and then the other, allowing each nostril to taste the air.

"There is a strange scent, though I can barely discern it," he said finally.

Bluesky couldn't smell a thing, try as he might, so he used his eyes and looked farther away over the dead birds.

His gaze traveled over the field and the small pine trees growing here and there in the tall brown grass. Again he noticed the houses, closer now that they were perched in this tall pine tree. His gaze traveled beyond them to some treetops in the distance.

"What is beyond those trees way over there?" Bluesky asked, nodding his head in their direction.

"That is where the crazy man lives with his monster dogs, the man with the death-sticks." Blackfeather craned his neck forward and ruffled his feathers with distaste.

Bluesky gazed at those distant trees and shuddered.

"Have you noticed the wind here? I hadn't realized it before because we were among the trees all this morning." Blackfeather looked around slowly.

Bluesky lifted his head higher to allow the wind to caress his feathers. He sensed the wind, felt its coolness wash over him.

And, he realized, it came from the direction of the rising of the sun.

"Yes, it comes out of the east today. That is not common," Blackfeather said with surprise in his voice.

"It normally comes from the north and west," Coolbreeze added.

"Yes," Blackfeather agreed with a low and mysterious tone. "Yes, an uncommon east wind -- and death rides on it."

"It was an east wind several days ago," another Crow called from above.

"Yes ... Yeeessss," Blackfeather said. "And birds flew in fear that day, although I did not personally hear the cry 'death on the wind' called by the Chickadees like today. I think they've learned what the danger was since then ..."

"I'm -- I'm going home," Bluesky said.

"Yes, we should all go home," Blackfeather said, "but first, I think I'll visit our friend Nightwind."

Bluesky watched Blackfeather fly off alone while the other two Crows traveled in another direction. He and Coolbreeze made their way back to the familiar trees and houses of their home.

The rest of the day, Bluesky ate and flew with somberness. He kept seeing the lifeless bodies of the three birds in his mind no matter where he went.

After the sun had set into the west, he found Ol' Gray Mama and her small flock of Doves.

He sat a little closer to Ol' Gray Mama that evening as the stars glittered in the night sky above. The warmth of her feathers comforted him. He snuggled closer.

Just as sleep started to cloak his mind, he jumped awake at an eerie and haunting cry piercing the darkness.

"What was that?" Bluesky asked fearfully.

"Hush, baby," Ol' Gray Mama said in a comforting tone.

While they both listened to the silence of the night, the same haunting cry was answered from another direction. The eerie call rose and fell. In another moment, another bird answered.

From every direction in the darkness, the same

haunting calls echoed.

Bluesky shivered.

"It's the Owls -- they're calling to us," Ol' Gray Mama said.

"Calling us? But most birds are sleeping," Bluesky said.

"They know all birds are quiet right now, just before sleep. That's why they're calling. They know every bird will hear their call."

"It sounds so scary."

"That is how they call out to each other in the night. But the Screech Owls have another cry, a terrible wail that will make your feathers stand up all over your body." Ol' Gray Mama chuckled in the darkness beside him.

"What are the Owls saying to us?"

Ol' Gray Mama paused a moment. Bluesky heard her breathing rapidly, almost like she was preparing herself for flight. But she remained motionless, listening intently to the haunting calls echoing in the darkness.

"They're calling all birds to come together at the ancient oak near the stream."

"Why?" Bluesky asked.

"It must be something important. They're calling for the heads of each family of birds to come for a council."

"Who will go for the Doves?"

"I will go. I am one of the eldest and matriarch of this flock."

Bluesky smiled.

"As a matriarch, I get to choose who will accompany me as my second. I would like you to go

294

with me."

"I will." Bluesky felt a flurry of excitement.

"Good. I knew I could depend on you," Ol' Gray Mama coo'ed comfortingly.

"What is this meeting called?" Bluesky asked.

"The Council of Birds."

"Do you think this meeting is about the *death on the wind*?"

"Yes, I do."

Chapter Twenty-Two

He awoke famished the next morning.

"Meet me back here after the sun reaches its highest point in the sky," Ol' Gray Mama said. "We'll wait here until the sun sets low in the western sky. After that, we'll join the other birds and fly to the Council."

"I'll meet you then!" Bluesky took wing and soared into the cool freshness of the morning air.

While he flew, he thought about the events of yesterday.

He shivered, remembering the Chickadees' warning cries and how everyone took flight to escape. And then he saw the dead birds lying on the ground again.

Bluesky shook his head, trying to erase that terrible sight.

He turned his thoughts in another direction ... to Tootight.

It had really surprised him to learn Tootight had a mate. He knew the Robin was about the same age as he was, and he had just assumed he was ... well, that Tootight was still a bachelor like him. He couldn't recall Tootight ever mentioning a mate. But then again, they had mostly laughed and joked and never really talked about anything serious.

Why was he so amazed to find out Tootight had a mate? Did he think the Robin too young? Or ...

Bluesky tried to picture Tootight with a mate.

It was true; Tootight was a hefty bird, but he was a cheerful and handsome bird too. And he was a fun bird, always laughing. Perhaps a female would be drawn to those qualities? After all, it was the natural thing for a boy bird and girl bird to meet ... get to know one another ... and ...

Bluesky suddenly felt a strong stirring inside his breast. His heart pounded, and he thought about meeting a pretty female ...

But even as he felt this wonderful sensation -- this deep and yearning desire to seek a mate -- a pervasive sadness choked it out instantly.

After all, what Mockingbird would ever want to be the mate of a one-legged bird?

The laughter of Robins interrupted his sad thoughts. The happy sounds rose from the front yard while he soared above more rooftops and trees. A Towhee called out with a bright 'towww-eeeee', and another answered cheerily in the distance. It was probably his mate ...

Bluesky sighed and continued on alone.

As he flew over a large man-road, he heard a familiar squeaking behind him.

"Where are you going, Bluesky?" Coolbreeze zipped up beside him, laughing as he squeaked.

"I'm going to find some juicy bugs. After that, I'm going to the 'Council of Birds' with Ol' Gray Mama at the ancient oak tree."

"I think I'll go too."

"I thought only the heads of the bird families and those who accompany them could attend?"

"Others can sit in the trees around the Council as an audience. Didn't you know that?"

"Oh! Well, no, I've never been to one."

"They're only called for special reasons."

Coolbreeze flew circles around Bluesky as he flew along at a steady pace.

"I think this one is about the *death on the wind* that's killing the birds," Bluesky said.

"It kills animals too. My friend, Flowersipper, told me some rabbits and other animals got sick and died yesterday."

"KC told me that Katie, a little girl, got sick the other day when it happened then."

"Yes, this *death on the wind* is bad. It can kill anyone if they breathe it."

"What will the Council do tonight?" Bluesky asked.

"I'm not sure, but I'm sure the smartest and wisest birds gathered there will think of something," Coolbreeze squeaked confidently.

Bluesky found a yard that looked like it would have lots of juicy bugs. He was famished. He landed in the grass that was still wet with morning dew. After a few moments, he spotted a bug and quickly gobbled it down. In quick order, he ate another and another.

Coolbreeze hummed around in the air for a while, going from flower to flower at the edge of the house and drinking his fill of sweet nectar.

"Uh-oh, I need to go protect my water-flower! I've been away too long!" Coolbreeze shouted. He zoomed off in a flash of iridescent feathers.

Bluesky laughed at his little friend and continued eating breakfast.

After he satisfied himself, he flew up to the highest branch of a tall pine tree. He perched in the crook of the highest branch to rest a few moments and digest his breakfast. He surveyed the world around him, satisfied and content.

He noticed two Blue Jays flying slowly over the trees toward the east. Over toward the south, he watched several Carolina Wrens playing among branches.

A squeaking noise caused him to look toward the ground.

At first, he expected to see Coolbreeze or another Ruby-throated Hummingbird. Instead, he saw two young squirrels scurrying across the grass. Suddenly, they paused to sniff the air. Satisfied all was well, they searched slowly through the grass for food.

Bluesky wondered what kind of food squirrels ate.

Suddenly, a large shadow shot across the ground. Before Bluesky could take another breath or even blink his eye, a large bird landed on one of the small squirrels.

The bird was huge!

As he watched in shocked horror, the bird's head shot down several times while it sat on the ground with its massive wings spread wide.

The second squirrel stood frozen a moment, simply staring. In the next moment, it fled in terror toward some bushes and disappeared.

Bluesky finally took a breath.

In that instant, he recognized that the huge bird was a Hawk.

The raptor raised its head and leapt into the air, beating its mighty wings. Held tight within the grasp of its talons was the limp form of the squirrel.

Bluesky gasped.

The Hawk beat its huge wings methodically. With each mighty downstroke, it rose higher into the air while carrying the dead squirrel.

Bluesky watched in a mixture of horror and fascination as the Hawk flew toward the bare branches at the top of a dead tree. The Hawk landed right at the top. He stood tall and straight for several minutes, surveying the world like some fearless conqueror.

Bluesky turned away when the Hawk reached down to its prey with its curved beak. For several minutes, he was afraid to look.

He knew what was happening in the tree across from him. He knew the Hawk was feeding on the squirrel. And he knew once the meal was finished, he had to fly over and talk with this terrible, terrible bird.

Still, he refused to look over and see what was happening. It was enough to know what was happening -- *he didn't want to actually see it.*

Long minutes passed as the morning breeze ruffled his feathers. He heard other birds singing all around him as if life were continuing exactly like normal. And as the birds sang and flew around him, he realized life *was* continuing exactly as before.

Bluesky turned and peeked.

The Red-shouldered Hawk stood tall and silent in the tree.

Bluesky looked and looked, but he no longer saw any sign of the squirrel. He strained his eyes and searched the black talons that gripped the branch, searched some of the lower branches below the Hawk, but there was nothing ...

He decided the Hawk must have eaten the animal and perhaps discarded what was left ...

At least, that was what he hoped.

The Hawk stood straight and tall and silent. He turned his head and peered in one direction for a long time. Then, he turned his head and stared long and hard in another direction.

Bluesky's heart pounded inside his breast. He tried to move, but he couldn't.

He was afraid.

He remained frozen, staring in awe at the mighty raptor. In contrast, the Hawk seemed afraid of absolutely nothing, standing boldly in the topmost branches of the tree -- visible to everyone and everything.

As the minutes passed, the pounding of Bluesky's heart slowed. In his mind, he heard the words of Nightwind and Blackfeather again, urging him to seek out this great raptor of the sky.

He realized there would be no better time than now.

Bluesky flew.

When he neared the great Hawk, he saw it turn and stare at him with unblinking eyes. He flew around the tree and carefully watched to see if the Hawk would come after him.

The mighty Hawk ignored him completely.

Bluesky flew lower and circled around the tree a second time, just to make sure. Still the Hawk stood silent.

Although his heart pounded again inside his chest and a terrible fear filled his entire being,

Bluesky landed on a branch just across from the Hawk.

Bluesky was astonished at the Hawk's size. The raptor towered over him, at least three times larger than himself if not more.

What amazed him most were the Hawk's eyes ...

They were huge and almost pure black. It seemed to Bluesky that its eyes were much too large for this bird -- for any bird. They seemed so intense, so powerful.

And when the Hawk turned his head and stared at him with those big, black eyes, Bluesky felt like the Hawk could see right through him.

The Hawk's baleful gaze froze Bluesky.

Without realizing it, Bluesky held his breath, waiting for the Hawk to make the next move.

"Why have you approached me, young Mockingbird?" The Hawk spoke in a clear and deliberate manner, his deep baritone voice confident and sure.

"My name is Bluesky. I ... I am on a journey ..." Bluesky's voice was just the opposite of the great Hawk's -- unsure and unsteady and edged with fear.

"You have chosen the best time to approach me. I perceive that either an Owl or a Crow has advised you.

"A Crow named B-b-blackfeather."

"I have met this Blackfeather. I know him." The Hawk lowered his head, and his black eyes stared right through Bluesky. "You may speak."

Bluesky introduced himself and explained his journey, how Nightwind had sent him to seek out the beauty and goodness of each kind of bird. He told the Hawk of the birds he'd met -- and the beauty and goodness he'd discovered in each. As he continued, he felt his fear slowly slip away.

Finally, he paused.

"My name is Thundercloud. I am a Red-shouldered Hawk. My mate, Morningsun, and I have lived here for many seasons. This is our territory." The Hawk's unblinking eyes peered slowly around the horizon a moment.

"As far as you can see, this is Morningsun's and mine."

Bluesky gazed at the mighty Hawk with respect and awe.

Thundercloud stood on the branch with his great wings folded, Bluesky noticed the red-barred pattern of feathers across his chest. He guessed the same pattern of red feathers must stretch to his shoulders under his folded wings.

His wings were covered with black feathers intermixed with small patterns of white feathers. The Hawk's back and outer shoulders were covered with the same pattern of black and white feathers.

Thundercloud was a magnificent raptor. Everything about him -- his immense size, his razor-sharp talons, his hooked beak, and his large, baleful eyes -- cast an aura of strength and power.

"You are a magnificent b-bird," Bluesky stuttered. "Please tell me, what is good about your kind?"

Thundercloud chuckled to himself. He lowered his head and smiled. "We are fiercely loyal -- Hawks mate for life. Most of all, we protect what is ours -- even to the death."

"What makes you so courageous?" Bluesky asked after a long pause. "Is it your great size? Or your strength? Or your talons?"

"It is none of those," Thundercloud replied simply.

"Then, what is it?"

"Love."

"Love?" Bluesky repeated in disbelief. "How can love make you courageous?"

"Only love can strengthen one's heart and enable a bird to fly into the face of death." Thundercloud preened the feathers on his left wing with his hooked beak a moment. "Love fosters loyalty. And both together are more powerful than the strongest force in nature. In the power of love, anything is possible. And only love enables one to give up his life for his friends -- that is the strongest love."

"Wow," Bluesky whispered with profound appreciation.

"We see far. We see all -- nothing escapes our notice. This enables us to have great foresight. We are quick to adapt. The great forests of the past are long gone. My generation hunts among the houses of men and the small stands of trees around them now. What few fields and small forests are left I hunt among as well."

Bluesky remained silent.

"My cousin, Silenthunter, hunts at the great place where men fly inside metal machines of thunder and smoke. And yet, he is unafraid and feeds on the birds and other animals that live in the shadow of the great man-machines. I myself have seen him sitting on the man-trees of steel silently scanning for his prey."

"I'm not sure if the greatest good about you is your great strength or your far-seeing eyes. Or is it your courage ... or your loyalty ... or your strong love?"

"It is all those things. Every creature is the sum of all he knows and all he has experienced. It is a wise bird who seeks out the best in others and then makes such noble qualities a part of himself." Thundercloud raised himself erect and stared toward the distant horizon.

"You speak like Nightwind and Blackfeather," Bluesky said with a hush.

"I have conversed many times with the wise Owls, and I have enjoyed the riddles and thought-puzzles of Crows." Thundercloud turned his piercing eyes directly upon Bluesky.

Bluesky shuddered under the Hawk's baleful glare.

"I know Nightwind the Wise, and I know Blackfeather, the great Trickster." Thundercloud paused a moment in thought. "It is interesting that we share the same circle of friends, young Mockingbird."

"I-I am glad I've finally met you, Thundercloud." Bluesky's beak hung open a moment in shock at his own words. "I wish that I was strong like you. And most of all, I wish I could have loyal love like you."

"I have heard of you, Bluesky. It made me angry when I heard that your kind had shunned you." Thundercloud nodded approvingly at him. "But you have lived on in spite of them, and you grow with each day. A one-legged bird must by necessity be stronger, more courageous, and wiser than a normal bird just to survive."

"I don't know." Bluesky lowered his head and sighed. He stared down at the stump of his leg.

"You have shown great courage simply by coming here to talk with me, young Mockingbird. Few birds would ever attempt such a thing. I commend you."

"I am just a one-legged Mockingbird. I could never --"

"You have more heart than any bird that I've ever met." Thundercloud smiled, and his dark eyes twinkled.

Suddenly, Thundercloud spread his massive wings and held them out to each side. He stood tall and silent, his eyes unblinking while the gentle breeze ruffled a few feathers here and there over his muscular body. In the distance, another Hawk cried out.

Bluesky leaned backward in awe of Thundercloud's massive wingspan.

"Morningsun calls to me. I must go."

"Can I ... can we ... I mean, I really want to talk with you again," Bluesky said hurriedly.

Thundercloud stood as motionless as a statue with his huge wings spread wide.

Bluesky involuntarily leaned further away; the sheer presence of Thundercloud seemed to emanate power and fear until it almost overwhelmed him.

"Yes, I would like that too. I want to learn more about you, young Mockingbird. I want to hear more about your journey. Heed this warning -- when you seek me, only come when I show myself plainly as you found me now. It means I am fed and content, and only then can you safely approach."

"Thank you." Bluesky watched Thundercloud leap into the wind and glide effortlessly a long distance, flapping his great wings from time to time to maintain his altitude.

"What a magnificent bird!" Bluesky said out loud.

He spent the rest of the morning hunting bugs and singing. After the sun reached its zenith, he flew back to the familiar house and trees where Ol' Gray Mama waited patiently.

They spent the remainder of the afternoon together. The old Dove walked around hunting seed, her head bobbing in rhythm with her every step. Bluesky sang from a nearby tree while his excitement grew and grew.

He sang a new song: a song about the Hawk and its great strength, its powerful eyes, and its powerful love.

Finally, the time arrived to leave for the 'Council of Birds.'

Bluesky and Ol' Gray Mama flew along at a leisurely pace. As they flew, Bluesky noticed a great crowd of other birds flying in the same direction. Birds of every kind and every feather flew under the late afternoon sky, all heading for the same destination.

They crossed the wide man-road, but much farther north from where Bluesky, Coolbreeze, and the Crows had spotted the dead birds. This was a place with no houses, only fields of tall, waving grass and wildflowers bordered by a large stand of trees.

Bluesky could smell water and knew a sizable stream flowed among those same trees. As he and hundreds of other birds flew among the shadows of the forest, the sound of a greater multitude of birds echoed from within.

He followed Ol' Gray Mama as she flew over and around limbs and tree trunks. The constant babble of birds grew louder with each beat of his wings. Soon, the multitude of voices became so loud it seemed to Bluesky that every bird in the world must have come to this place.

His heart beat faster while his excitement mounted and the sounds overwhelmed his senses.

Suddenly, they entered a small clearing.

Bluesky gasped.

The ground was alive with thousands of birds moving and hopping side by side. As he flew on toward a great oak, he noticed that the branches of every tree were filled with birds too.

The cacophony grew deafening.

Almost out of instinct, Bluesky called out to join his voice with theirs.

He was surprised that Ol' Gray Mama didn't find a spot to land in a tree near the ancient oak. Instead, she flew up to the gnarled trunk and thick lower branches of the oak itself. Although many birds perched on this centerpiece of the great Council of Birds, the birds on this tree did not line it as thickly as they did the trees that encircled it.

Ol' Gray Mama landed on the lowest branch alongside many other Mourning Doves. Bluesky landed and smiled shyly when another Dove glanced at him in surprise.

"He's with me," Ol' Gray Mama said quickly to all the Doves around them. "He's part of my flock."

Bluesky smiled proudly at their astonished faces.

He looked over at another branch that curved away from the thick trunk almost level with this branch. That branch was as thick as the one on which he sat, but it was filled solely with Owls, whereas this branch was filled with Doves, Chickadees, and several other different families of birds.

Glancing up at the higher branches, he noticed a branch filled with Mockingbirds, Brown Thrashers, Catbirds, American Robins, and many other kinds of birds. In fact, every branch up to the highest seethed with groupings of families of birds.

It was only the one branch filled with Owls that seemed to contain a single species of bird.

On all the other branches, various families of birds crowded close together in groups; no other branch contained just a single family of bird like the one with the Owls.

"The heads of each flock and their seconds sit in this oak," Ol' Gray Mama said with a smile. She looked around. "The field and the other trees that surround it are filled with birds who serve as audience to this Council."

As Bluesky looked around, his eyes were drawn back to the branch filled with Owls. Sure enough, he recognized the familiar face of Nightwind.

Nightwind nodded at him with a twinkle in his

eyes.

An especially large Barn Owl sitting near Nightwind lifted his wings high.

The intense wall of sound grew silent, and every bird turned his head to the branch filled with Owls.

"I call this Council to order," the Barn Owl cried with a commanding call.

Chapter Twenty-Three

"A great danger has come on the wind."

The largest and most distinguished-looking Barn Owl paused a moment to allow his words to sink in. Silence filled the air while he looked slowly around the gathering of birds. The silence grew more intense as every bird fixed their gaze on the Speaker.

"Many birds have reported death and sickness recently. Even animals and people are affected. This unseen danger threatens us all!"

"This poison is from man!" a single bird shouted from the crowd.

"Yes," another shouted. "It is man that kills us!"

"Man poisons the air we breathe and the water we drink. He fouls the very world we all live in!" a third shouted.

"Man is stupid!" a large group of birds shouted.

Great shouting erupted from everyone all around the ancient oak. Soon, the shouting coalesced into a single sentence, a single thought that gripped the minds of every bird in attendance. They repeated this single phrase over and over again.

"Man fouls his own nest! Man fouls his own nest! Man fouls his own nest!"

The leaders of the Owls remained silent, gazing stoically at the mass of angry birds. The chant quickly rose to a crescendo.

After it reached its angry climax, the large Barn Owl raised his wings once again for silence.

The chant faded instantly; every bird obeyed the signal.

"It is true -- this poison is from man. But it endangers our lives and the lives of our future hatchlings. The wind has brought this poison many times in the last two years, and it grows stronger each time. We cannot wait for man any longer. Birds must act, or the next wind might kill us all ..."

"What can birds do?" a robin shouted back from the ground.

"That's right -- what can we do?"

"We can find its source. Once we locate it, perhaps we can determine the next step," the Barn Owl said calmly.

"Man must fix this problem!" the same robin shouted again.

"Perhaps we can get some animals to assist us. After all, it is killing them too. Once we locate the source, we can analyze the situation and determine our options." The Barn Owl raised his white face and looked around at the gathering.

"Man must fix this problem they created!" a Wren twittered angrily.

"Then we must help man to fix it. Somehow, we must try," the wise Owl replied.

Bluesky listened in respectful silence. As he pondered the Barn Owl's words along with the cries of those gathered in audience, he thought of KC. He remembered how KC had told him her dad's daughter had gotten sick with the poison the last time they'd experienced *death on the wind*.

He remembered how KC had said that '*Dad would know what to do*' -- he would know how to protect them. And he was a man!

Bluesky wondered how KC communicated with her dad and the other humans in the house. KC was his friend, and if somehow he and the cat could get the man to help them ...

"Who shall go for us? I propose we pick a special flock to seek out the source of this poison, birds of many feathers who shall combine their unique skills and go forth to save us. But first, there must be a leader, a bird of great insight and courage who will lead this flock on this most dangerous mission." The Barn Owl narrowed his eyes and gazed at the crowds with a stern expression.

"Who shall lead this special mixed-flock of birds and find the source of this poison?" The Barn Owl and every Owl on the limb looked slowly around at the great gathering. But as their eyes passed over the thousands of birds gathered, not a single bird raised a wing to volunteer.

The thick silence of the thousands gathered filled the air with a heaviness, a palpable tension, as if a terrible storm were about to burst forth. The eternal seconds dragged on, and the very air seemed to vibrate with uneasiness and indecision. In the minds of all present, it seemed the problem had grown insurmountable -- impossible. The fear of everyone present seemed to come alive with a sudden blast of wind. While the trees swayed and the leaves danced, many birds cried out as if the terrible and unseen poison were attacking them that very moment.

The same thought occurred to everyone at once -- was death on this wind too?

Now their fear turned to an urgent need to flee!

The sound of hundreds of birds fluttering their wings as they prepared to flee added to climax of fear.

"I will go!"

Everyone froze. The bold words of the volunteer had somehow evaporated the climate of fear in a single instant.

Surprised murmurs filled the air, and everyone looked around for the brave bird who had spoken.

"Who said that?" the Barn Owl cried out as the strong breeze continued to ruffle the feathers across his head.

Nightwind turned and looked directly at Bluesky perched with the Mourning Doves on the other side of the ancient oak. The other Owls followed his gaze.

"Here I am! Send me! I'll go for all the birds!" Bluesky cried out courageously.

"Fly over here, my good Mockingbird," the Barn Owl said in a calm and deep voice.

Bluesky flew over and sat next to the large Owl.

"What is your name?"

"Bluesky."

"My name is Moonlight," the Barn Owl replied. "You are a brave bird to answer our dire call for help."

"I-I will do what I can," Bluesky said with a bow.

Moonlight turned to the crowd. He raised his wings high in the air and now shouted to all, "Bluesky the Mockingbird will lead this expedition to find the source of the poison. Give him a cheer for courage, my fellow birds!"

Instead, a new silence filled the air.

This silence was one of surprise and shock.

"He's that one-legged bird!" an unseen bird shouted in disappointment.

"Yeah, what can he do? He can't even walk like a normal bird," another shouted.

More began shouting insults when they realized it was Bluesky sitting alongside Moonlight.

Even Moonlight looked down in surprise to see that indeed Bluesky had only one leg. The leader of the Owls sighed and looked at the other Owls with a questioning expression.

Suddenly, Ol' Gray Mama soared through the air and landed next to Moonlight. She gazed at the large Owl with a fierce and determined expression.

But Moonlight remained mute.

All the other birds grew silent at the seeming confrontation among the leaders.

Ol' Gray Mama turned to the crowd. "Let me tell you something about this one-legged Mockingbird. This young Mockingbird has more heart and more courage than any bird here. I didn't see any of you raise a wing to volunteer, now did you?"

Ol' Gray Mama looked sternly around at the thousands of birds.

A shocked silence was the only reply.

"That's right -- he's already done more than any of you. And now you bunch of hypocrites ask, 'what can a one-legged bird do?' He's already shown he's willing to find this poison -- for us! For you! And all of you just sat there on your feathered rumps.

When would you volunteer? Tomorrow? When the poison kills your mate? Or your first offspring?"

Throughout the crowd, every bird remained firmly silent, though now the air was filled with shame and embarrassment.

"Now, I just want to know one more thing. And what I'm going to ask will give you the opportunity to show that you can measure up to the courage of this one-legged Mockingbird." She paused, once again looking slowly around at crowd of stunned birds.

"Are you going to let this bird fly alone? Are you going to let him face this terrible danger all alone?" She raised both her wings and shouted her next words.

"Is this one-legged Mockingbird the only brave bird perched here tonight?"

Another Mockingbird flew down from the high branch where all Mockingbirds were gathered. The young Mockingbird cocked his tail boldly and stared at Bluesky.

Bluesky recognized Funwind instantly.

"It was this same poison that caused his deformity!" Funwind shouted. "We now know this poison has caused many eggs to never hatch. And it has caused many other deformities in others. Perhaps it is fitting that Bluesky find this poison!" Funwind hopped closer and looked Bluesky straight in the eyes as if in challenge.

But Bluesky did not return Funwind's angry glare. Bluesky simply gazed back with compassion.

"I will go for you too, Funwind," Bluesky whispered softly.

Funwind's beak dropped open in shock.

Moonlight opened his huge eyes wide and nodded in approval. He raised his wings again to speak. "I perceive that this is no ordinary bird standing here on one leg."

"I agree," Nightwind added quickly. He hopped over next to Bluesky and Ol' Gray Mama. "I've come to know this bird, and I believe he is the right bird to lead this expedition. He will find the source of the poison. And what's more, he'll find a solution too!"

"You're kidding," Funwind sneered. "I've known this bird all my life too. And I know that he's a loser. Why, where's his family? They all left him, didn't they? Where does he live now? The only birds who'll tolerate him are a bunch of old, crotchety Doves!"

Bluesky's heart shuddered with pain and sadness. In an instant, his gladness turned to dust.

What made it worse was that he knew Funwind was right.

His father and siblings had left him. His mother had died. If it hadn't been for Ol' Gray Mama and the other nice old Doves ...

Bluesky fluttered his wings nervously, almost losing his balance.

Moonlight and the other Owls peered questioningly, as if unsure now.

Suddenly, Ol' Gray Mama leaped high in the air with a flash of wings and a whistling of her tail feathers. She flew right over Funwind before he had a chance to move.

A hollow thud echoed clearly as she pecked his

head with a sharp thrust of her pointed beak.

"Owwwww!" Funwind shouted, covering his head with his wings. "That hurt, you old bird! Owwwww!"

"You say another mean word about my Bluesky, and I'll peck you so hard you won't be able to fly straight the rest of your life!"

She landed right next to Bluesky and glared at Funwind, daring him to open his beak again.

A ripple of laughter sped through the crowd. Funwind took wing and returned to sit with the other Mockingbirds.

Bluesky smiled sheepishly at Ol' Gray Mama.

"You never mind that mean old Mockingbird. I love you. I believe you can save us. And many others do too!"

Bluesky nodded, but inside his heart, it still felt heavy with sadness.

"Ol' Gray Mama is right," Moonlight shouted to the crowd. "It will take more than this one brave bird to find the solution! Who will join Bluesky?"

Once again, a thick silence hung in the evening air. But this time, the silence contained fear mixed with shame.

"I will fly with him!" a deep voice shouted powerfully from the very top of the ancient oak.

"Show yourself, brave bird!" Moonlight called back.

A gasp swept the crowd as a Hawk glided down with his great wings spread apart. He perched beside the one-legged Mockingbird, and his huge chest swelled, revealing the red-barred pattern of rust and white feathers. The Hawk turned his head

318

and leaned toward Bluesky, his impressive hooked beak bare inches from the Mockingbird.

Bluesky reached up and patted the Hawk's shoulder with his wingtip. "Thank you, Thundercloud. I couldn't have wished for a braver bird to join me."

Thundercloud looked up at all the birds now staring in total disbelief at the pair.

"A Hawk and a Mockingbird flying together?" someone shouted in awe from the crowd.

"I will go too!"

A humming filled the air, and Coolbreeze zoomed from a far tree at the edge of the field toward the pair. Every bird in the crowd gasped as his urgent squeaks filled the air while he flew in circles above Bluesky and Thundercloud. With a final victory squeak, Coolbreeze perched beside them.

"Well, the largest and the smallest of all the birds have joined our brave Mockingbird. Now, who else will make up this mixed-feather flock?" Moonlight asked.

From several directions the sound of birds in flight echoed in the air. The bright scarlet of a Cardinal and the black and rufous and white feathers of a Towhee came from one direction; Daymoon and Bushhopper joined the three birds on the branch of the oak.

Tootight joined next, his laughing twitters filling the air and bringing a smile to many.

A small Sparrow landed right next to Bluesky and smiled.

"But you're a girl," Bluesky said to Treeflower.

"And you have eggs. Who'll look after your eggs if you go with us?"

"My mate has agreed to take over all those duties," Treeflower said with confidence. "I think at least one bird in this flock needs to be a female, just to ensure there is some common sense!"

"I am glad you joined us, brave Sparrow," Thundercloud said in a deep voice. "Courage is courage -- it makes no difference if you are male or female."

"It seems to make no difference if we're a Hawk or a Sparrow either!" She laughed joyfully.

Thundercloud's hearty laughter shook the air.

Bluesky and all the others laughed along with them, but as the others continued laughing, he searched the sky for a Bluebird he hoped would also join them.

Try as he might, though, he saw no sign of Dancingleaves.

"We need a Chickadee to join this group," Moonlight said. "Every bird knows that Chickadees are the first to recognize danger. It was the Chickadees who first gave voice to the danger we now face."

"I will go!"

A Carolina Chickadee flew across the field in undulating flight, flapping her wings a few times and falling forward while she held them folded. She landed next to Treeflower. The black cap, black bib, and white stripe of feathers across her cheeks marked her kind. She hopped up and down excitedly, walking before Bluesky and then to Thundercloud, Daymoon, Bushhopper, Coolbreeze,

Tootight, and back to Treeflower.

"My name is Highclouds. I will fly with you and warn you of danger, and I know the scent of the poison. I will help make you successful!" she cried proudly.

"My, what a cheeky bird you are," Tootight said with a laugh.

"I do have bold cheeks, so I should be cheeky!" She laughed back.

Tootight laughed even louder. "I tell a joke, and you one-up me. I like this bird!"

The others laughed in agreement.

"We need to assign an Owl to this expedition to act as counselor." Moonlight's glance fell upon Nightwind. "I submit Nightwind, since he gave his personal recommendation for Bluesky!"

The other Owls hooted agreement.

Nightwind hopped closer to Bluesky and the others.

"My first bit of counsel is this -- this is a difficult assignment, and it will require keen insight and careful discernment as well quick thinking." Nightwind smiled. "But more than that, it will require the highest degree of trickery! We need a Crow on this team, and not just any Crow. We need the best!"

"CAW! CAW! CAW!"

A large group of Crows perched high with the Falcons and Hawks continued their insistent cries as they called out for one Crow in particular.

Moments later, Blackfeather swooped down.

"This team is now complete!" Blackfeather shouted with a glint in his eyes.

Nightwind and the others cheered loudly, as did every bird gathered.

While the cheering slowly subsided, a single voice pierced the air.

"But what will they do when they find the poison?" Funwind shouted down from above. "We agreed that only men can solve this problem in the end."

"I have a friend who is a cat!" Bluesky shouted back at Funwind. "KC talks to a man she calls Dad! I will get KC to help us too!"

"Say what?" Funwind's eyes opened wide.

A murmur swept the crowd like wildfire -- whispers of total surprise.

"A cat ... helping a bird?"

"What is the world coming to? Poison on the wind, and now birds and cats are friends?" an old bird cried out.

A new tidal wave of murmuring filled the air.

"Yes, yes!" Nightwind said. "Perhaps your friend KC can help us. I had not thought of that!"

"I will talk to KC before we fly our first mission to seek out the source of the poison. I will ask her to help us. And KC will ask the man, her dad, to help us too. I'm sure of it!"

A great shout went up.

After the cheering and shouts finally subsided, Moonlight raised his wings.

"When shall you leave, my brave birds?"

"We will start tomorrow, when the sun is highest in the sky!" Bluesky shouted bravely.

The cheering and chirping now rose to a new crescendo, and at that moment Moonlight leaned

322

over and whispered in Nightwind's feathered ear, "This is the most bizarre mixed-flock of birds I've ever heard of, Nightwind."

"It is true. Who would have ever dreamed it possible?"

"And yet, the skills and talents of each of these different species may be needed to face this terrible poison at its evil source," Moonlight acknowledged.

"I am sure of it." Nightwind nodded somberly.

"But as surprising as it is that a Hawk and a Sparrow, a Hummingbird and a Crow -- as unthinkable as all these wildly different birds joined together, it surprises me most that a cat and a man may also join!"

"Not really, if you knew Bluesky." Nightwind chuckled.

"Really?"

"Yes. But all the other birds are most surprised over the one thing that should not matter at all," Nightwind said.

"What is that?" Moonlight asked.

"The fact that ... *a one-legged Mockingbird will lead them all*."

***

Keep reading for a sneak preview of the conclusion of the Song of Life trilogy: *The Singer*

Can Bluesky and his mixed-flock team
find the source of death on the wind?
Enjoy this sneak preview of
The Singer (unedited)

Chapter One

Bluesky sang louder as the first golden rays of the sun streamed through the trees.

He felt so happy inside! In fact, he was filled with such pure, unbridled gladness that it even made him feel a little giddy, like he had eaten one too many overripe berries. And yet, he wasn't quite sure why he felt so wonderful. All he knew was that his heart was filled with joy and he just had to sing out for the entire world to hear.

The sky grew lighter while the golden orb of the sun rose steadily higher. The sky gradually, almost imperceptivity, transformed to a deeper and deeper shade of blue. In the distance, a line of large, mountain-like clouds became visible in the west. The eastern flanks of these sky mountains glowed pure white from the light of the morning sun. But underneath, they were swollen and purple-black with the promise of heavy rain.

The sky finished its transformation into its normal blue, but the distant storm clouds grew more ominous. The air quickly grew laden with humidity and soon became sticky with a pervasive wetness that blanketed every creature it touched. And more, the air itself grew heavy, pressing against each living thing like an invisible vise from the pressure of an impending storm growing ever closer.

Every creature knew these signs; this would be a day of thunder and lightning, a day of storm and high winds fueled by the blazing heat of the summer sun.

A brisk morning breeze caressed the leaves and sent them wildly dancing as the world fully awakened.

After the sun rose above the tree tops, Bluesky flew up and perched on the highest branch in the tallest tree and then sang even louder.

After an especially long and melodic trill, he looked down and noticed KC watching from the ground far below.

He flew down to talk with his friend.

"Guess what? I'm part of a team that is going on an expedition! And a lot of my bird friends have joined me!"

"That sounds like fun," KC purred.

Bluesky's expression turned serious. "Well, actually it won't be that much fun."

"Oh, why not?"

"Our mission is to locate the source of the poison that is killing so many birds and animals."

KC stopped purring. Her green eyes narrowed, and she leaned closer to Bluesky.

"It makes humans sick too. It might even kill them. You're right -- this could be very dangerous." KC paused a moment, obviously contemplating these things over in her mind. "Yes, very dangerous indeed! Why were you picked?"

"Well, I... uh... I volunteered."

"That was very brave thing to do," KC said with

awe. "I am proud of you."

"Thank you. And, um, I have a favor to ask of you too ..."

"Oh really? Go right ahead."

"Um, didn't you say your dad would help you -- if you needed help? And protect you?"

KC purred a moment in contented thought before she spoke. "Of course he would -- he's my dad."

"And, didn't you say Katie got sick from the poison?"

"Yes, it made me very sad. It made everyone sad in our house. Buddy and I stayed near Mom and Dad all day to provide them comfort."

"Do you think you could get your dad to help us if we find the poison?"

KC froze in shock.

She raised her paw and carefully licked it for several, long seconds as she considered the matter.

The silence continued for a long time.

Bluesky began to wonder if she had heard him.

"I don't know. I mean, I'm not sure. What do you have in mind?" KC finally asked.

"Our mission is to find the source of the poison. That is the first step. We hope after we find it, a solution will present itself." Bluesky wagged his long tail nervously as he gazed hopefully at KC.

"That is a good plan. Hmmmm." KC continued licking her paw deep in thought.

Bluesky waited nervously, wagging his tail continuously with his growing excitement.

Finally, KC spoke. "If the poison is not too far away, I think I could lead my dad to it. He will follow me. And when I show him the poison, I'm sure he'll know what to do."

"That's great!" Bluesky shouted.

"But, what if it is far away?" KC asked.

"I'm not sure. We'll have to fly over that tree when we get to it." Bluesky shook his head slowly. "But, you will help us no matter what, right?"

"You tell the other birds this exact message, okay?" KC purred louder. "Tell them, 'KC the kitty cat will help the birds!'"

"That's wonderful!"

"Do you want me to go on the expedition with you today?" KC asked.

"No, we're going to fly far and fast and try to cover a lot of territory. But when we find it, I'll take you to see it. Then we can decide how to get your dad to follow you to it."

"Sounds pretty easy," KC purred.

"We can only hope."

Bluesky flew off feeling even better. KC had agreed to help, and it seemed she could get the man she called her dad to follow her to the poison. Bluesky felt deep inside that KC was right -- if her dad saw the poison, he would fix it and everyone would be safe.

Now, Bluesky flew off to find one bird in particular -- Dancingleaves.

He soon spotted a familiar flash of bright blue feathers against the green leaves. Bluesky was happy he had found his friend so easily.

But Dancingleaves sat on the branch looking lonely and sad.

"Hi, Dancingleaves." Bluesky settled on the

branch next to the Bluebird. "I kept looking for you at the Council of Birds. Were you there?"

"Yes." Dancingleaves averted his eyes.

"I was hoping you'd join us yesterday."

A pained expression filled Dancingleave's face. He stared at the ground far below for a long moment. Finally, he spoke. "I'm ... I'm too scared."

Bluesky put his wing around the shoulder of his friend. "I'm scared too. See, we're both scared."

"But you volunteered. And I thought you were very brave for doing so." Dancingleaves finally looked straight into Bluesky's eyes. He smiled a brief moment and quickly turned away.

"Believe me -- I was scared when I did it. But I kept thinking, I want to help. I want to do something." Bluesky shrugged. "I thought about my sister, Songjoy, and her eggs that will hatch soon. And Treeflower has eggs. So, although I felt scared, I also felt determined to help them and their babies. I don't want any more birds to die!"

"You were scared?" Dancingleaves asked hesitantly.

"Yes, but I focused on my desire to help. And somehow, I wasn't quite so scared any more."

"You're a brave bird, Bluesky." Dancingleaves smiled shyly.

"And today, we fly our first mission." Bluesky smiled hopefully at the Bluebird.

"But how will you find the poison?"

"We're going to search off toward the eastern fields and woods first. After that, well, we'll just have to wing it." Bluesky chuckled at his play on words.

328

Dancingleaves nodded absent-mindedly, oblivious to Bluesky's pun.

"I'd like you to join us. KC said she'd help too." Bluesky squeezed Dancingleaves' shoulder reassuringly. We need another good bird, like you."

"I'm too nervous around birds I don't know. I'm too shy. And ... I'd just get in the way."

"You flew with Tootight and Coolbreeze when we all went up inside the clouds! You weren't scared then," Bluesky said in a warm, encouraging tone.

"But there are lots of birds on your team. There's a huge Hawk. And a Crow too! I-I just couldn't do it. I would be so scared the whole time. I wouldn't even know what to do ..."

"I'm not going to pressure you, but if you decide you'd like to join us, you can." Bluesky patted Dancingleaves on his back. "I would value your help."

Dancingleaves stared in puzzlement at Bluesky a moment. Finally, he smiled. "I'll think about it."

"Good! I'll come back and tell you what we find ... if you want." Bluesky looked questioningly at him.

"Y-yes. Let me know what you find."

"I'll see you tomorrow then."

"And Bluesky ..." Dancingleaves' eyes grew wide as if something had suddenly frightened him.

"Yes." Bluesky replied.

"Please be careful.

Chapter Two

Bluesky flew off toward the tree at which they all agreed to meet. Deep inside, he felt bad for his friend, but in his heart he knew Dancingleaves could help. In fact, somehow he knew the team would not be complete without the shy Bluebird.

"Why don't you just fly away, you weird little bird!"

Bluesky's heart thumped in panic on hearing the all-too-familiar words.

He recognized a Mockingbird's voice shouting in a demeaning tone. The happiness and joy that had filled his heart evaporated. A haunting sadness enveloped him. Bluesky sighed as he looked to see who was taunting him now.

He didn't really want to face them, but he felt he must. After all, he was trying to help them too. Didn't they understand that? He was risking his life in trying to find the source of the poison. Didn't he deserve some measure of kindness from even the Mockingbirds now?

He gazed about a moment.

He finally noticed four Mockingbirds in a nearby tree and flew over. As he got closer, he realized they had no idea he was there, so they hadn't been shouting taunts at him. He also realized that all four were young females.

One of them was very small. Actually, she was tiny.

The other three were taunting her.

Bluesky landed above them and decided to

observe in silence a moment in order to discern this situation.

The petite female hung her head sadly as the other three continued to throw insults at her.

"You're not even big enough to be a sparrow!"

"She's too thin! She's all feathers and bone!"

"We don't want to play with you anymore -- none of the other Mockingbirds like you either!"

The diminutive Mockingbird remained silent, not even raising her head. A moment later, she began to cry.

Bluesky had heard enough. He flew down and landed right beside the little Mockingbird.

"You three leave her alone -- don't you see you've hurt her feelings!" Bluesky said firmly.

The three Mockingbirds gasped in surprise.

"Who are you?" the small Mockingbird asked as if in a daze. "I-I don't know you ..."

"He's that one-legged Mockingbird!" one of them suddenly shouted.

"Yeah, I guess it takes one weird bird to like another weird one! Ha!"

"Right! No self-respecting Mockingbird would be seen with him either. He's a loner. He's weird too," shouted the third.

"They make quite a pair, a midget and a one-legged Mockingbird."

Bluesky flew right up in their faces and flapped his wings at them in order to make them leave. All three leapt into the air in shocked surprise.

The three flew off as Bluesky gave chase.

He turned around after he was sure they wouldn't return. He wanted to make sure the little

Mockingbird was all right before he continued to the meeting.

"Are you okay?" Bluesky asked after he landed on the branch beside her. "I can take you to your parents if you like."

"I'm one season old already. I don't need you to take me to my parents like I'm a new hatchling!" she replied with a defensive tone.

Bluesky gulped. He hadn't meant to offend her.

Bluesky looked at her closely and quickly realized that although she was the size of a Mockingbird who had just left the nest, her eyes and her manner revealed she was his age at least. She was just very petite and small, which made her seem younger at a glance.

"I'm sorry -- I didn't mean to insult you. I only wanted to help. I'll just go then ..."

Bluesky turned to fly.

"No, wait!" she shouted earnestly.

Bluesky was so surprised he almost fell off the branch and had to flap his wings vigorously in order to regain his balance. He started laughing at himself as he settled down, knowing how close he came to falling flat on his beak.

As he continued laughing, he saw the young female laughing right along.

"I guess I looked pretty silly, eh? Right in the middle of launching into the air and suddenly stopping right in the middle -- flapping my wings just like a Hummingbird!" Bluesky laughed harder.

"Yes." She laughed "It was hilarious!"

Their laughter gradually faded.

She looked down at his leg.

Bluesky steeled his heart, expecting rejection.

She looked up at him and peered deep into his eyes a moment before she spoke. "You're the Mockingbird who volunteered to find the poison, aren't you!"

"Um, yes," Bluesky said tentatively.

"I think you're very brave. And, well ..." She looked away as if embarrassed, but she quickly looked back at him. "I want to thank you for helping me just now. I don't know what to do any more. Those birds are always making fun of me, and nothing I do seems to stop them. So I was just trying to ignore them, hoping they'd go away. But I started crying. And then, you arrived ..."

"Um, yes ..." Bluesky's thoughts suddenly became jumbled in confusion as he realized how pretty she was. And her eyes, they were so beautiful.

"Yes ... I did ... er, sort of ... um ..." Bluesky stopped speaking. He couldn't remember what they were talking about. All he could think about was how pretty this tiny bird was.

She giggled.

Bluesky smiled in dumbfounded silence as he continued to gaze into her eyes.

"You don't even know my name!" she exclaimed suddenly.

Bluesky hopped back in surprise. "Um, my name is Bluesky." He smiled at her with a kind of quirky, dreamy expression.

"Yes, I know. I remember your name from the Council of Birds," she said with a twinkle in her eyes. "My name is Windwhisper."

"Windwhisper," Bluesky repeated breathlessly. "Windwhisper! What a beautiful name. It's such a nice name ... yes, nice ... very ... nice!"

Windwhisper giggled again.

Bluesky stared at her with that same dreamy look in his eyes.

"Have you found the poison yet?" she asked as he continued to stare at her.

Bluesky shook himself. He suddenly remembered the search. He looked up and realized the sun was at its highest point in the sky for the day.

"Oh, I've got to fly. I'm going to be late." He leapt into the air and flew toward house where KC lived.

A moment later, he realized Windwhisper was flying beside him.

"Um ... I was wondering." She flapped her wings harder to keep up with Bluesky.

Bluesky slowed his speed to make it easier for her.

"Wondering what?" Bluesky asked. He was filled with amazement that she was flying beside him.

"I was hoping ... that we could be friends!"

Bluesky almost fell out of the sky.

He flapped out of rhythm -- almost as if this was his first flight out of the nest. He fell a dozen feet, flapped his wings so hard he lost his breath and fell forward again toward the ground.

It took him several seconds to regain his normal flying motion and regain his flight speed. Finally, after what seemed an eternity of struggling to remember how to fly, he again flew in a steady, normal motion.

He looked over at Windwhisper, dumbfounded.

A profound sadness spread on her face.

"Well, you probably know that I don't have many friends because I'm so small. Birds don't like me, which makes me sad. And if you don't want to be friends, well, I understand." Windwhisper turned to leave.

"Oh, no! I want to be friends. I'm just ... surprised ..."

They flew side by side a distance without speaking.

Finally, Windwhisper spoke. "Do you really want us to be friends?" she asked hesitantly.

"Yes, I do! Absolutely!" Bluesky shouted joyfully.

All the birds in the nearby trees turned in surprise at the loudness of his outburst.

"Ooops, I didn't mean to shout. Sorry."

"That's all right." Windwhisper laughed.

"It's just ... well ... I'm just not used to others asking to be my friend ... especially a girrr ... um ... a bird not a boy, I mean ..."

Windwhisper giggled -- a happy, trill-like chirp that made Bluesky's heart happy.

Bluesky felt his face grow warm with embarrassment, but the happiness inside his heart grew with each new stroke of his wings through the clear air. In fact, it wasn't just her pretty laughter that made him happy. He felt happy just flying alongside her!

"I saw you when you volunteered yesterday.

And I think you're the bravest Mockingbird in the entire world."

Bluesky lost his flight rhythm again.

This time he didn't quite fall right out of the sky like before.

But he came close.

"I'm ... I'm glad you feel that way. I just want to help."

They talked a long time. They didn't talk about anything in particular, just different things, whatever came into their mind as they flew.

Bluesky discovered that Windwhisper loved to watch the clouds too. And she loved to sing, though most of the time she sang by herself because no other birds would sing with her, with the exception of her siblings and parents.

"At least you have your family!" Bluesky said after she mentioned again how lonely she was with no real friends.

He then explained how his family had scattered, though he had recently found his sister again.

Sadly, he spoke of his mother's death.

As he saw her eyes fill with tears for him, he quickly told her of how he met Ol' Gray Mama and that she was now his second mother. Then he told her how he met Dancingleaves and Tootight and Nightwind and the other birds he now called friends.

"Wow! You have lots of friends. I'm surprised you want another friend like me," Windwhisper whistled.

"A bird can never have too many friends!" Bluesky laughed out loud as he repeated the oft-

spoken proverb.

They flew onward, each one sharing what was inside their heart with the other.

All too soon, Bluesky reached the meeting tree.

"I've got to go now. When the other birds arrive, we've got to go find the source of the poison." Bluesky's voice was full of regret at their imminent parting.

"Can we sing together tomorrow? And you can tell me what you find!"

"Yes, I'll meet you in the dogwood tree that grows over there." Bluesky pointed to the nearby tree.

Windwhisper flew into the air. But as she started to go over the top of the house, she looked back and whistled a happy little tune back to Bluesky.

Bluesky closed his eyes and almost fell off the branch.

He opened his eyes as he caught himself. He looked up, hoping Windwhisper hadn't seen.

She was out of sight now.

Bluesky whistled the tune Windwhisper had sung to him, a little melody filled with joy and happiness.

He repeated it a second time with a little embellishment of his own.

Suddenly, the most exquisite feeling filled his heart -- something he'd never felt before. As he breathed deeply, his heart quivered with the joy rushing through his entire being.

He was so happy!

Bluesky spread his wings and flew from branch to branch. All the while he sang the new tune --

Windwhisper's tune -- creating variations on the melody until he filled the air with his joyous trills and warbles.

In less than five minutes, he had flown to every branch in the entire tree. He started over again, singing non-stop. As soon as he landed on a branch, the feeling inside seemed to erupt like a volcano and he leapt into the air, flew to another branch, and sang Windwhisper's melody again.

He couldn't stop singing!

He couldn't stop flying!

He didn't want this joyous, wondrous feeling that filled his heart to ever go away! It was like he had dreamed the most beautiful dream and woke up and realized it wasn't a dream -- that it was real.

"What exactly are you doing?"

Daymoon's black face and scarlet form suddenly appeared next to him.

Bluesky stopped singing in mid-melody.

"You've got the silliest smile on your face, you know," Tootight said with a chuckle. "You look like the bird that ate the biggest bug ever!"

Bluesky laughed out loud.

"I think I know what happened," Bushhopper said with a wink at Daymoon and Tootight.

"You know what?" Coolbreeze squeaked happily as he zoomed up and hovered before them. The bright sunlight caught his red gorget and caused it to sparkle like thousands of tiny rubies.

"I know why Bluesky has that silly smirk on his face,' Bushhopper chirped. The Towhee's sleek black feathers glistened in the sun and contrasted with the white of his belly and the reddish feathers

338

on his sides.

Coolbreeze hovered closer to Bluesky and stared at him a moment.

"You're right. And look, he's got a goofy look in his eyes too."

"Oh yeah, I see it now," Daymoon said with mock concern.

Bluesky looked from one bird to the other in total shock.

"What is it?" Bluesky asked with a hush.

"It's quite serious, you know. It happens to every bird sooner or later," Daymoon said very solemnly.

"What? What?" Bluesky asked urgently.

"But the good news is -- it's not usually fatal," Bushhopper added with a sly smile.

"Fatal?" Bluesky gasped.

"But it will change your life forever!" Tootight chuckled. "Like it or not!"

Bluesky froze in anticipation of the dire calamity about to be revealed.

"What?" Bluesky asked.

"You met a girl," Bushhopper said simply.

"Yes, as obvious as the sky is blue," Coolbreeze squeaked.

"There'll be no living with him now!" Tootight laughed.

Coolbreeze, Bushhopper, and Daymoon laughed along with Tootight.

Bluesky's beak dropped open in shock. But after a few moments, their mirth became contagious and he laughed right along with them.

"What's all this laughter about?" Thundercloud's

deep, bass voice boomed. "We've got a job to do."

"It's time to focus, birds. This is not a laugh festival," Blackfeather added with a serious tone.

"Oh, boys will be boys," Highclouds twittered from a branch above all of them.

"Yes, unfortunately, we had to endure the entire spectacle," Treeflower added with a wink at Highclouds.

"It was quite educational." Highclouds laughed.

Treeflower joined her, and soon every bird was laughing again.

Everyone was laughing except for Thundercloud and Blackfeather, who simply looked at each other with exasperated expressions.

"Birds! Focus!" Thundercloud boomed again.

The songbirds instantly became silent.

Thundercloud nodded at Blackfeather.

Blackfeather hopped over to Bluesky and the other small birds. He opened his shiny, black beak and spoke in a deadly, earnest tone.

"We're all here, Bluesky. It's time to search out the source of the *Death-on-the-Wind* ..."

Did you miss the start of the Song of Life trilogy?
See how the one-legged mockingbird's story began
in
Bluesky and Sunshine

Chapter One

A brilliant shaft of light flashed through the trees and announced the long-awaited appearance of the sun.

The birds sang out in celebration.

The early birds had been singing for almost an hour with the first hint of the brightening horizon. As the stars faded one by one and the sky transformed from velvety blackness to pale blue, more birds awakened and joined their voices to the chorus.

But as the golden rays multiplied, the melodic phrases and twinkling trills took on a real urgency. Birds sang out from every direction and increased their volume ten-fold when the blinding orb of the sun revealed itself at last through the leafy canopy.

A new day began exactly as every other day -- and yet as unique as an individual snowflake.

The sun's golden light gleamed across a street named Willow Hollow and into the yard behind the house located at number 3477. A particularly bright beam pierced through the leafy canopy of a dogwood tree and lit up a single branch like a spotlight. Two Mockingbirds sat on the branch and waited expectantly as three eggs shuddered with life.

And in that very moment, the miracle of birth

occurred.

Small chunks of eggshell cracked and fell away from one egg as it rocked excitedly. A tiny voice called out with heartwarming urgency as the outside world became visible for the very first time.

Sunshine's heart quivered with excitement.

The female Mockingbird cocked her head to one side and peered intently. She flicked her long, graceful tail as her excitement reached a fever pitch. She then hopped from side to side and opened her beak in a smile.

Sunshine couldn't contain her emotions any longer. She stretched out her wings and held them out wide. With her face toward the sky, she sang her happiness for the entire world to hear.

Suddenly, the egg rocked side to side as more eggshell crumbled away. Seconds later, a tiny beak and face peeped out.

The first baby emerged from the shell.

The two lifelong mates stared with open beaks as the tiny form pushed the remaining section of eggshell back and wriggled itself free.

The fragile creature shuddered with the first brush of air across its wet body. Its head seemed far too large compared to its tiny body in that first minute of life outside the egg. Struggling to lift its head and discover its new surroundings, the baby moved with jerky, unwieldy motions as it used its muscles for the first time.

Both parents leaned closer with eager expectation.

Lifting its head up, the baby cried out its first, precious words.

"I'm cold, and I'm hungry!"

Sunshine turned to her mate and laughed out loud.

Treetop smiled as he flicked his long tail proudly.

"Feed me! Feed me! Feed me!" the baby Mockingbird peeped urgently.

"Oh, Treetop. It's a little male. And he looks just like you," Sunshine trilled happily.

Treetop sang out joyfully as he leapt into the air and flew far above the trees, his song filling the air.

The birds in the nearby trees stopped their own singing to listen with awe and respect, realizing that a proud new parent was singing about the birth of his babies. Treetop's vibrant voice echoed throughout trees.

As the golden sun rose steadily into the clear blue sky, the other two babies slowly worked their way free.

Three newborn babies now cried out to their parents with constant calls for attention.

Sunshine and Treetop got to work.

First, Treetop reached into the nest and picked up the largest empty eggshell with his beak. He leapt into the air with it and then flew far away from the nest before he dropped the eggshell into the middle of a large bush.

He quickly flew back to the nest to remove more egg debris.

While he and Sunshine flew back and forth and carefully cleaned the nest, they recalled the two oldest sayings of nest-wisdom that all families of bird held dear.

The first: '*A clean nest means a clean bird.*'

This oldest bit of wisdom applied first for the parents as they sat long hours warming the eggs before the young hatch. But its primary meaning applied to the parents after the young hatched -- keeping the young clean and quickly disposing of all waste, external and internal.

Of course, caring parents by and large kept the nest and the babies clean; it was simply a part of being a good parent. But keeping a nest clean was not just important for appearances; it was an essential part of protecting the babies from potential predators. Snakes, possums, raccoons, and other birds would relish a meal of tender babies if they could find the nest hidden among the leaves.

If parents allowed waste to fall to the ground directly underneath the nest, they might return to the chilling sight of an empty nest and a few scattered feathers -- and no babies.

The second proverb had a similar meaning, but it applied more broadly to the everyday life of all birds. On any given day and in any given tree, a bird would likely hear this bit of wisdom chirped and chided by a parent to its offspring ...

'*A stupid bird fouls its own nest.*'

Treetop and Sunshine had been mates four seasons now. Together, they had successfully raised six sets of young. Their first nestlings usually hatched in early spring. After these babies were taught how to fly and how to feed using their own skills, Treetop and Sunshine would build another nest and raise another set of young, these usually being born during the heart of the summer.

The babies born in the nest this bright, wonderful day were their second set of hatchlings this season.

Sunshine flew back to the dogwood tree to feed her babies for the first time. Their cries for food touched her heart and urged her to fly faster.

But as she approached, Treetop glanced up at her with a strange expression, and she felt her heart seize with dread.

"There's a problem," he said simply.

"What's the matter?" she asked with a frantic tone.

"Something's wrong."

"What? What is it?" Sunshine gripped the branch tightly.

"It's ... it's one of the babies."

"What is it? Tell me!"

But Treetop turned away and shook his head.

"Tell me!" she pleaded urgently.

Treetop sighed heavily. He spoke with his back still turned. "He's deformed."

Together with his sister Virginia,
Tony Chandler has also written a story of dragons
and dragonslayers, honor and danger:

The Last Dragon of the North

Prologue

The clanking of mugs and the muffled sound of conversation drifted throughout the pub as the sun cast its last rays. Most of the local men had come to seek out friendly conversation over a few pints before returning to their homes for the evening. But off in a corner, one man sat alone with his ale.

He sat in a relaxed slouch with his back to the wall, facing the room before him. One hand grasped his mug while the other rested on the smooth wood of the table. A suggestion of a smile rested on his handsome features.

The conversations drifted into silence after the main door opened. A single man filled the doorway. Unlike the country folk gathered under the flickering lanterns of the pub, he wore a sword on his left hip, while on his right a dagger hung ominously. He waited while his eyes adjusted to the darkened room. After a few moments, he walked over to the bar and leaned over. Everyone took note as the pub owner nodded toward the corner of the room. After a quick glance, the stranger walked directly toward the corner and its lone occupant.

"I'm looking for a man named Owain Armstrong," the intruder stated in a deep voice.

The man seated at the table picked up his mug and took a drink. His other hand dropped off the edge of the table to rest on the handle of his own dagger strapped to his belt.

"You have found him."

They eyed each other carefully.

"You seem a bit young to be a dragonslayer."

A half smile crossed Owain's face as his hand relaxed on the handle of his dagger. He thought a moment, and then he slowly stood up. He stood even with the stranger, though he was only of medium build to the other's larger bulk. Owain began rolling up the sleeve that covered his left arm. The light from a lantern hanging on the wall gleamed on the bared forearm and the terrible scars that ran down the entire length.

"Ugly scars, mate," the stranger said, his voice tinged with awe.

"Dragon clawed me, right before I killed it. And it was a small one at that."

The stranger nodded silently, his eyes still fixed on the deep scars that disfigured Owain's entire forearm.

Owain sat back down, rolling down his sleeve.

"Well, I guess you'll have to do. You dragon hunters are hard to find these days. My master has placed notices from the coast all the way up to the highlands, and no one has answered them." The stranger raised an eyebrow. "Then some of the locals here sent us word a dragon hunter was passing through."

"Good thing dragons aren't that common any more."

"Common or not, we've got one. And we have to get rid of it, quick like." The stranger shook his head and sat down opposite Owain.

"My master, the earl of this land, is willing to pay handsomely." He reached into his shirt and pulled a small bag out. It jingled with coin as he sat it down in front of Owain.

"There's more where that came from -- if you can do the job."

A knowing smile crossed Owain's face as he picked up his mug and drained it. He signaled the pub's owner for another. Then he reached over, opened the bag, and inspected its contents. It held gold coin.

Owain looked evenly at the stranger while he set the bag back down between them.

"Perhaps you would like to accompany me when I hunt it. To *see* if I can do the job."

The eyebrows of the stranger rose questioningly.

Owain sat back as a woman placed a full mug before him. The stranger remained silent as the woman stepped away.

"I thought not," Owain said with a smug grin.

The man stared at him.

"What's your name?" Owain asked

"My name is Will Tate." The man paused. "So then, are you going to take the job?"

Owain took a short sip of the ale and then set it down. He gave Will a shrewd look. "How do you know it's a dragon? Could be wolves, eh?"

"I've seen what wolves will do. This is much worse."

"How so?" Owain's voice betrayed his growing

excitement.

The stranger took a deep breath.

"Bloody mess, really -- not much of the poor sheep or cow left. In fact, there's nothing left when it kills a sheep except the head and a great pool of blood on the ground." The stranger shook his head. "It doesn't *just* break their necks making the kill either."

The big man paused and looked straight at Owain.

"It pulls the head clean off! Even when it kills a young cow," he said with a whispered dread.

"What about any tracks?" Owain asked quickly.

"Not many."

"Can you follow them?"

"No. The tracks are only around the kill. There are none coming, nor any going. They seem to appear out of nowhere."

It was now Owain's turn to nod silently. He rubbed his left forearm, thinking deeply.

"One last question. On the tracks around the kill, how many toes on each foot?"

Will held up three fingers.

"How big are the hind feet?"

Will held up his hands and spread them almost two feet apart.

Owain leaned back against the wall and took a thoughtful drink from his mug.

"I will have to go and get my weapons first, but I can be ready to travel with the morning light." He sat upright. "And I will want to talk to your master myself. My price will depend on how big the beast turns out to be. The bigger and nastier they are,

349

well ..." He shrugged.

"So it shall be, young dragon-killer."

Will began to chuckle.

Owain gave him a slightly puzzled look.

"Share your humor, Will."

The man rose from the table, still smiling.

"It just crossed my mind, about dragon hunters and all -- why there's not many of you. And especially why the only one I find is so young."

"And ..." Owain prompted.

"I guess not many of you blokes live long enough to grow old!"

Chapter One

Later that same night, the gentle silver light of the waxing moon illuminated a rolling pasture twenty miles from the pub and revealed a large herd of sheep. Most were settled down for the evening on the soft grass, but others remained awake; their 'baaing' sound echoed from time to time into the darkness that enveloped the world beyond.

Two old shepherds kept a vigilant watch over their charges. As they stood under the starry sky a fresh breeze began to blow, causing the knee-high grass to wave to and fro much like some vast, grassy sea. The sheep that were still awake were relaxed and comforted by the shepherds' familiar presence.

All their lives Geoff and Arn had been shepherds. And though but humble shepherds, they could fight with courage to protect their helpless charges.

Once they had fought off an attack by five hungry wolves. Armed with only their staffs, they had placed themselves between the sheep and the fangs of the wolves. The shepherds battled almost an hour with the vicious brutes as they lunged again and again. In the end, the wolves retreated bloody and bruised. And though both men were exhausted and bled from their own wounds, they had lost not a single lamb.

The good shepherds watched their flock this moonlit night, but this night brought something more terrible than wolves. Yet unseen to either man, a huge and dark shape flew over them again and again ... The huge predator flew silently on leather wings while it surveyed them and planned its attack.

As Geoff and Arn leaned on their heavy staffs, the horned predator picked up speed and began to circle closer.

The older of the two shepherds wrinkled his nose in disgust when the breeze brought a whiff of hot stench.

"Come now, Geoff. Been eating too many beans tonight, have ya!"

Geoff twisted the staff in his hands as he eyed his companion.

"It's not me fouling the air tonight -- you walking outhouse," he shot back.

Arn began chuckling as the breeze changed directions, taking the rank smell with it.

"Good thing the wind has changed -- see there how your farts are disturbing my sheep." He pointed.

Indeed, the once settled flock was now quickly getting to their feet. And even in the low light from the moon, it was easy to discern their growing fright as they stumbled around and cried out from their broken slumber.

"Aye, it's nothing to worry over, Arn," Geoff replied, keenly surveying the fields for any predator that might have come near. Still, he kept his old eyes sharp and his grip tight on his stout staff.

But though he wished to remain silent and watchful this moment, his friend would not hold his wagging tongue.

"I've heard the widow Simmons has taken a

352

shine to thee now." Arn's gravelly voice chuckled. "You might want to take a bath early this week and pay her a visit tomorrow. That is, if you haven't forgotten how to court -- "

"Shut up now! There's something not right here," Geoff said curtly, cutting him off. But his friend did not take the hint.

"Aye, I know what it's like to be shy annn ..." But his words trailed off, and his smile evaporated.

The strange stench returned ... and the sheep grew jumpy with a panic that reached through the darkness and even gripped the shepherds as they each held their breath in tense anticipation.

For some unknown reason, they lowered their bodies closer to the ground as they eyed each other.

"What is it, Geoff? What is it? Wolves?"

"Hush, I said."

The hundred or so sheep now seemed blind and confused. While the shepherds stared in wonder, a small group of sheep would begin to run in one direction, but as soon as the rest of the flock began to join them, something unseen seemed to block the way. The unnerved animals retreated in another direction as if fleeing from something.

Both men stared hard into the darkness.

"Could something be out there we can't see ..." Geoff froze as something caught his eye from above. Then he heard a sound that made him cringe.

He heard the flapping of wings. But the sound, faint as it was, bespoke some nightmare creature of immense proportions.

"What was that, Geoff?" Arn asked fearfully.

Both men looked upward into the dark sky

above.

It was too fast to make out, and it was worse only half-seeing it like that. Did they actually see the large, leathery wings blotting out a few stars, or did their own rising fear trick their poor night vision?

The flapping of huge wings came near, and the sheep now began running in a blind panic. The sheep all cried out at once and ran as one.

The mysterious thing in the air was herding the sheep and fueling their overwhelming fear. Now the sheep, thoroughly confused, seemed one mass of moving, jumping blurs of white fleece. There was nowhere for them to run, no protection, and the ones too slow or stricken with fear fell beneath the feet of their peers and were quickly trampled to death.

"What are we going to do, Geoff? Something is up there! I can't see what is, I can't ..."

They saw it at the same time.

It crossed just below the edge of the moon. The saw clearly the jagged wings of leather stretched out wide, they saw the beast, and they even felt it. And if they had been frozen by their fear of this unknown thing before, this brief, clear sight of it took the breath straight out of their lungs as if they had been struck the heaviest of blows. It was as if they had forgotten how to breathe now.

The very air trembled with the stomach-churning sound of a monstrous roar.

Arn fell to the ground, covering his eyes with his hands; Geoff watched in disbelieving shock. And then the evil visage disappeared into the darkness again.

354

But now they knew it was up there --
somewhere. The beast flew, invisible in the dark
skies above them.

And there on the open grasslands, both men
suddenly felt naked and exposed.

They found themselves straining their old eyes
first in one direction and then another. They could
no longer tell if the faint sound of wings flapping on
the breeze was actually the thing they had seen or a
trick of the rushing blood pounding in their veins
and in their ears.

Arn, as he crouched fearfully close to the
ground with his hands over his bent head, finally
found the breath to speak.

"I can't remember how to pray, Geoff! *I can't
remember ... !*"

Geoff shook his head in stunned silence, still
staring at the black sky.

"It's a demon, isn't it?" Arn's voice grew shrill.
"It's come to take us, Geoff! I seen its wicked
wings! I seen it! Only a black demon has wings like
that, Geoff! *Only a demon has wings like that!*"

Arn's fearful shouts became mixed with the
pitiful sounds of the sheep. Every noise seemed to
melt into the cries of the doomed.

Geoff turned, just in time to see a large ram
suddenly bolt from the mass of animals. It ran faster
as it neared a small hill.

But it could not outrun what hunted it from
above.

Geoff saw the serpentine form drop out of the
black sky and cover the whiteness of the sheep
completely. He strained, trying again to make it out.

But his limited vision only gave him the impression of some huge, winged snake.

The pinned ram gave a shrill cry of pain, its shoulders pushed into the ground by the sharp and merciless talons. As the animal looked up for the last time and brayed its desperate fear, it saw the pointed snout part to reveal hideous fangs that glistened in the moonlight.

The long neck arched back, and then it struck.

Geoff heard the horrid growl rumble through the darkness again. And then came the sickening sound of bone snapping.

A tense silence filled the air.

Suddenly, he heard the muffled sound of something thumping onto the ground just before him. His body stiffened, but he forced himself forward a few steps -- afraid to look, but just as afraid not to look.

He cried out when he saw the wide-open eyes of the ram's severed head staring up at him from the ground.

Arn's stricken voice behind him mixed with the sound of his own pounding heart.

"I can't remember how to pray ... I can't remember ... I can't remember ..."

Geoff knew what it was now, though he had believed it was only wolves taking sheep from his neighbors' flocks these last weeks. He had heard the word *dragon* before, but only in tales used to scare children at night. He had also heard the earl's warning about a dragon, but Geoff had not believed.

Now he did.

"Keep it away ... keep the demon away ..."

"It's worse than that, Arn," Geoff said in a low voice. His eyes focused on the dark form over a hundred feet away.

The writhing creature began to stir, ready to take to the air with its prize.

Geoff's protective instincts took over, and without thinking, he stepped forward with his large staff raised. He shouted in rage as he realized one of his precious sheep had been killed right before his eyes.

And from between the two large wings, the long neck twisted back around towards him.

The glaring red eyes fixed on Geoff as its fangs dripped blood all across the scaly snout. The earth-shattering growl caused Geoff to go silent.

Geoff stopped and groaned in fear, but the beast was angry now.

Geoff watched in horror as the great beast drew itself up on its hind legs. Staring helplessly, he felt Arn stumble up beside him still whimpering. But Geoff stared as if in a daze while the creature drew itself fully erect with its great leathery wings completely extended.

It became deathly still in that position, its jagged wings wide and its short front legs curled in front of its scaled chest. The slender tail alone writhed with tense excitement as the pointed snout smiled with bloody fangs in the moonlight.

It was so unreal.

They both jumped when the noise began.

It sounded like a windstorm rushing quickly from the distant netherworld. Louder and louder it grew, this rushing wind of death, until the terrible sound filled their senses.

As suddenly as it started, the loud rushing of air stopped.

Everything grew fearfully silent, and even the panicked cries of the sheep were now silenced as everyone -- man and sheep -- stood still as stone.

The heaviness of the silence gripped their hearts in a stranglehold.

Geoff, still staring at the beast, spoke once more.

"Pray now."

Flames exploded down upon the two helpless and crouching forms. Their clothes were ripped off their bodies and hurtled like flaming meteors towards the fleeing sheep. The seconds seemed eternal as the fire licked and devoured and burned even the very earth itself, so powerful was its intensity.

Dragon's fire lit up the entire area like a beacon.

Its fiery breath finished, the beast grasped its kill in its powerful talons. With a mighty sweep of its jagged wings it leaped back into the night sky.

And it feared nothing.

Read more about Tony Chandler's books

Mothership Series
Mothership

In the midst of Galactic War a new life form is born -- an AI starship. But with all its weapons and sophisticated programming, the sentient starship is not equipped for its greatest challenge -- that of becoming the mother to the last three children of humanity.

Borne On Wings Of Steel

The much anticipated sequel to *MotherShip*! Traveling to the farthest known worlds of the universe, Mother, Jaric, and Kyle continue their search for other survivors of the human race. They soon find themselves caught in a web of intrigue, deception, and danger ...

Other Books
Lost In Time

Gordon Smith and Sarah Nightingale are lost in time... And most disturbing, they have no memories of their lives prior to time traveling. As they journey through Earth's timeline, they search for clues to their previous life and to the most important question of all -- what happened to wipe out their memories?

One thing they do know -- they are being chased throughout time by dangerous Shadows and the faceless Anon. However, they have a plan. They travel back to meet Jane Austen and set their strategy in motion, but events quickly spiral out of control.

Gordon and Sarah are forced to travel again to rescue William Shakespeare. When a new and greater enemy threatens Earth's timeline with an evil act that could change history forever, they find themselves in a desperate race against time itself!

The Last Dragon Of The North
(written with Virginia Chandler)

Owain Armstrong is used to hunting dragons on his own, but then he meets up with the famous dragonslayers of the Northern Band. The band of weary slayers long had been on a quest to kill the last dragon of the north. They soon hear strange tales -- tales of the Green Dragon Inn and the monster that lives inside the mountain.

And for a price, anything is possible...

Song of Life Trilogy
Bluesky And Sunshine

The 'Song of Life' is a tale about a one-legged Mockingbird named Bluesky. At its heart, it is a story of how love and friendship ultimately conquer hatred and prejudice - and how a hero is born.

The Journey

Orphaned and outcast, Bluesky despairs of ever finding acceptance and friendship, but then the wise Owl Nightwind sends him on a journey of discovery. The one-legged Mockingbird discovers that perhaps birds of a feather *don't* have to stick together.

The Singer

In the exciting conclusion to the Song of Life trilogy, Bluesky must turn a mixed flock of birds into a team that can solve the mystery of what is causing *death on the wind.*